MW00685166

The Canine Handler

SETBACK

M.C. HILLEGAS

Topographical map courtesy of CalTopo.com, California

ISBN 13: 978-1-945670-93-0
ISBN 10: 1-945670-93-2

Year of the Book
135 Glen Avenue
Glen Rock, Pennsylvania

In Remembrance of
T. Madaline Schumacher.
Mom, I miss you every day.

Dedicated to the
souls of the forever lost.

LOST REFLECTIONS

How I mourn the value of would be reflections

Stolen, as our lives took on different directions.

My heart mourns for time forever lost

A mother's heart endures the greatest cost.

With all my body and soul, I wish, I pray

As I hold tight to thoughts of you each day

Yearning you found the arms of a mother

Holding hope she adored a daughter of another.

~From Sarah to the daughter she never knew

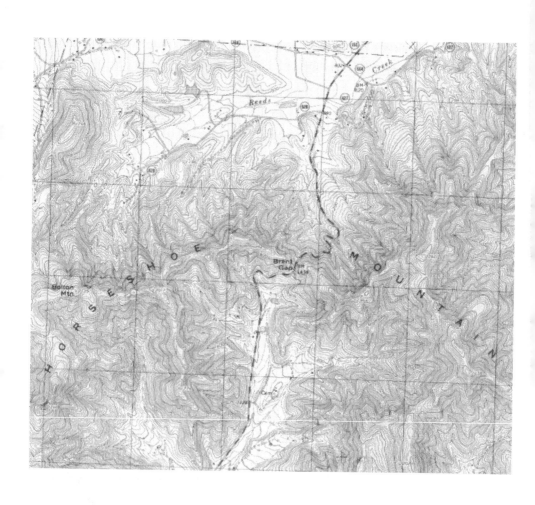

PROLOGUE

The hiker and his dog trekked along a ridge within the Horseshoe Mountains. Mid-March weather cooperated, showering the woods with bright sunshine. With a positive outlook and a soft eye, he scanned the forest floor for deer sheds. Hoping to find a handful leftover from late winter that critters hadn't chewed or damaged, he continued to hunt among dead leaves and fallen branches.

Heading down a ravine with his dog in the lead, he threw a branch into the broad creek below. The canine bounced into the chilly waters after the stick. Shoving his snout into the shallows, the dog thrashed about, clawing at the water.

"Ben, what're you up to? Get your stick buddy," the man called.

For a moment the dog looked up, but then went back to his excavating. Quickly, he pulled out what appeared to be a thick, but short branch from the creek bottom. Grasping the treasure in his jaws, he headed back up the hillside toward his owner.

Dropping the new trophy at his owner's feet, the dog backed up. The man bent down to pick it up.

The dog wagged his tail in anticipation, but the man stopped abruptly, running his fingers over the smooth texture of the object. Turning it over in his hands, he inspected it closer. After a few moments, he realized what it was... but was unsure if it was animal or human.

He stuffed the object in his backpack and called for the dog.

CHAPTER 1

ASHLEY

Tilting her head against the stained pillow, Ashley pushed strands of damp hair from her face and neck. Within the confines of the hot, stuffy isolation trailer, she inhaled in shallow breaths. It was the only thing that helped keep the chronic smell at bay.

Alone, Ashley took stock of her situation. Even if it were possible to escape by breaking through the ceiling or floorboards, they'd be watching. Checking every possible area for another option, in the back of her mind she knew there would be eyes on her. *No way out.* It was defeating.

Windows, blackened with crusty cardboard held in place by duct tape, remained secured by rusty bars. Sweat and blood mingled with urine, and other bodily fluids mixed amid the tangled and filthy pile of bed coverings she straddled.

Sparse clothing stuck to her in places she hadn't been allowed to clean in days, maybe a week. Ashley couldn't remember. Shifting onto her back, with her arms and legs spread, she tried to stay as cool as possible, and weighed her circumstances.

Punished. Labeled a troublemaker and a known runner by her captives, they were teaching her a lesson. The beating and solitary confinement were part of the price of her attempt to flee, but only fueled her determination to break free. *Hardheaded, entitled,* they had called her, remembering the first time they caught her trying to escape. *Why?* Her bottom lip quivered as she tasted salty tears. Her body was sore, used-up. *So thirsty.* Hunger pangs erupted from an empty stomach.

Baking in a layer of sweat as the humidity continued to rise, Ashley imagined the sun directly over the trailer. *Midday.* No air conditioning or fan graced the mobile home.

Shards of light splayed through cracks in the torn cardboard coverings. Dust danced in the bands of light each time she rearranged her position on the bed. She tried not to move much. *What was so hard about life back home? How is this any better? I wish I'd known what I was getting into.* They had told her she was beautiful... promised a career in modeling.

Lethargic, she leaned her head over the edge of the bed and closed her eyes. Dizzy, slightly incoherent, maybe from dehydration, her thoughts drifted. Her mom's boyfriends had always come first. From the very beginning, even as a small child, she could remember the abuse, the alcohol, the disappointment. *Was I three years old? Or four? Does it even matter at this point?* She racked her brain. She always knew the molestation was wrong.

Recalling the first time she was old enough to tell her mom, Ashley closed her eyes. It had been so hard. She had been so ashamed. When she finally found the courage, her mother's reaction was different than she had thought it would be. The woman had beaten her black and blue... told her to quit lying. Said she was only looking for attention. "Jealous." After that, Ashley didn't say another word to anyone.

When she was ten or eleven years old, her mom married Todd. He was much older. A well-seasoned, conniving salesman. He had been nice in the beginning of their relationship. What Ashley thought would have been considered *normal.*

A couple years passed without incident. But by the time she hit her teens, Todd eyed her up and made perverted remarks when they were alone. She tried to avoid him. The first time he approached Ashley, he grabbed her hand and held it on the crotch of his pants. She felt him move beneath her. He grinned and laughed.

Knowing what was surely to come, she fled. Her mother reported her missing to the authorities—an underage runaway.

Returning home a few days later, Ashley once again tried to tell her mom what was going on. Her mother only berated her. *"We're lucky to find such a good man to take us in. Why're you always stirring things up? Can't you just leave it be?"*

After strained relations with her mother and several more "encounters" with Todd, Ashley left for good.

This time, her mother never reported her to the authorities even though she was still underage.

Ashley's eyes flew open. The sound of gravel crunching under the weight of vehicle tires startled her. Terror surged through her. Jerking her head upward from where she hung over the side of the mattress, she gasped for air, choking on saliva. Sharp pains crisscrossed her forehead.

Holding her breath, she listened with paralyzed intent. *Oh fuck!* Worn brakes squealed as the driver stopped, jamming the vehicle into park. Feeling faint, the arteries in her neck ticked with a quick, erratic pulse.

Several car doors slammed. Loud, lewd male voices carried through the humid air. She could hear them as they pounded up the front porch steps.

Pulling her knees up to her chin, Ashley closed her eyes and wrapped her arms around her legs. She tried to draw a deep breath but only succeeded in hyperventilating. Keys rattled in the damaged and dented metal door that had offered no way out. Knowing the abuse in store for her, she tried to mentally prepare herself.

I need to find a way of out this shit hole!

CHAPTER 2

SARAH

Several months had passed since Sarah's arrest and indictment for the Codorus Murders. The state had served the warrant before she'd even been released from the hospital.

With Sarah's past, growing up in the Pennsylvania foster care system and the trail of paperwork from her state-appointed psychologists, she had been sent to Danville State Hospital. As a state prisoner, she was able to continue treatment and physical therapy for injuries sustained in the shooting incident. Beyond her immediate doctors and physical therapist, she initially refused to meet with anyone from the outside.

Eventually, Sarah had no choice but to receive visitors. The prosecutor's office sent their experts to interview her. They needed to determine whether she had been mentally competent at the time of the murders and if she could withstand a trial. The defense team argued she suffered Dissociative Identity Disorder or DID. "Absurd and ridiculous" was the prosecution's psychologist's view of her multiple personality diagnosis. No one from their side believed DID even existed as her defense team was trying to claim.

The public defender's office countered with their specialists to maintain just the opposite. And the Pennsylvania Office of Internal Affairs sent investigators to ask leading questions about her time in the York County foster care system. Everyone seemed to want to probe and prod into her life.

Delving deep into her past caused Sarah's mood to spiral. A migraine pierced her thoughts. The weight of the situation was suffocating. Shades drawn, the overhead light off, Sarah lay in bed, facing the wall. She drew the covers over her head to shut out the world.

"Go away," she growled, hearing the door to her hospital room open followed by footsteps.

Her lawyer entered. With the physical portion of her recovery concluding, the real drama in court would begin soon.

"You'll have to do more than that to convince me to leave," Elliot Roth replied in his normal dynamic manner. "Come on, it's afternoon. What're you still doing in bed?"

Sarah turned toward her attorney and sat up, letting the covers drop to her waist. "I'm rebelling." Sarah peered up at him with a wry smile. She let her guard down with Elliot. He was one of the only people in her world who cared and had a stake in the outcome of the trial.

With neatly trimmed good looks and well-fitting suits offset by huge, thick glasses that made his eyes look bulbous, Elliot appeared sharp, intelligent. Empathetic with a comical tendency, he made her feel at ease.

"You need to eat," Elliot suggested eyeing the cold, congealed food on her bedside tray.

"You try. Let me know what you think of their culinary delights." Sarah turned away. At first, she'd been happy to see her lawyer, but it also made her think of the trial which hung over her world like a dark, angry cloud.

Sarah eyed the sterile ceramic blocks that formed her room. A television set hung from the ceiling, and a small cluttered table and chairs filled one corner.

Following her gaze, Elliot asked, "More fan mail?"

"For once, a letter from Dave. Not much, but he says Gunner and Sam are doing fine." Sarah almost choked. It broke her heart knowing someone else was caring for her beloved German Shepherds. "He's keeping their training up to date," she managed before sniffling.

Elliot walked to the bed and laid his arm around Sarah's shoulders. "He's doing the best he can. At least you don't have to worry about the dogs' care."

Sarah pushed him away and wiped her nose on the bed sheet. Swinging her legs over the side, she stood and smoothed out her clothes and hair self-consciously. "So, what brings you here? No one told me to expect you today."

"I was in the area researching another case. We have a lot to prep for the trial. The state's in a bit of a quandary, Sarah. Committing you to Danville allowed them to delve into your past foster care experience. They're pulling out all the stops to cover their asses before we go to court."

Sarah chuckled. "Foster care *experience*? That's a fucking nice way to put it."

"Well, they're backpedaling. Pennsylvania's foster care system is under federal investigation, as well as the state's internal investigation into your case, and the missing children from your foster home. Children's Services are feeling the heat. Massive corruption has already been exposed. I think if we work the jury just right, you may have a fighting chance."

"A chance for what? There's no way in hell I'm ever going to be free."

"Sarah, you need to fight for yourself. The state acted in haste processing your arrest warrant. They only have circumstantial evidence, but the judge allowed it. There also seems to be some issues with the evidence collected."

Pulling the cord to the shades, a few rays of sunshine spilled into Sarah's barren room. Dust particles floated and resettled on the windowsill. The frozen outdoors bristled through her soul until she spied a few early warblers on the naked trees below.

"The state attorney believes you're a smoking gun. Responsible for the two Codorus State Park murders as well as the foster care mother, and they're preparing to prosecute accordingly. But we won't know more until the criminologist's report comes back. I'm on their ass about it. Even brought in outside professionals to take a second and third look. State's budgeting more for your defense because you were brought up in their foster system."

Sarah knew what the charges were. They'd stared her in the face every second of every waking hour she had spent in Danville. Two counts of Murder I, one count of Murder II, Arson I and Trespassing weren't easy to forget.

Looking at her young state-appointed attorney, she let a smile escape. He was energetic, ambitious, and upbeat. He had a few years' experience defending criminals and had already gained a tenacious reputation, climbing his way up through a justice department career.

Her case seemed to bring out his inner wolf. A hunger. He radiated energy for the controversy. And here she was in the middle of it all. She felt like she had won the lottery with Elliot Roth.

The mail cart came through while she and Elliot were strategizing. The orderly danced into her room, his long dreads swaying. He pulled one earbud out, smiled and handed her a letter. "For me redhotchachi lady friend in room seventine." He danced back out without waiting for a thank you.

The man's island burr and carefree attitude brightened her mood somewhat.

Looking down at the envelope, she spied her friend and mentor's return address. A guilty twinge stirred deep within. Kellee still supported her, even after learning Sarah had been indirectly linked to the murder of Kellee's daughter. The state had tried bringing conspiracy charges against Sarah, but the accusations hadn't held weight. Sarah laid the unopened envelope on the small table alongside the letter from Dave.

"Guess it's time for me to hit the road." Elliot gave Sarah a bear hug, sweeping her up and crushing her. "Jesus, girl, you need to eat."

"Yeah, sure. Just love the food here." They both looked at the hardened mass still sitting on the tray and laughed. It felt good to laugh, even if only for a moment.

Elliot opened the door and turned to leave. "Call if you need anything, okay? Next time I come, I'll bring you a pizza with all the toppings."

"That would be great." Sarah's eyes trailed after him as he disappeared down the corridor. Her heightened mood left with him. Darkness settled like a constrictive shroud, suffocating and depressing.

Limping on her injured leg, Sarah dragged a chair to the window. Plopping down, she stared out at the still frozen world. Locked away from other patients, prisoners, the general population. *Probably a good thing.* Only recently had she been moved to a lower security wing. But it hadn't mattered to Sarah. She didn't care to see anyone or socialize. And she couldn't get far in her condition anyway.

Sarah had wasted so much energy trying to put her past behind her. The life she'd built with her canines, her small circle of friends... Dave. Her job with the county communication center. It all evaporated. Sarah wasn't as optimistic as Elliot about her trial. She couldn't see past a lifetime of incarceration.

She'd fought so hard to make a life after her dysfunctional upbringing in the state's foster care program. She never wanted to look back. All her studies, schooling, cramming for the FBI academy's testing had been for naught.

And here she was, once again a ward of the state.

CHAPTER 3

DAVE

"Dammit, Graves. You know this puts me in a bad position." Langenberg locked menacing eyes with him. With high cheekbones and full lips, she had a gorgeous face, but his lieutenant carried a cool military edge about her. "Why didn't you come to me first with the information you acquired? What is it about this girl that has you so fucked up? You're walking a double-edged sword, rusty and bent for hell. I'd watch my back if I were you."

Swallowing hard, Dave looked away. He knew she meant the comment in more than one way. He also knew she might be right. Staring out the large, grimy diner window, he pretended to concentrate on the small birds fluttering against the late winter winds. He took a moment to gather his thoughts.

Langenberg was doing him a favor—meeting him outside headquarters and off the record. They had history. And it was apparent she still had a small claim on him.

"I didn't uncover much. I couldn't substantiate what I found. I wanted to give Sarah a chance to prove me wrong, I guess," was all Dave could muster up. He looked away again.

"But the information you tracked down was accurate—at least what I know of it. Your hunches have always been spot on. You're a damn good cop and have good intuition. Just like the rest of your family."

As a cop, Dave had followed in the footsteps of his father, who'd followed those before him. His mother and siblings were also involved in the criminal justice system in varying capacities.

The lieutenant leaned across the booth, closer to Dave. In a muted tone, she asked, "So what's your family think about all this shit?"

"I haven't involved them. Not at this point. I mean I haven't even spoken to Sarah in weeks anyway. There's really nothing to tell."

Dave wanted to detach Sarah from this conversation. It really wasn't about her or their relationship, anyway. It was about information he had kept to himself and how that would impact his job as a trooper with the Pennsylvania State Police.

"Well, I'm sure they won't be happy. But that's not the point of our meeting today."

"No, no it's not. I just wanted to find out where I stood with the agency. Get your advice on my future with the state."

"Future?" Langenberg leaned back against the padded booth seat. Her eyes widened with a hint of surprise, a smirk. Her raised brow and grin expressed open sarcasm.

"What's this gonna cost me?" Dave was coming to terms with his position.

"I'm sorry, Dave, but if you stay, I'm going to have to report everything I know."

"Really?" He looked away from the lieutenant's smirking glare. It was if she enjoyed the discomfort she was inflicting on him.

"You'll be reprimanded. Possibly terminated. This is me giving you a chance to resign and move on without tarnishing your reputation."

Dave folded his hands in front of him on the table. He knew she was only speaking the truth. It wasn't fair for him to put her in this position.

"I appreciate you being up front with me. I still have to give a deposition for the trial, but so far, neither team has actively courted me as a witness. Guess I have a few things to be thankful for."

"God, no," Langenberg snorted. "The defense doesn't want a state trooper on the stand if they can help it. They would be worried you might say something to incriminate their client. And the prosecutor is afraid you'll defend her actions. I don't think you have to worry about sticking around for the trial."

Langenberg stood and rearranged the pink and black Glock on her hip. Dave realized the meeting was over. She reached into her lined leather jacket, pulled out a couple dollar bills, and threw them down on the table. Dave slid out from behind the booth and stood. "How long do I have?"

"I'll give you two weeks to tie up loose ends. Then I expect your resignation on my desk. That'll give you until the end of February. Do you think you can get this done?"

Dave nodded, averting his eyes from her dominating stare.

"I'll have a letter of reference typed up for your file." She turned and started toward the door without a hint of emotion.

"Sure, thanks," was all Dave could think to say as Langenberg and his career walked out the diner's door.

CHAPTER 4

SARAH

Sarah filed into the courtroom, eyes focused on her lawyer's backside. A county deputy followed close, unlocking the cuffs before she took a seat. Absentmindedly, she rubbed her wrists made raw from the strict metal restraints. Stealing a glance around the packed room, she was overcome with nausea and gripped the table top. Although she and Elliot had spent hours preparing for this day, she found the initial proceedings overwhelming.

Sarah took her seat at the defense table. She twisted around in the stiff wooden chair and gazed into a sea of prodding eyes. Her chest constricted. Sarah sucked her breath in and swiveled back around. *Cornered, like a trapped animal.* She could feel the sting of hardened expressions with their already formed opinions pressing against her. Bile rose up in her throat.

There wasn't an empty seat in the courtroom. Sarah suspected only a few attended because they were interested in the case, but the rest were there for the show. From her past as a 911 operator, she knew some people craved drama, and would take solace in the pain of watching others struggle. *Human nature, nothing personal.*

Near the front of the room, evidence lay neatly labeled on tables opposite the judge's bench. Sarah and Elliot had discussed every piece in detail during their trial preparations. The judge allowed prosecution to pre-admit each article. A rusted and dented five-gallon fuel can lay alongside a leather fanny pack, black wig, and a kitchen knife stained with dried blood. Faint gasoline vapors wafted toward the defense table.

Drawing in a sharp breath, Sarah faltered when the prosecution team filed in. From the discovery process, she knew they had pictures that had been taken during the fire. But she wasn't aware they would be exploited in large, blown up portraits lining each side of the courtroom.

Alarmed by the grandiose display, Sarah fixated her gaze on candid shots of her and her two search and rescue dogs, amid gruesome images of victims at the other murder scenes. One caught her full attention. Positioned on an easel, the full-length glossy drew her in. It revealed a woman with short-cropped black hair, dark makeup and gothic style clothing. Sarah didn't recognize her, but knew the person under the façade was, in fact, her. *Who was this Eva person?*

"All rise," the bailiff called, breaking the spell.

Elliot gently took Sarah's elbow and guided her upward to a standing position. She looked ahead as the judge entered the room from a hidden door behind the bench. Heavy-set, with thick black hair and graying mustache, the Honorable Judge Brocklehurst made his appearance.

Reality set in, fear replaced uncertainty. Sarah swayed slightly, so Elliot grasped her arm as the bailiff told them to be seated.

"You okay?" he whispered.

Sarah took a deep, shaky breath and nodded. She wouldn't look him in the eye. She was far from alright. Pain seared through her injured leg. Her head throbbed with the threat of a migraine. *How am I going to get through this?*

Listening as the judge declared, "The State of Pennsylvania vs. Sarah Gavin," he then read the multiple charges and stated Sarah's entered pleas of 'not guilty.'

Sarah attempted to re-focus. After both sides replied they were ready and the jury was sworn in by the clerk, the prosecuting attorney made his way near the juror's box to deliver his opening argument. *Odd.* After majoring in criminal justice, Sarah had never thought she'd find herself on this side of the courtroom.

Hot, stuffy air closed in around her. Beads of sweat formed along her hairline. She couldn't shake the mix of emotions, so she took a deep breath and held it for a moment, calming her nerves. Totally exposed, it was all so surreal as the state's attorney began his opening statement.

Rigid at the defense table, Sarah was captivated by his theatrics. Planted in front of his audience, the prosecutor waved his arms wildly over his head. He spoke loud and confidently, often pointing toward her and the evidence table. Sarah drew back in her seat.

Hearing the state's side, up front and in person, verbalized in such a manner, made her more than uneasy. She didn't remember. Couldn't remember. And had no knowledge of Eva or her activities.

There had been discussion regarding a plea of insanity. Sarah had undergone weeks of testing from both sides to declare whether she could use that ploy. The state's side had eventually won the ruling and found her competent to stand trial.

It hadn't mattered to Sarah, either way—a plea of insanity wouldn't mean freedom. Neither side could conclude what had happened in her past, at the time the murders were committed. Character witnesses who had been deposed shed light on Sarah as dependable, reliable and a stable individual. "Helpful" and "social" was how they described her.

The intensity of the juror's glares weighed heavy on Sarah. Numb, she fixated on a wood knot in the railing. Steeling herself, she held a poker face, not wanting to reflect emotion. She fought to stay in control.

The prosecutor finished his opening statement with a flare. Spinning around on well-shod heels, he spouted his devotion and dedication to the safety of the community. He declared how he would prove to the jury, without a doubt, Sarah Gavin had committed all three murders in heinous and horrific ways. There would be no question as to her guilt.

In great detail, he'd spoken facts about the murdered subjects. Each victim had been mutilated in some dark and sordid way. Every attack, each homicide, proved it had been personal. The drowned victim's tongue had been partially mutilated within the subject's mouth. Some of the specifics surrounding Sarah's foster brother—whose body had been discovered in Codorus State Park's forest—already made headlines months ago, facts the investigators hadn't been able to keep under wraps. Information regarding the dismemberment of his penis had filtered through the ranks, quickly becoming public knowledge. Her foster care mother's autopsy showed multiple stab wounds to the heart... another fact that found its way out to the public before the police released the information.

Sarah hadn't realized how hard this was going to be. Her future, her life was on the line. *Will there be anything left of me?*

Yawning, unimpressed, the judge barely looked up from his podium and asked if the prosecutor was finished.

"Yes, your honor."

"Please be seated," the judge directed him, then turned to Elliot. "Will the defense be delivering an opening statement?"

Elliot stood, faced the judge and answered, "No, your honor, the defense will not."

The overflowing gallery of spectators erupted in whispers. Hushed comments grew louder in response to Sarah's defense lawyer's decision.

Sarah trusted her attorney, even though it felt wrong not to serve up a rebuttal right on the tail of the prosecutor's opening arguments. *"Trust me,"* Elliot had told her.

"Order, order!" the judge yelled in a deep baritone, slamming his gavel on the desk of his bench. Sarah flinched. "The prosecution may call its first witness."

The prosecutor swung around in his chair and made eye contact with a middle-aged man seated behind the bar. Standing, he announced, "My first witness, Carl Dorrell, is a consultant from the Pennsylvania State Police and an expert witness in the evaluation of fingerprint evidence."

From the gallery, a large man rose from his seat. He had the typical militaristic authoritarian look written all over him, from his buzz-cut to the detail in his dress and the assertive way he carried himself. A look Sarah had always admired, it was quite different from what she had grown up alongside in her foster care home.

Dorrell was sworn in and formalities regarding his background were established with great weight upon his knowledge.

Pointing to an oar labeled "Exhibit A," the prosecutor addressed the jury and went into detail about the latent print found on the object and identifying who it belonged to. He also discussed what the item was, where it had been found and what it was used for normally... and that it could've been used to attack a fellow boater.

Elliot shot up from his chair yelling, "Objection," before Sarah understood what was going on.

The judge rolled his eyes to meet the defense lawyer's.

"The prosecutor is alleging that my client used this object to murder the first victim. This is all speculation!" Elliot fumed, waving his hand toward the prosecutor.

"Objection overruled. Prosecutor, you many proceed."

Sarah watched as an Elliot she had never seen in action huffed and slammed down in his seat.

With a smug look, the prosecutor returned to his witness. "Mr. Dorrell, can you tell me, in your expert opinion, what was found on this exhibit and where it was located?"

"Of course," Dorrell responded with a certain professionalism. He restated the facts, "Exhibit A is a red, plastic composite kayak oar that could be found in the boat rental area within Codorus State Park. On this particular oar, we found a partial palm print that was identified as the defendant's, Miss Sarah Gavin."

"There!" the prosecutor swung around with overstated emphasis. "This places the defendant at the scene of the first murder. We have proof she was in the area!"

The prosecution prattled on again, speculating how an oar might possibly be used in a murder. Finished with his tirade, he turned the witness over to the defense.

Elliot stood, introduced himself and thanked the witness for taking his time to attend the trial. He made quick work of Dorrell, asking him if he could prove how old the latent print was, how long it might endure the elements and whether he was aware that the defendant frequented the park regularly and rented kayaks from that location.

"No, I can't age the print, and yes, the partial palm print is in the portion along the shaft of the oar in accordance with how it would be used to row."

"So, folks, there you have it. This confirms that my client was in fact in Codorus State Park and used this oar, but the prosecution cannot prove when or how that oar was used other than to row a kayak on Lake Marburg!" Elliot went a step further and held up copies of receipts documenting Sarah's kayak rentals on several occasions in the days prior to the murders.

"Objection!" the prosecutor yelled, moving forcefully from his position at his table. "This should've been entered into discovery! How come we were never advised?"

"Objection sustained," the judge ordered. Turning to Elliot, he said, "Explain yourself."

Appearing smug, Elliot answered, "I'm sorry, we just located this information last evening, your honor. The prosecution is welcome to look it over at their convenience."

The prosecution brought in more expert witnesses over several days. A retired morgue employee who dealt in body trauma, a civilian canine handler, and another expert in latent prints. Elliot cross-examined each witness, leaving more unanswered questions.

Sarah's attorney had begun the process of sewing doubt into the minds of the jury. Sarah observed how well received he seemed to come across to the jurors. She was good at reading people, their expressions, their body language. She saw jurors' jaws tense when the state's prosecutor took the stage and visibly relax when Elliot entered. *Do I detect a fracture?*

Sarah grinned. It was entertaining to watch the dance between both sides, a delicate balance that was intriguing. She watched as Elliot found legitimate fault with each piece of evidence and why it couldn't be used against her.

"Do you have any additional witnesses to call?" the judge asked the prosecutor.

"No, your honor, not at this time."

"Do you wish to give a summation at this time?" the judge proposed.

"Yes, your honor, I would."

"Please go ahead."

Standing front and center, the prosecutor gazed around the crowded courtroom. He held a serious expression with pursed lips, planting fists firmly on his hips. He appeared to be gearing up to deliver a sermon. Sarah caught the judge exhaling in exasperation.

Two more pieces of evidence lay on the table, the knife and gas container. The knife was the only item that was completely tied to Sarah and the last victim. It had been recovered from her hand, at the scene with the victim's blood. The container held a partial print.

"There is no doubt..." the prosecutor gave a pregnant pause. He paraded around the bar area holding up the plastic baggy containing the bloody knife, "...that the defendant used this knife to stab the victim multiple times which culminated in the victim's death. Only a cold blooded, sociopathic individual could carry out such an act!

"She was placed in Codorus Park where the other two murders occurred. There is numerous evidence that ties Ms. Sarah Gavin to all three victims and the murder scenes. Don't be fooled into what the defense will bring forth to speculate that his client may be innocent. She is guilty of three, well thought out monstrous acts and should be found accountable. I rest my case for now, your honor."

Whispers started among the gallery again. The judge took control of the courtroom slamming his gavel on the bench, "Okay, that's all for today," the judge grumbled. "I expect you to be ready with your first witness tomorrow, 9:00 A.M. sharp," he spoke directly to Elliott. Elliott nodded his head at the judge.

Sarah's skin crawled. Her anxiety level rose a notch with the increasing noise in the courtroom as everyone prepared to exit. *Am I ready for this?* Petrified, she knew she would have to take the stand and the prosecutor would work her, grill her. She and Elliot had spent weeks preparing, but it still sent terrifying thoughts through her mind, wondering what the prosecutor would dredge up to expose her.

CHAPTER 5

SARAH

Staring out the van window, Sarah braced herself for the day's events. Elliot would begin her defense this morning. Unable to sleep the previous night, she had laid awake staring at the walls. Internally, she tried to summon enough energy to help see her through the day.

She squinted as they drove to the courthouse, the early morning rays stretched across the horizon piercing the vehicle's tinted windows. The sun promised warmer weather, elevating her slightly, re-vitalizing her soul.

"You ready?" the female county deputy sitting beside her asked. The same officer had accompanied her each day, checking her in and out of the facilities.

Sarah nodded. The women exited the vehicle and headed into the courthouse. *Ready for this to be over!* Deep down, Sarah wanted nothing more than to be finished with this mockery of her life.

"All rise," the bailiff announced. Everyone in the courthouse stood as the judge entered, took his seat, and excused the room from standing.

"Today, the jury will hear the defense's side. York County Public Defender, Elliot Roth, representing the defendant will now have the floor."

Taking front and center of the courtroom, Elliot gave a short overview. He addressed the jury, "I want you all to pay close attention to the details of what transpired and of each piece of evidence that was entered into exhibits. I'll show you where the fault lays in the state's weak case against my client."

At the conclusion of his opening declaration he prepared to move forward with testimonies.

"I call my first witness, Phillip Fyock, Fire Chief of Penn Township, Station 41."

Sarah watched as a middle-aged gentleman with thinning hair made his way from the gallery seating. Vaguely familiar, she racked her brain trying to figure out how she knew him.

Jumping right in, Elliot asked the Fire Chief if he remembered everything that had occurred the day the foster mother was found dead, the day of the house fire.

"Sure, sure, that's not a day I'll forget anytime soon."

"Good, good," Elliot gave a reassuring response. He paced back and forth in front of the witness stand as he spoke. "Do you remember speaking with Pennsylvania State Trooper Graves about the events when he arrived on scene? About what had taken place?"

"Yes, yes, of course. He showed up just as we were finishing extinguishing the house fire."

"And why was he called to the scene?" Elliot stood just to the side of the witness, leaning toward the chief in a friendly manner.

"Because a body had been discovered inside the burned house."

"And this is normal protocol?"

"Yes, State Police have jurisdiction over suspicious deaths in our township."

"And this death was suspicious?"

"Yes, the subject appeared to have injuries to her chest area and her throat as well."

"Okay, we have the suspicious death, and following protocol, you called in the State Police. Was the body guarded as per protocol of chain of custody?"

"Yes, we contained the area and had a fireman and regional police officer in charge of the scene where the body was found. They were stationed there until the medical examiner showed up on-scene and took custody of the body."

"Good, good. Now there was another piece of circumstantial evidence located at the scene as well. Can you describe that?"

"Yes, the gas can that is sitting on the table." The fire chief pointed to the evidence table.

"Where was that gas can located, exactly?"

"It was found in the backyard of the burned house."

"How far was that from where the dead subject was being guarded?"

"Outside of the house."

"And was there a chain of custody guarding this evidence as well?"

"No, I just told my guys to leave it, not to touch it."

"Could the person watching over the body see the gas can outside?"

"No."

"So, anyone could have touched or moved this can?" Elliot's expression changed to a more serious look as he cupped his chin in his hand.

"Well, I don't think so, but we weren't watching it the whole time."

Sarah listened as Elliot walked the witness through that day's events. She understood her lawyer was exposing gaps. What the state had on her might appear solid, but that's not always the case. Turning in her seat to look at the gallery, Trooper Dave Graves caught her eye. Seeing him stole her breath, her heart beat faster. She quickly turned back around.

Elliot established that this was the same house where Sarah had grown up and at some point, could've encountered the can. He also pointed out that the print found on the can was only a partial, difficult to lift, and the state had only found it to be likely Sarah's, as they couldn't say definitively it was hers. It appeared several of the print's ridges and whorls were smeared and unreadable.

The prosecutor took his time cross-examining the fire chief and reiterated the point that the victim was deceased, and had a neck wound.

Moving forward, Elliot said, "I call my next witness, Dr. James Moxley, retired medical examiner and an expert witness in self-defense wounds."

A stooped over, white-haired gentleman was sworn in and took the stand.

Elliot took his time as he proceeded with questions. Sarah could see an excitement build in Elliot as he moved forward.

"Dr. Moxley, have you had a chance to go over the medical examiner's reports from the autopsy for this victim?"

"Yes, in detail."

"Can you give me your opinion whether the victim had any other injuries to her body than the stab wounds to her chest and the injury to her neck?"

"Yes, indeed she did. It appears as though she had been in a struggle of some sort prior to the inflicted fatal injuries."

"Can you go into more detail?"

"Of course. The victim had blood and cuts on both knuckles. There were also skin follicles and blood found under her nails as if she had scratched another person."

"And did you find anything unusual about that?"

"Not necessarily unusual for someone who was inflicting injury or defending themselves."

"What else were you able to conclude about the blood on the victim and skin found under her nails?"

"That it belonged to the defendant. We found the skin under the victim's nails and the blood on her knuckles were a positive match to Ms. Sarah Gavin."

"And what did you find with the pictures you viewed from when the defendant was first admitted to the hospital?"

"It was noted from the defendant's hospital photos that she appeared to have injuries sustained that would correlate with the evidence found on the victim."

"So, someone might conclude that the victim and my defendant had been in a close, physical altercation? Perhaps, my defendant was fighting for her life in self-defense?"

"Yes, one could come to that conclusion..." Dr. Moxley started to respond.

"Objection! Objection!" the prosecutor leapt to his feet.

Comments from the gallery brought the noise level up a notch in the normally hushed courtroom.

"What are you trying to prove here?" the judge questioned Elliot.

"I'm not trying to prove anything, your honor. I'm only showing that the defendant may have acted in self-defense, and the situation got out of hand."

"Objection overruled," the judge responded.

Elliot handed the M.E. over to the prosecutor. Sarah gave Elliot a quick grin as he sat down beside her to prepare for his next witness.

Trying to stay positive, she braced herself for what she knew Elliot was about to do to Dave. She also wondered why Dave was dressed in a suit and not his trooper uniform. *Odd.*

"The defense calls its next witness, former Pennsylvania State Trooper David Graves to the stand." Smiling, Elliot stood and approached the front.

Former? Dave and Sarah had minimal contact the last several months when she had been incarcerated. His letters were always upbeat and mainly stuck to the care of her dogs. Why didn't Elliot fill her in? *What else are they keeping from me?*

CHAPTER 6

DAVE

Suffocating in his business attire, Dave sat perched and ready. He understood it would benefit Sarah's situation if he took the stand, but he knew it could hurt his reputation as an officer of the law. He loved her and would do anything to help her out, but this was stretching that bond.

Once called by Sarah's lawyer, he stood and flexed taut muscles before walking through the bar where he would be sworn in. After Dave was seated, a staff member rolled a large screen TV into the center of the courtroom. *Great.* He knew Elliot's plan, and had tried to prepare himself to watch the video *again,* but it never got any easier.

Dave listened as the defense attorney went through the formalities—introducing Dave, his profession, and where his expertise did... or as Dave expected, *did not* fall.

"So, Mr. Graves, I understand you were a Pennsylvania State Trooper? How long did you work for the State of Pennsylvania in this capacity?"

"Yes, for six years. I resigned earlier this year and now work with another law enforcement agency."

"Oh, I see. When you were employed as a PA state trooper, what were your duties?"

"I worked as a patrol officer and as a liaison with the York Communication Center until my last year when I was transferred into the canine unit."

"So, you were only in the canine unit for one year?"

"Yes."

"Would you call yourself an expert on canines and the police work they are trained for?"

"No, not exactly, but I am very experienced in training and working tracking canines."

"Okay, so you were called to the scene of the final victim, correct?"

"Yes, my canine partner, Bella, and I responded to the call."

"I'm going to go over this recording that was filmed by the News 8 camera crew." Elliot pointed to a staff member and she turned on the video.

Dave cringed in his seat.

With the volume turned up, the video began rolling. Although many cell phone videos had been posted to social media outlets, this film captured the event completely and in the best quality. The news team had turned the tape over to the investigators, but it had never been aired to the public.

A camera man had followed and began videoing Dave as soon as he pulled his bloodhound Bella from his SUV. The film captured all that transpired including the moment Dave set the dog on the gas can, to Bella ranging around, catching some sort of scent and heading toward the crowd, where it all culminated with the shooting incident.

Dave eyed Sarah as she sat at the defense table, her attention glued to the screen. She looked pale, like the blood had drained from her. She didn't look like the Sarah he had come to know and love over the last couple years. The spark had gone missing from her normally vibrant green eyes.

Displeased when Elliot pressed the pause button, Dave knew the interrogation of his actions would begin. Tightening his jaw, Dave was acutely aware he was becoming defensive.

"Following your trail here from the gas can, anyone from that crowd or neighborhood could've come in contact with, or moved it," Elliot said, facing the jury to make sure they were taking in his words. "We watch as your leashed canine partner is casting about while you follow her out of the yard. Do you agree with this statement?"

"Yes, but I believe the defendant's scent was on the can and that's what Bella, my canine partner, was scenting and following."

"Okay, but we cannot prove that, correct? And please stick to only answering the question."

Flushing a little, Dave answered, "Correct."

Elliot let the video roll until they came to the part where the dog pulled the leash from Dave's grip and ran toward Sarah. The entire scene that followed—where Sarah raised a knife at Bella and Dave shot her—aired for all to see. Gasps from the jury and gallery filled the room. Sarah abruptly turned away, tears sliding down her cheeks.

Dave bowed his head. He hadn't wanted to revisit that scene. Ever.

"So, we understand it was protocol to protect the canine because Bella carries the same weight as human law enforcement officers do. That is not in question here. What is in question is, did the canine know Sarah prior to this event and could the dog have been looking for Sarah and not actually following a track at all?" Elliot's voice grew louder as he spoke.

"Yes," Dave answered flatly, annoyance clearly present in his tone.

"And how did the canine know, or meet the defendant prior to this event?"

"The defendant and I trained canines together on occasion. We were also deployed on the same search missions in the past."

"So, by stating that your canine was following Sarah's track from the gas can to where she was standing, can you, without a doubt, tell the jury that this canine only tracked her scent on the ground and did not pick up on her as a familiar person standing in the crowd outside a burned home that held the deceased subject?"

Elliot's skepticism was unmistakable. Dave looked at him for a moment, trying to quell the rising anger over being questioned about his dog. About Sarah. About that damned day.

"Can you answer the question, Mr. Graves?" Elliot pushed.

"No, I can't say without a doubt that the bloodhound only followed the track that led to the defendant. But I believe—"

"So, we have here a gas can," Elliot interrupted, "that anyone could have touched, or moved, because it was left unguarded. No chain of custody. A tracking canine working a scene it was not trained nor certified for, and the canine and handler also had past relations with the defendant. That is all for now." Elliot stepped away from the stand quickly. His point had been made. "Prosecution, your witness."

Dave contained his anger when he was dismissed from the stand. He knew Sarah's eyes were on him as he made his way out of the courtroom. He hoped he'd helped her case. Feeling ridiculed in front of a courtroom wasn't something he had planned on in his career. Or lifetime.

CHAPTER 7

SARAH

Sarah stared at the witness stand. A deafening roar filled her ears. After finally becoming almost comfortable at the defense table, it was time for her to be questioned. Air caught in her throat. *Breathe.* But she only succeeded in sucking in short gasps of air. *Settle!* Her thoughts were stern. *I got this.*

"For my next witness, I call the defendant, Sarah Gavin, to the stand." Elliot announced her name as a daring ringmaster would broadcast the next act. The gallery appeared restless. Background noise rose for a moment as spectators shifted in their seats, murmuring whispered comments to one another.

Guess I'm the headliner, she mused as her mood darkened.

With measured movements, Sarah pushed the chair out from behind her. She used her cane to calmly walk to the clerk and lay her hand on the leather Bible. Repeating, "I swear by Almighty God that the evidence I shall give shall be the truth, the whole truth and nothing but the truth," was the first lie. It felt peculiar swearing to a God she didn't believe in. For reasons unknown, maybe because she was apprehensive, she found it humorous and smiled.

"Please state your name and where you are from," the judge barreled down to her after she was seated.

"Sarah Anne Gavin. From Penn Township in York County, Pennsylvania, your honor."

"Thank you, your honor," Elliot nodded his head toward the judge. With Sarah seated, Elliot walked up to where she was on display, rooted in front of the courtroom.

Silence replaced soft mumbles. No one wanted to miss a word.

"Ms. Gavin, I'll be asking you a series of questions concerning the three murders that took place in and around Codorus State Park and Lake Marburg. I need you to be completely honest with your answers. Do you understand?"

"Yes, I will try and answer to the best of my ability."

"Is it true that you knew each one of the murdered victims?"

"Yes, I knew them from my former foster care home where I grew up." Sarah's voice was hoarse, her throat dry. She took a sip of water from the bottle that was provided to her by the clerk.

"And how long has it been since you had seen any of the victims?"

Looking down at the polished wood, she answered as honestly as she could. "Well, I was forced out of the foster home at age eighteen." There had been one moment prior to the murders where Sarah thought she had seen her foster brother as she jogged through the park. She looked up at Elliot and answered, "It's been at least four or five years. I don't remember exactly." It wasn't a lie; she wasn't sure who it had been that day she passed a man in a hoody several months ago.

"You don't remember seeing any of the victims over the past year or prior to their deaths? You haven't had any contact with them?"

"No. I have no recollection of seeing any of them since I left the home. There was no reason. No reason for me to stay in contact," Sarah answered in a monotone.

"You have entered a plea of not guilty for each murder even though there is circumstantial evidence connecting you to the crime scenes." Elliot paused, looking around, giving an inviting expression to the entire courtroom. "Would you have this court of law believe that you are not guilty of these crimes?"

In a small voice, Sarah answered yes. She felt conflicted, unsure, since she couldn't remember what happened.

Low whispers could be heard from the gallery as they commented on Sarah's testimony. Sarah tried to stay focused, keeping her eyes on Elliot as he paced around the area between the defense table and the witness stand.

"And why would you have us believe that you are, in fact, not guilty of these crimes?"

"I don't remember any of the events that transpired regarding these murders."

"What do you mean, you don't remember?" Elliot prodded.

"I mean, I don't remember! That's what I'm trying to say! I have no memory of any connections to these people since I left the confines of the abusive situation that was called my foster care home!" Flustered, Sarah spat out her answer.

Elliot was dredging up long buried memories. She felt herself overheating.

"Objection!" the prosecutor shouted, jumping up from the table.

"Yes?" the judge inquired.

Waving his hands, the prosecutor decided against pursuing his objection. "I apologize, pass."

The judge eyed Elliot. "You may continue."

Turning toward Sarah, Elliot asked, "Are you saying that you have no memory of the events... or no memory of seeing the victims?"

"Both. There are times I haven't been able to account for. Time lost. I'd wake up and I'm someplace else."

"So, what you are saying is that you've experienced lapses in your memory or blackouts? Is this something new?"

Sarah watched as the prosecutor raised his shoulders in disbelief. She knew he completely doubted her. "I experienced bouts of blackouts when I was younger while living in the foster home. But they started again last year."

"Was there anything that might have triggered these 'blackouts'?"

Sarah shook her head. "No. I have no idea what triggers them." Her mood continued to darken as Elliot's questioning persisted.

"What do you remember from previous blackouts in the past, when you were living in the foster care home?"

"Not much. The home was an abusive situation. Physically—"

"Objection! Objection!" the prosecutor bellowed.

The judge looked at the prosecutor and waited.

"This trial is about the victims—the Codorus Murders—not about the defendant's foster care home and how she was raised!" Spittle flew from the prosecutor's lips.

"Objection overruled. You may proceed. Just clarify your line of questioning," the judge told Elliot.

"Yes, your honor. I'm trying to establish a line of reasoning regarding my client."

The prosecutor coughed loudly. He grinned to let everyone know what his thoughts were of the line of questioning.

Elliot continued to ask Sarah about her past, and the events that happened in the home. Sarah knew he was pushing the limit. Both lawyers had been warned that an internal investigation into her background and into foster care in the state would begin after her trial and not to involve it in this case. But Elliot wasn't refraining from any opportunities to expose how she was raised and what she had suffered. Sarah had expected some of the questions, since they had discussed strategy prior to trial.

"These blackouts or bouts of time that you don't remember, do you remember when you first experienced them?"

Sarah turned to her lawyer. Gathering up courage she replied, "The first time I remember waking up from a period of lost time was when I was fifteen. Fifteen and pregnant."

Gasps escaped a few jurors and several of the spectators. Sarah's lawyer waited until the courtroom quieted.

"And what exactly do you remember from that first experience?" Elliot asked.

"Not much. I remember waking up at another student's home. The police were looking for me, said I was reported as a runaway from the foster home. I didn't remember anything."

"Have you ever had any kind of medical workup like an MRI of your brain? Or counseling?"

"Counseling yes, no medical intervention."

"Thank you, Ms. Gavin, for your testimony. I will now turn the witness over to the prosecution." Elliot walked forward to Sarah. He reached over the desk and took her hand. "It will be okay. Answer honestly." Without a word, she nodded and watched as he walked back to the defense table.

Sarah steeled herself as the prosecutor approached. He unbuttoned his suit, showing off his vest and pocket watch. Taking a stance in front of her, he planted both hands on his hips and pushed his jacket back. He reminded Sarah of a used car salesman. He was just missing the mirrored sunglasses and a gold incisor.

"So, in accordance with this recent testimony, you established that you knew each victim and there was a history."

"Yes," Sarah replied bluntly.

"You stated this was an abusive situation, yet there were no formal complaints or references filed with the county or state regarding abuse in this home. If you can conjure up blackouts, I'm sure you can conjure up past abuse."

Starting right in, he was trying to make a mockery out of her character. "Conjure up?" Sarah questioned back. Ears ringing, she could feel blood coursing through tightened veins.

"Yes, aren't you inventing stories to taint the victims' character? Do you really have any abusive situations you might share with us?" he taunted.

Dredging up long buried memories, Sarah hissed, "Yes."

"I'm sorry, could you please repeat your answer?" the prosecutor demanded.

"Where would you like me to begin?" Sarah's cheeks flushed red. "What I first remember as a young child? Or later in my teenaged years when I was used to service clients?"

Sarah sat up tall, rigid in her seat. Without taking her eyes off the prosecutor, she pushed a sprig of curls out of her face.

Spectators in the gallery shuddered at the outburst. The jurors nodded their heads and commented to each other.

"Order, order in the courtroom," the judge demanded, pounding his gavel. Slowly, the people settled, and the buzzing subsided. "Okay, let's move on with your questioning, prosecutor."

"Thank you, your honor." The prosecutor turned from facing the judge to Sarah. "When was the last time you saw any of the victims or encountered them?"

"We went over this already. I don't remember," Sarah replied. "It's been years. Since before I turned eighteen and was removed from the foster home."

"Years? How can you say it's been years when here you are..." the prosecutor pointed to the picture of Sarah in the black wig, "...not even a block away from the foster home wielding the knife that murdered your foster mother!"

Stunned, Sarah spouted back, "That's not me, I don't recognize that person!"

"What do you mean, you don't recognize the person? Who else could it be?" he asked in a mocking tone, almost laughing.

Sarah knew he was trying to make a joke out of the possibility of another personality hidden deep within her. "I'm not sure who it is, but it's not me."

"Well, can you tell us who you think it is?" his mocking tone attempting to bury Sarah in the eyes of the jurors.

"I... I think it's someone who was called Eva." Sarah spoke not to the prosecutor or the jury, but rather she spoke into the wooden desk of the stand. It was unknown territory to her. She didn't remember Eva. She didn't know her.

Feigning exasperation, the prosecutor threw his arms up in the air. "Eva? Your other, made up personality? Who you thought you could pin all of this on? Tell us more about this Eva person. No wait, let me explain it further."

As the prosecutor droned on with his theory, Sarah spied a man standing in the door jamb of the courtroom. Just out of the light. She recognized him for an instant. But the memory was faded, distant, and she couldn't place him. He was tall, thin with a ragged, worn look. Gray spun like cobwebs through his unkempt shaggy hair. His beard and sideburns appeared rough and disheveled.

Sarah turned her head toward where Elliot sat at the defense table, caught his eye and looked back to the door. The man was gone. *Who was he?*

Elliot caught her drift and swung around to look where Sarah was focused but didn't seem to understand. He shook his head.

"Please answer the question, Ms. Gavin," the judge ordered Sarah once again.

"I'm sorry, could you please repeat the question?" She squared her shoulders to compose herself.

The prosecutor looked toward the spectators and the jury as he said, "I asked, when was the first time you believe you 'encountered' this other person, this Eva?"

Sarah's face reddened in a flash of anger. Emotions boiled to the top, overflowing with a rush of heat. "When I was fifteen, used up, abused and pregnant in that hellhole the state called a foster home!" She held the prosecutor's eye. *Challenge accepted.*

Leaning in close to her, the prosecutor glared and accused, "You mean when you were a promiscuous teenager living under the roof of the state?"

"Promiscuous? We were sold to service clients. Raped, sodomized, beat, tortured, whatever word you want to call it." In a fury of emotion, Sarah lost control. Tears streaming, she continued, "There were times I blacked out, for hours, days sometimes, and when I awoke, I would be dressed differently, bruised and bloody. Sometimes they would call me Eva..." Sarah trailed off.

"You'll have me believe, and the court believe, that you were part of sex trafficking? Right here in York County at the hands of your foster parents?" With a look of feigned shock at this outrageous claim, the prosecutor raised his brows. Shrugging his shoulders, he set off again to bury Sarah and her fake character deeper.

"Objection, objection!" Elliot jumped from his seat at the defense table, knocking his chair to the floor. Voices from the gallery rose, disrupting the courtroom. The jurors looked at each other in disbelief.

"Order, Order!" Spittle flew from the judge's lips as he banged his gavel over and over. "Where are you going with this line of questioning?" he directed toward the prosecutor. Turning to face the jurors, the judge instructed the clerk to strike the last exchange from Sarah.

Sarah read the jurors' expressions and knew her words hadn't been lost. It was too late to erase them from their memory.

The prosecutor faced the judge. "The state rests."

With the weighty words of her past spilled out into the open, Sarah's mood lightened. *Who knew?* It was like a cleansing for her soul to release the issues she had kept bottled up for years.

Now nearing the end of the trial, a sense of relief washed over Sarah. Glad to be off the stand and back at the defense table, she and the rest of the courtroom waited as Elliot prepared to deliver his closing argument.

CHAPTER 8

DAVE

"Hurry, Sam. Hurry!" Dave yelled at the dog. "Gunner's gonna get it if you don't hurry up!"

His energy motivated the dog to swim faster so Gunner wouldn't be the first to reach the orange bumper floating in the spring-fed pond. Dave smiled as he watched the dogs vie for the toy. Always a competition between the two shepherds, Gunner usually came out on top. Dave silently pulled for Sam to win for once. He always rooted for the underdog.

He stood on the grassy knoll beside the water and scanned the area around him. The cabin, the barn, the pond. *Perfect. Just perfect.*

Dave was satisfied with the decision to move south from Pennsylvania to the quieter, rural Nelson County nestled in the Virginia mountains. The property he decided on was located a few miles outside of Lovingston, a small town and the county seat. The area had been devastated by Hurricane Camille in '69 and was still trying to recover.

More than a hunch, something lured him toward the natural beauty of the Shenandoah and the Horseshoe mountains' landscape.

He couldn't put it into words. But other variables played into the decision. He couldn't even make sense of his feelings, but even without the undefined pull, Dave realized Sarah would love the area. Sam and Gunner already approved.

His decision to move had started with the background research on Sarah's foster family. He'd found the foster mother's roots ran deep in Nelson and other counties surrounding Charlottesville.

The note Eva held the day of the shooting incident had given Dave the idea to research Sarah's past and her foster family. He suspected a tie between the missing children from the foster home and this area—the biggest reason he chose to relocate. It put him right where he needed to be to act on his instinctive, and usually correct, hunches.

He had no idea whether Sarah would be in his future. The trial was not yet complete, and there appeared to be problems with the state's prosecution, but still, so much clear-cut evidence was stacked against her. They hadn't been able to use the plea of insanity, which would be better for Sarah in the long run. No defendant had successfully pleaded insanity in a murder case since The Zoo Man back in the early '90s. At least not in the states. And Thomas Dee Huskie, aka The Zoo Man, had walked away due to a mistrial, not by winning his court case.

Sam bounded out of the pond with the retrieving dummy in his mouth. "Good job, Sam!"

Gunner was hot on the other dog's tail, trying to grab the dummy away. Both dogs shook the water violently from their coats, soaking Dave in the process.

"Thanks, guys! Really appreciate it," Dave laughed as they ran back toward the pond again.

His phone pinged with a text. Wiping damp hands on his shirt, he retrieved the cell from his back pants pocket. Dave read the lines from Sarah's lawyer:

State's case falling apart. Closing arguments start next week.

No words of hope or anticipation had been connected to the statements. Dave gauged whether the lawyer was trying to stay balanced and unemotional, or just not jinx the outcome.

Dave sent a silent prayer up to the clouds and shoved the phone back in his pocket without responding.

CHAPTER 9

SARAH

Nearing completion, the trial raised more questions than answers. Several weeks of arguments and heated discussions were coming to a close.

After the judge re-read the charges following closing arguments, the jury retired to deliberate behind closed doors. They had been given specific instructions on what each verdict meant, while Sarah returned to her lockup within the state's mental facilities.

The two weeks of deliberation were the longest of Sarah's life. During her wait, she had been allowed a few approved visitors—Kellee, a few of her search and rescue teammates, and some friends from the communications center. She wondered where Dave was. Why didn't he visit? Did he still care for her or had he moved on with his life? These were questions Sarah desperately needed answers to regardless of the trial outcome.

Finally, the jury reached its conclusion. Sarah was shuttled back to the courthouse for the reading of the verdict. It would be a formal setting just as the trial had been.

Overflowing, the courtroom was packed, and tension was heavy as the judge entered. The jury foreperson—an older, slight-built woman, dressed in a drab brown suit—slowly approached the bench.

"Have you reached a verdict?" the judge inquired.

"No, your honor. We have not. The jury has not been able to come to an agreement after two weeks of deliberations. We, the jury, have come to an impasse."

"Is the jury positive they cannot come to a decision? Does the jury understand the implications of what a 'No Verdict' decision will mean in this case?"

"Yes," the foreperson responded.

Motioning to both lawyers to approach the bench, the judge called the jury foreperson over. The foreperson motioned for the rest of the jury to come forward to the bench. The group disappeared through a door behind the stand into the judge's chambers.

Sarah could barely maintain herself. Her mind raced in overdrive. Voices from the gallery began at a whisper, but the decibels quickly rose. Soon the courtroom was awash in conversation. Sarah continued to stare straight ahead at the door where judge, jury and both lawyers had disappeared.

Several minutes later, the jury members filed in and took their appropriate positions. The conversation quickly died down when the judge returned to the bench. Both lawyers quietly returned to their tables where they continued to stand. Elliot motioned for Sarah to rise as well.

Still standing, the judge waited for the noise in the courtroom to dissipate. "Due to the complications of a No Verdict delivered by the jury, this trial is now considered a mistrial." The judge took his seat with his last statement, and the jury, lawyers and Sarah followed suit.

Gasps resounded from courtroom spectators. News reporters pulled phones and tablets from their bags and typed furiously.

Sarah felt the floor give way. She couldn't catch her breath. Grabbing the chair rails for support, she tried to steady herself. *Is this really happening?* For the first time since she had been moved from the hospital to lockdown in the psych ward, she felt a wave of hopefulness.

The judged banged his gavel several times to regain control. "Please rise again," he ordered. With a furrowed brow he asked the prosecutor if any new discovery information had appeared to present to the court.

The prosecutor hung his head. "Not at this time, your honor."

"On that note, I declare this trial of the State of Pennsylvania vs. Sarah Gavin as a mistrial." The judge turned and spoke directly to the prosecutor, "The state has five years to return with new evidence." He then turned toward Sarah and her lawyer. "At this time," he locked eyes with Sarah and continued, "this means you are free to go and live your life as you see fit until, if ever, another trial date is set."

Sarah stood, discomfort radiating across her back and down her leg. The soreness made her think of that day, many months ago when she'd woken up in the hospital terrified. The pain somehow kept her grounded and in the moment.

Her lawyer gave her a quick hug. "We need to take you out the back way," Elliot whispered in her ear. "The media is going to have a field day with this."

Sarah didn't care. Silent tears fell as she realized she had been given a second chance. She wasn't sure why, but now, it didn't matter.

One person continued to claim her thoughts. She wondered if he still cared for her and where he had been these past several weeks. Sarah knew how difficult the situation had probably been for him, with his background in law enforcement, but she still clung to a sliver of hope.

CHAPTER 10

DAVE

Dave had distanced himself purposely from Sarah during the trial for professional reasons, but personally, he needed to be there for the reading of the verdict. Quietly sneaking into the back of the courtroom, he'd made it just in time to watch the proceedings and hear the verdict read.

Dave wiped sweaty palms along his jeans. Bouncing from foot to foot, he couldn't stay still. Impatient, he slipped out through the heavy courtroom doors and into the lobby. Pausing in the main hall of the old building, he scrutinized the activity. Several cameramen and newspaper reporters—beyond the local channels—stood rigid in the narrow space, making Dave picture lions poised for the kill. *What a clusterfuck.*

A subtle vibration emitted from his phone as he contemplated where he should go next. "Back entrance," was all the message stated from Sarah's lawyer. *Short and to the point as usual.*

Dave slipped the phone back in his pocket without replying, then headed toward the rear of the building where his vehicle was already parked. He needed to retrieve a couple items.

Making his way to his vehicle, Dave could hear Gunner and Sam barking. The car's interior was getting warm. Even with the windows down, they were protesting. Spring brought the warmer weather and humidity. The sun was reaching its highest point in the sky. He had scored a parking place under a large maple tree beginning to fill out with neon green leaves. It provided some shade for the dogs but apparently not enough.

Dave found a covered spot and sat down on the cool stone steps behind the old courthouse. Scratching each dog behind the ears, they leaned into Dave's body. Both appeared to be tense, picking up on Dave's elevated emotions.

Anxious and excited, he was full of the unknown that fell between him and Sarah. A nervousness about the situation plagued him.

Suddenly, Dave witnessed the dogs become very still and focused. Their eyes glued to the back of the building. *How do they know? Intuition? Extra sensitive scenting ability*? Dave looked from the dogs to the back door. Gunner quivered. Low, meager whines escaped each dog.

As Sarah emerged, Dave stood and smiled. He watched her step out of the courthouse from fugitive to freedom. Relief replaced his concern.

Gunner and Sam shifted their noses skyward reading the air. Both dogs turned their heads simultaneously in the direction as the breeze rolled down the marble steps. Lunging at the end of their leashes, they pulled Dave off balance.

Standing at the landing, with no one else nearby, Sarah looked down the steps to Dave. A broad smile graced her face. Releasing the leather leashes, he set the two German Shepherds free. "Go get her, guys."

Sarah fell to her knees embracing the over-zealous animals as they scrambled up the steps to meet her. Pain seared through her thigh, but she was overcome with emotion. Nothing else mattered. Barking and whining, the dogs slobbered her with wet kisses. Turning in tight circles, ears pinned back in elation, the dogs tucked their tails and jumped up, knocking into her hard. Pure chaotic bliss.

After the dogs settled down a notch and were under control, Sarah walked to Dave. She reached out to him. Arms open wide, he pulled Sarah into him, embracing her wholeheartedly. His body completely engulfed her.

Melting into his large muscular frame, she looked up to face him. "I can't believe you're here. I can't believe I'm here." Tears began to fall freely. Months of pent up emotions flooded out.

Shaking, Dave held onto her.

"Where do I go now?" Sarah spoke between sobs.

"It's okay, we got this," Dave whispered as he buried his face in her feral, penny-colored hair. Pressing several curls behind her delicate ears, he whispered over and over it was okay. He wanted her to let it out, let it all go.

Leaning back, she looked up at Dave. She studied him for a moment, looking deep into his dark eyes. "*We* got this? Is there even a *we* anymore?" Sarah asked. "I've lost almost everything." The tears launched again.

Dave knew the weight of the world bore down on Sarah as the realization of her situation materialized. He let her cling tight to him.

Biting her lip, Sarah shuddered. "I don't even have a home to go home to," she asserted. Sarah's eyes filled with tears once again.

Dave cupped her face in his strong hands. The smoothness of her soft skin mollified the roughness of his worn ones.

"Where've you been? Why haven't I seen you?" Sarah asked. She held her face against his hands. Closing her damp eyes, she pressed her face deeper into them. Finally, opening her eyes, she looked up into his. "What am I going to do now?"

"I got this, Sarah," he replied. "I have a plan. You need to believe in me. You have to trust in us."

Dave put his hand out to take one of the dogs' leashes from her.

Sarah begrudgingly let him take Sam and followed him down the weathered steps. Dave knew she had much to think about. She would need time to sort everything out.

The dogs were lean and fit, but with the double coats German Shepherds carried, direct sunlight from the asphalt roadway heated them quickly. "It's getting kind of warm out here for these guys," Sarah broke the silence. "We really should get them in some shade."

Both dogs panted, tongues hanging low as they walked obediently next to Sarah and Dave.

"Maybe we can take them somewhere to swim and cool off," Dave offered.

"Can we grab a bite to eat on the way?" Sarah asked, acknowledging her appetite was back. She had lost a considerable amount of weight, mainly muscle since her injury and being confined.

"I know the perfect place. We'll pick up something on the way. We can let the dogs swim as we eat and discuss our future," Dave offered.

Sarah smiled. He smiled back. He wasn't sure how it would all play out. He wanted their relationship to be open, upfront and honest. Dave needed to make sure this was what she wanted and eventually he knew everything would be okay. *But really, who knew what their future would hold?*

CHAPTER 11

SARAH

Sarah allowed Dave to take the lead. They loaded the dogs into his Ford Explorer. *I wonder where Bella is?* He only had two crates in the back of the vehicle, and no bloodhound equipment, search gear, or police paraphernalia. No normal, greasy smell bloodhounds were so well known for...

Then she noticed the SUV had Virginia license plates. Had he moved? *Does he still care for me? Even after he realizes what Eva did?*

Sarah closed her eyes. Contemplation cut deep into her soul. Inhaling sharply, she realized if she persisted to press herself mentally, she would end up hyperventilating and with a migraine.

They climbed into the front and Sarah realigned her leather bucket seat as well as her frame of mind. She stared out the window as Dave pulled away from the curb. Turning a few times in their crates before finally settling, both dogs lay down with a heavy thud.

"Good job, guys," Dave called to Gunner and Sam as he looked at them in the rearview mirror.

Sarah flinched. These were her dogs, not his. *Or were they?*

Dave glanced over at her. "Sorry, it's a habit. I've talked to them a lot lately."

Sarah stared out the passenger side window, not wanting to look at Dave. She should feel grateful he cared for them so much. But it still hurt.

"They're still your dogs," he said, as if reading her mind. "Gunner and Sam only put up with me because I was the one feeding them. Don't think you can be so easily replaced."

Sucking in her lower lip, she bit down hard. Maybe the physical pain would somehow stop the emotional one.

So out of place, so out of control. She had no idea where she belonged or what she was supposed to be doing, a feeling of detached buoyancy. "I've lost so much, almost everything, including time," she squeaked out. "I don't have a clue what to do. What life even holds for me now. Where do I go from here?"

Dave reached out and placed one hand over hers while negotiating through congested city streets. "Look at me, Sarah."

Sarah turned to face him as he drove along. She pushed a few stray curls away that hung in her eyes. Humid air had caused them to escape in every direction, which only made her feel even more out of control.

"We're in this together. I'll tell you a million times if you want me to. Whatever you need to do, I will be here to support you. Understand?"

Sarah only nodded.

"So much has happened with me as well over the past several months," Dave continued. "There's so much we need to talk about. Things I need to catch you up on."

"It's all overwhelming right now. I feel disconnected from everything, everyone,"

"Let things work out. Just let the pieces fall into place. Try not to worry about everything," Dave countered.

"It's hard not to think or worry about the future. About where I fit into the picture or what will become of me and my life."

Dave's jaw tightened.

"*Our* life," Sarah said, barely audible, still not completely convinced.

She had reservations. Dave didn't truly understand what he'd gotten involved with. Deep down within, she considered Eva gone. She believed that part of her had died when Sarah took the bullet. But still, the deeds had been done and carried out with Sarah's own two hands.

"Things will work out. Just give it time," Dave repeated.

Maybe he was right. She was free, at least for the time being. The state prosecutor had no clue if they were going to push for a second trial. New evidence would have to be found and presented. Other than being available for the state's ongoing internal investigation into her foster home, she was free to go and do as she pleased with her life.

Eventually, she would have to come back for interviews, depositions, and to testify to the abuse she and the others in her foster home had suffered. She would also have to testify on what could've happened to several of the children who disappeared from her foster home. For now, she was free to move on and had no obligations or restrictions on where she could go or what she could do.

Changing gears, she said, "I'm dying for a huge, greasy hamburger and fries. The food on the inside was pretty dreadful." She smiled at him as she used her shirt to wipe her nose and tears from her face.

"I know the best place to pick up a heart attack on a bun," Dave replied with a smile.

She knew he liked to cook healthy foods, and he worked out on a consistent basis. Sarah liked junk food and her La-Z Boy recliner. But she also used to like to run—something she hoped to be able to do again when her back and hip fully healed.

With their takeout and water bottles, the foursome headed to a small picnic area along the western bank of the Susquehanna River, just outside the city. A safe, shallow area extended several meters out into the river and ran parallel along the picnic area. They could sit at a table and eat while the dogs romped and cooled off in the water.

For the moment, neither dog was ready to leave Sarah's side. They both leaned into her body, making sure they were touching her, connecting with her in some way.

"So, a lot has happened," Dave started. "Nothing like what you've endured over this past year, or the years prior, but I've taken a different and unexpected path."

"Because of me." Sarah stood. The dogs were making her hot, leaning against her. She moved away and sat on top of a worn picnic table, resting her feet on the bench. The dogs followed and parked in front of her again, this time begging for food. She tossed fries intermittently to each dog.

Gunner tried to keep his rear end on the ground in a sit, but continued to offer up other behaviors and would lie down, only to pop right back up into a sitting or standing position. Sam sat, but lifted one front paw and then the other.

"What's this?" Sarah asked with a smile. She hadn't taught her dogs to shake.

"Oh sorry," Dave said sheepishly, "I tried to teach them some tricks when they were rooming with me. Sam was an astute student and learned how to shake. Now Gunner on the other hand, he wouldn't have any of it."

"Good boy, Gunner! Way to stick to your guns and stay true to the serious working canine you are." Sarah stepped down from the picnic table and wrapped the dog in a quick hug. "Shame on you, Sam, for giving in!" Sarah teased as she took Sam's paw in her hand and lightly shook it, rewarding him with a fry. "I'm sorry. I cut you off," Sarah apologized to Dave. "I can't help but feel responsible for your decisions, for getting mixed up with me."

"Stop taking the blame for me, for us, okay? I'm a grown-ass adult. I have a choice in this matter, and I chose you. I believe in you, and I want us to have some kind of life together. Any kind of life together..." Dave trailed off.

"Why would you want to be tangled up with me?" *After everything Eva did?* "I appreciate what you've done for me. For Gunner and Sam. For us. I care for you deeply, but it's going to take time to unravel everything I've been through. Hell, my body is barely healed."

Dave stared off into the distance. He had been the one who had shot her, almost causing her death. Even though his action had been justified, he still carried the guilt.

"I don't blame you," Sarah backpedaled. "I only meant to say, I have a lot of sorting out to do. Layers of baggage just to find myself. And that's not all." Sarah's voice quivered as it caught in the back of her throat, "I don't know what you expect out of life, but I'll never be able to conceive or carry a baby to term again." Sarah looked down, memories of backroom botched abortions came flooding back. Tears welled behind red rimmed, swollen eyes. "I... I just want you to know everything up front."

She watched as Dave processed what she had just said. He would want children someday, and she wanted to make sure he fully understood what a life with her might mean. He looked away from her for a moment.

"It's fine," Dave responded. "I'm good with everything you're saying. It'll take time for you to process everything... You don't owe me anything either. It's not the type of foundation for a relationship I want to build on. I accept you fully, who you are... if you fully accept me for who I am."

"That's only fair. So where do we begin again? Where do we go from here, from this starting point? I need to know what's going on with you, your plans." Sarah took a step back. Closing her eyes, she took a deep breath trying to control her emotions. She opened her eyes facing Dave. "You didn't give me much detail in the letters you sent. Where is Bella? Your patrol vehicle? And why are you driving an SUV with Virginia tags?"

CHAPTER 12

DAVE

Dave looked beyond Sarah, crossing his arms over his chest. He'd known the question was inevitable. "I had to resign. At least I was given that option. It could've been worse."

"Resign as a trooper? Why?"

"They believed I'd tampered with information about you and your case. That I'd withheld important facts."

"You didn't, did you?"

"Yes and no." Dave hesitated. "I found information linking you to the foster home when I was researching the second victim." He skipped the name, knowing what the monster meant to Sarah. "I stumbled across more than I'd bargained for."

"Like what?" Her jaw tightened.

"Nothing that matters now. Nothing that changes how I feel about you and our relationship."

"I want to know," she insisted.

Dave looked out across the river. It had meant something to him at the time and he had felt betrayed. But with time to sort it out... he was positive Sarah had wanted to keep her ties from the past, in the past.

"You and the victims shared an address years ago. You never let on that you were familiar with any of them."

Faced flushed, she looked away. "I never told you I didn't know them either," Sarah shot back.

"I understand you didn't want anyone knowing your history. But that was a huge piece of information you withheld from me, from the lieutenant running the searches, from everyone."

Dave closed his eyes and took a deep breath to maintain his composure. He was okay with it now, but at the time he hadn't been.

"When I first found the information, I panicked." Taking a step closer, Dave reached out and lightly brushed Sarah's cheek with his hand. He shifted his weight back on his heels, but looked her squarely in the eyes. "I believed you might be in danger. I kept trying to call you, to get ahold of you, but you never picked up. I wanted you to explain it first, before I told the lieutenant. But then everything turned into a big mess, and I got caught in the crossfire."

"We both got caught in the crossfire," Sarah returned in a whisper.

Stepping down from the picnic table, her cheeks were still flushed, her jaw set defensively. She walked over to the parking lot and retrieved a ball from the car, then headed toward the water's edge with the dogs.

Dave trailed several steps behind, giving her space to digest what he was telling her. He stood back and watched as Sarah interacted with the dogs.

She pitched the ball into the shallows of the river, taking a few steps backwards as both dogs took off, splash-landing in the water. It was a competition as usual between Sam and Gunner to see who could win the toy.

Slowly, the faraway look in her eyes dissipated. Her rigid stance eased as she played with the dogs. Visibly relaxing, she smiled at their water romp.

After several minutes, Sarah called, "Come on in, guys! Game over!"

Sam obliged by dropping the ball at her feet and wagging his wet tail all over her. It took more convincing to get Gunner out, but he finally relented and both dogs settled down along the shoreline to rest.

Dave decided the timing was right. He followed her to the riverbank and said, "The state took Bella after the shooting and reassigned her to another canine handler. I was immediately placed on admin duty..." His voice faltered. Bella had not only been his partner, she had also been his best buddy and he missed everything about her.

Sarah faced Dave, tears beginning to form in her already swollen eyes. "I'm... I'm so sorry. I didn't even think about what would happen to you."

"No one knew what would happen once the dust settled. I don't blame you for me losing Bella. Or my position with the state," he added.

"But what about your family? Your mom and dad? What do they think of all this? How do they feel about you being involved with an indicted murderer?"

She'd finally said it.

Dave got the impression she didn't want to leave any skeletons in the closet, no stone left unturned. They both appeared to be on the same page, wanting everything out on the table.

"To be honest, they are not happy with me, but I have been completely up front and truthful with my parents and the rest of my family. Anyone who mattered, at least. It's up to them to come to terms with my decision. It's our life, Sarah, not theirs."

Sarah stared out across the river and stifled a cry with the back of her hand.

Encircling her shoulders, Dave could feel the rigidness of her muscles. "Look at me, Sarah."

She leaned her head back, but wouldn't meet his gaze.

"Like I said earlier, everything will fall into place."

They stood on a small outcropping of rocks beside the river. Relieved to have gotten that out of the way, Dave hesitated before springing his latest information. He didn't want to lose her again.

"I start a new position in Virginia next week as a deputy for the Nelson County Sheriff's Department. It's right outside of Charlottesville." He felt Sarah tense up once again. "We have a place there, just on the other side of the city limits. The area's intoxicating," he said. "Plenty of room for Gunner and Sam and more. I think you'll love it." Dave smiled as he pictured the area. His hands flew through the air describing the mountains and terrain. His mood lightened.

"Charlottesville?" Sarah finally asked. "We?"

He watched her expression morph as the full weight of the location hit Sarah.

"But that's where..."

"Yes," Dave affirmed. "That may have played a part in my decision, but it wasn't the only reason."

Dave knew Charlottesville was the only link Sarah had to where her daughter may have been taken as a newborn so many years ago. *I hope that's not the only element that will convince her.*

"Yes, that's the place. Will you come with me? We can start a new chapter. I'll give you as much time and space as you need. You'll have your own room. I'm willing to wait until you're ready."

Sarah allowed Dave to pull her into his arms. Her breathing slowed, became more even.

"I know this is a lot to take in all at once. So many changes. But I care for you with my whole heart."

Sarah leaned back and looked directly into his eyes. The sun reflected from her face and hair, showing off her high cheekbones and dimples. A hint of freckles playfully splashed across her nose.

Dave smiled down at her. She was so beautiful. Mesmerizing. There was a lure to her which he couldn't fend off. A pull so intense he couldn't, or didn't want to fight. Even after all she had been through, her green eyes regained their sparkle and that was one of the qualities Dave loved best about her.

He sensed she was looking deep within him, searching his soul. Sarah had never had family and few close, stable relationships. Would she allow another person close to her heart, especially with her fractured past? He hoped she was ready to take a chance. A chance on him and a new life.

Sarah gave a timid smile. She closed her eyes and let her full weight lean into him. Dave could feel the rhythm of her breathing steady. He closed his eyes and just held onto her.

Without looking up, Sarah whispered, "So when do we leave for Virginia?"

CHAPTER 13

ASHLEY

Used up, her body on fire, Ashley lay in the cubby hell hole. The men had deposited her there once they had finished with her. Shrouded in darkness, she shivered and pulled a threadbare quilt over her abused body. Curling up in a fetal position, she realized she wasn't hungry anymore.

The tiny slice of living space she occupied was one among several she shared with other captives in the double-wide trailer. Each small, sectioned-off cubby housed an imprisoned prostitute and contained a dirty twin-sized mattress positioned on the floor. A small end table or wooden crate sat beside it and held their few belongings—a defined boundary of the victim's precarious life.

The cubbies were where they serviced the men who paid for sex. Most of them were littered with used condoms, syringes, and spent needles, depending on the *guest's* needs. Clientele varied. The bulk of the customers were immigrants who arrived together. Far from their families, they came to blow a portion of their weekly paycheck for a night of partying, sex, and drugs.

Others were lower-class locals, but the girls also catered to a few higher-dollar clients, who earned the owners of the compound more money—as well as protection from the law. These clients rated special rooms in the main house.

Several of Ashley's customers wore wedding bands. Men who couldn't fulfill their needs within their own homes or were looking for a different kind of gratification. She was sure their partners had no idea, or if they did, they didn't care anymore.

A sort of relief washed over Ashley, aware her time in the torture box had finally been satisfied, and she was now back in an area where other women were housed. And she understood what to expect from her captors. Thankful for some unknown, absurd reason.

Exhausted and defeated, she closed her eyes and tried to make the most of the quiet moment and rest. She was sure she was suffering from a host of STDs because a fever had spiked. She had been violated in so many ways, she couldn't remember.

Soft cries crept through the hollow dividers, muffled moans escaping. The trailer shuddered. Harsh vibrations rocked the unit in response to someone being handled roughly. *Treated like a piece of trash, used up and thrown away. Disposable.* Empathy for the fellow captive filled her heart while determination filled her mind. She silently let the tears fall, shedding them for the captive as well. *Who is it this time?*

Even though the prisoners were not allowed to associate with each other, the predators who operated the compound couldn't keep track of every detail, every hour, and she'd been able to befriend a few of the girls. They had their ways of leaving messages for one another or quick exchanges when passing in the hall. Frightened of getting caught, they kept communications to a minimum.

Turning over, she pulled the tattered cover over her head to block out the sounds. Block out the world. She placed her right hand across her heart and touched the raised inked outline along her breast. A memory from a happier time a few years ago brought a smile to her face momentarily. She'd hoped it would bring her luck.

Ashley needed a strategy. An escape plan. It seemed like a mammoth task, too much to think about. It would have to wait. Right now, she was weak and closed her eyes. Rest and healing were what she needed first.

She recognized the sharp creak of the trailer door opening. Ashley froze. A sharp pain pierced her head as she lay frozen in fear. Holding her breath, she listened. Someone walked to the front of the trailer, inside the kitchen. Lights flickered on. A metal container clanked down hard on the counter, the contents jostled within—a sound she recognized. *"The Doctor,"* as he was referred to. *Please, please, please no*, she pleaded in frantic silence.

Rustling through the container, he searched for something. Footsteps echoed on the tile as he headed down the narrow hall in her direction. She prayed he would pass her by.

Although he often brought relief to captives who suffered from diseases, his main job was to keep them in an altered state. She could use something for her infected genitals, but she worried he would also administer a cocktail of mind-altering drugs. She'd rather suffer through the painful burning.

He stopped at the cubby before hers. The young girl in the next room greeted the doctor in a slur, "Heyyyyyaaa."

"Hold out your arm," he demanded.

"Stopppp. You're hurting me," the girl responded in a robotic voice.

"Can't find a clean goddamn place on you. All your damn veins are collapsed in both arms," he huffed. "Turn over. I need to check the back of your legs," he demanded in a thick accent.

The girl in the next cubby knocked against the thin wall as she flopped over on her stomach.

"There, perfect," he stated after a few minutes.

Ashley was next and lay in fear. Pretending she was asleep, she covered herself with the patch of fraying quilt. He stopped at her door and stood for a few moments before moving past her to the next cubby. She wasn't quite sure why he passed her by. Maybe he knew she had just gotten back from her punishment and wasn't sure what drugs she had been subjected to. Whatever the reason, she prayed he would finish with the other girls and leave soon.

The door to the trailer swung open again, hitting the wall with a loud thud. Ashley reacted with a quick jolt.

Heavy footsteps crossed into the kitchen where the doctor was busy shuffling through his medic box again. "There you are," the doctor said to whoever had just walked in. "I might need you to restrain one of the subjects."

Ashley shuddered in fear.

The Disposer, a man who never spoke, had joined the doctor. He'd been the one who was responsible for her and her punishment when she had gotten caught after her escape attempt. The other captives whispered stories, bits and pieces here and there, indicating he rid the compound of older, unwanted prostitutes or problems, thus earning him his nickname. Ashley tensed. The doctor moved through the tight maze of halls with the other man following.

The pair approached a newer captive who hadn't learned to cooperate yet. The Disposer held her down as the doctor shot her up with god-knows-what.

Overdoses were a weekly occurrence within the compound, but since the new opiate antidote became available, fewer captives died. That resulted in less overall loss for the compound's bottom line.

Hearing the doctor close his tackle box and the door slam shut, Ashley released a deep breath. Time to plan another escape. She had memorized the layout of the compound. She knew the normal schedule, the busy times and the lax times of the week. But she knew they'd be watching her.

She wouldn't befriend anyone this time, but go it alone. Last time, inviting someone to split with her did nothing but get her in trouble.

CHAPTER 14

SARAH

Packing up what few belongings she had left to her name in a rented trailer, Sarah stifled a laugh. A mural on the side of the truck portrayed a large man balancing the earth on his backbone—the condemned Atlas destined by Zeus to hold up the heavens on his hind side. Sarah identified with the heaviness.

With the trailer hitched and dogs loaded, Dave and Sarah started goodbyes to friends. Sarah clung to Kellee, unwilling to let go after their recent restraints and limited visits, but it was time to leave.

Releasing her grip, Sarah held Kellee at arm's length.

"Stop worrying, this isn't the end," Kellee voiced.

"I'm not sure about all of this," Sarah answered.

"It'll be okay.... You'll be okay," Kellee responded in a calm, but stern voice.

Sarah conjured up a nervous smile. "I'm scared, but I'm also excited."

"You're only four hours away. Don't stress so much," Kellee lectured. "I'm sure we'll see each other soon again."

"You promise?" Sarah asked.

"Yes. I've also been checking out the search-and-rescue teams in your area. When I find a decent, solid canine team who might give you a chance, I'll send you information. You should be settled in by then."

Maybe by the time I'm healed as well, Sarah thought, as the dull pain from her injured hip reminded her she still wasn't ready to return to any heavy type of physical activity.

"Wouldn't that be great? It's been difficult not training and working the dogs. But I'm not sure Virginia will accept me—with my history."

"You were indicted, not convicted. There's a difference."

"Another option would be to train Gunner and Sam exclusively on human remains," Dave piped in. "You wouldn't need a team. You could freelance with your dogs, once you got in good with a few agencies in the area."

Sarah considered the option. "Maybe, but I really like the camaraderie of a team and working other teammates' dogs. You learn so much. It's all about the dogs." It would be difficult to get accepted on a team, or even work her dogs again on deployments. Virginia required background checks, and she didn't think she would pass one. Most everyone who worked dogs knew who she was, her history anyway. She doubted another handler would even want to work with her.

"Just a suggestion," Dave reminded. "You don't actually have any convictions."

Kellee leaned in close to Sarah and whispered, "Dave's a good man. Trust him. The dogs do. Give him a chance."

A cold sweat clung to the back of Sarah's neck. It worked its way down her spine. She was moving away from the only place she had ever known. The only people she'd ever known. Struggling to stay strong on the outside, she squared her shoulders. On the inside, she was in complete shambles. *Look on the positive side. What could go wrong? What could possibly be worse than growing up in the foster home? AND getting shot and put on trial for multiple murders?*

"Time to get a move on, Sarah. Daylight's burning. I'd like to get there early enough to show you around while it's still light out."

Sarah topped off the dogs' hanging water buckets in the traveling crates and gave each a cow hoof to gnaw for the trip. She'd been surprised to learn that hoof offered some beneficial elements. *Hopefully, that will keep them busy for the drive.*

"Daylight's burning, woman!" Dave teased again. Jingling the keys, he shifted his weight from one foot to the other, eager to get on the road. "I want to make it to the foothills before the sun begins setting. I can't wait for you to see how breathtaking the area is."

Sarah knew he was excited that the first portion of their plans were beginning to take shape. She could tell he was also excited to show her what he was calling "hillbilly heaven."

His excitement was starting to rub off on her. She had never traveled, never visited other areas. It was overwhelming to her on so many levels.

"Okay, I've been ready," Sarah smirked. "Are you finally done gabbing? I'm tired of waiting!" she sparred back. It helped lighten her heavy heart.

"Me?" Dave returned a smile.

Making one last goodbye, they settled into the vehicle. Dave negotiated turning the SUV with the attached trailer. Sarah tuned in a decent radio station. She pulled out a Virginia map to study as they made their way south. She wanted to learn more about where they were going, the logistics of her new area, and what the surrounding terrain was like.

"I promise you're going to love the Charlottesville area. The mountains, the early summer colors. Spectacular sunrises and sunsets alone will make you fall in love with the area. And the people. They're a hard-working, religious bunch, but they're also the giving, neighborly type who go out of their way to help you." His energy was infectious.

"Well, let's hope they're still that way when they figure out where I'm from and who I am," Sarah spoke. Silently promising to give them and this new life a fighting chance, she worried how the neighbors would perceive her.

"Things will work out. Have faith."

Sarah determined to put her past behind her. Leave it in Pennsylvania and set her sights on the future. *What was there to lose?*

CHAPTER 15

ASHLEY

Opening her eyes to darkness, Ashley lay quiet, attentive to her surroundings. Crickets chirped. Mosquitoes droned. The insects could be easily heard through the thin, manufactured walls. She lay still, continuing to listen for a long stretch of time.

Yawning, she checked the small digital clock sitting on the floor beside her mattress. Blazing numbers declared the early morning hour boldly in red: 2:47 A.M. *Ready?* Ashley silently willed herself to go through with it. She had backed out several times already.

She rolled over on her side and winced. The punishment was still fresh in her mind and on her body from the last escape attempt. No telling what would happen this time if they caught her. Stories had drifted through the compound about previous runners and their punishments. Some had paid with their lives. The specter of The Disposer loomed over her. *I just won't get caught this time, that's all.*

Easing herself up from the floor, she moved in cautious steps. She pulled on a red halter top and matching red spandex shorts. Although small, it was one of her only outfits that wasn't dirty or in tatters. She tucked two crumpled, one-dollar bills in her bra. The only money she had, it had been a tip from a client.

She smiled to herself thinking of the irony. The money had been hidden in a hole in the side of the mattress—the same hole she had been hiding pills and other drugs they had given her. Antidepressants, anxiety drugs, recreational drugs... a cocktail of everything from Rohypnol and Ativan to cocaine and heroin.

Ashley moved carefully through the house trailer. In stocking feet, she headed toward the back door paying close attention to her intended path.

Stopping briefly to peer out a side window, it offered a broad view of the entire compound. She looked across the way to the main house and couldn't make out any lights burning inside. Only the yellowed front porch light was lit. The hound dogs tied to the porch posts were curled up, asleep. No one sat with them... *Please stay that way.*

Standing inside the back door she stalled, making sure no one was stirring. Turning the knob, she pulled the door open just wide enough to slip through. Ashley hurried down the few steps to the ground, rushing to the edge of the yard.

With caution, she negotiated the compound area she had committed to memory. Treading along the back fence that lined the property, she followed the tall wooden structure enclosing the property. Reaching the rotted-out area of the fence, she bent down and wiggled herself through the opening.

Ashley's long blonde hair caught in a crack of the fence. She managed to free it with a quick yank, leaving behind a few strands. Standing up, she brushed herself off, slipped her flats over her damp socks, and headed in the direction where she was sure a highway would be.

With renewed determination, she started down the mountainside. No moon hung out to guide her; cloud cover hugged the mountain. Darkness embraced her as she made her way through the rough terrain.

What was that? She paused to listen.

Behind her through the woods, she heard a sound above the pounding in her ears. There, again. She heard something and swiveled around, facing the direction she had come. Frozen in place, she listened. Several heartbeats later, a long, deep howl sliced through the night. Several hounds chimed in, echoing throughout the compound. Sucking in a sharp breath, Ashley tried to steady herself but panic set in. Terror swept through her. *They already know I'm gone!*

Move, dammit, move! she told her shaky limbs.

She tore down the mountainside blindly. The cheap flats broke free from her feet. Shale sliced through the soles of her feet leaving a bloody trail. Tree limbs smacked her, raising angry welts. Thorns from new underbrush dug into her skin and clothes. She ran oblivious to the pain. Pushing her body hard she had to continue down the mountain as fast as she could.

Swallowing gulps of air, her sides heaved and her lungs burned. Turning her head, she strained to listen for her captors. Somewhere in the dark abyss behind her, they were hard on her trail. Losing her balance, she stumbled over a downed log and let out a muffled gasp. Landing with a heavy thud, her leg twisted beneath her. She heard the crack. A rush of intense pain burst from her leg. *No, no, no, no!*

She held her breath, lying as quietly as possible. Tears streamed down her face. *Maybe, I lost them.* Then she heard her predators through the thick night air. The baying of the hounds traveled eerily across the mountainside. The men, the crack of branches, flashlight beams shone in her direction.

Pulling herself upright, the pain from her injured leg stole what breath she had left. She leaned against a tree and tried to regain her bearings. She set off, dragging her leg the rest of the way down the incline. Behind her, the men closed the distance. Hyperventilating, capillaries ruptured, blood ran from her nose. She could taste the metallic liquid as it seeped into her mouth. *Why? Why is this happening?*

Trees thinned out as the mountainside gave way to an even slope. As the ground leveled out, it was easier to maneuver her injured leg. Arriving at a paved road, she grew positive she would succeed. Someone would come along. She prayed hard to a God she never knew as she hauled her injured limb along the asphalt.

The road came to a bridge which spanned a vast, deep gorge. Ashley could hear the rush of angry white water below. She'd dragged herself halfway across when the men spilled out of the woods. Oncoming car lights cut through the darkness in front of her. A glimmer of hope. *Maybe I'll make it out this time!* Praying, she pulled herself across the metal overpass toward the oncoming headlights.

CHAPTER 16

SARAH

Grumbling, Sarah rolled over and buried her face in the pillow. Still twilight, Dave's showering had woken her. *Early shift.* The dogs heard her move and prodded her with their cold wet noses. "Okay, okay." Sarah stretched, then stood to make her way to the kitchen. "Come on, guys."

The dogs followed her to the side door where she let them out.

"You didn't have to get up," Dave said as he entered.

"Right," she smiled. "Like those two are going to sleep after one of us is up and moving." Opening the door, both dogs busted back inside excited, hungry for breakfast.

"Sorry," Dave offered sheepishly. "But thank you for getting up and making breakfast. What're your plans today? Will you be able to work on the stalls in the barn?"

"Not exactly a subtle hint there, Dave. I'll finish emptying out the stalls today. Don't understand the rush, that's all."

"No rush, really, just want to get it done." David downed a piece of toast and topped off his travel mug. "Gotta go," he said, still chewing. He leaned down and gave Sarah a peck on the forehead. "I'll stop by at lunch if it's slow," he promised as he headed out the door.

Sarah's face stiffened as she stood up from the table. Shifting her weight to her better leg, she took a deep breath and followed Dave to the front door. Leaning against the door jamb, she watched him climb into the county cruiser. Soft hues broke across the sky, barely illuminating the mountain ridgeline as Dave drove out the rutted lane.

Raising her hand in a half-hearted send-off, she missed him already. "Bye," she whispered in a faint breath.

Dave's position with the sheriff's department took him away for long hours. As one of the most recent hires, he worked shifts during the normal work week as well as some weekends and nights, but he was never far from their small farm and cabin. He patrolled in and around their property and took the opportunity to stop in and check on Sarah during breaks.

The property needed upkeep and repair. Sarah busied herself during the day working on projects in the cabin and around the farm. She had more than enough to do. Between the lawn and garden work and the barn repairs and clean-up, she spent a good deal of time in the fresh air. Gunner and Sam reveled in the large outdoor area and followed her as she went about her work. The environment and work had become Sarah's therapy for the time being.

Dressed and ready to head out, Sarah opened the side door once again. Sam and Gunner bolted through first. She followed, smiling at their antics as they raced across the yard.

The trio found time to hike around the farm and swim in the pond when Sarah decided she'd had enough and needed a break. She was still limited to how much activity she could handle due to the injury to her hip and left leg, but she slowly grew stronger and increased her distances daily.

She wasn't sure if she would ever be physically strong enough to handle working her dogs on a large-scale wilderness search again. The possibility weighed heavy on her mind. Dave kept telling her to take her time, she was making progress. He advised her not to push too hard, it takes time to let your body fully heal. He was only a few years older than her, but in many ways, much more mature. And she was thankful for that. She trusted his judgment, most of the time.

Stopping to pry open the rusted latch to the front paddock, she looked back over her shoulder at the cabin, admiring the setting.

Nestled between mountains, it appeared serene; tranquil. The image brought a peacefulness to her soul.

Years ago, the property had been a working cattle farm. Portions of it had been sold off and what remained was the carriage house—the two-bedroom cabin they were living in—the barn, some other out buildings on ten acres bordering a small running creek to the east, forest on two other sides, and a road directly in front of the farm.

Sarah let out a sigh as she entered the barn. The old structure was made of oak boards on a foundation of fieldstone, set just below the cabin on a knoll overlooking the pasture fields. There were a handful of livestock stalls in its interior, a huge hayloft, and a large loafing shed jutting off the back side that had been used for cattle. The entire structure was solidly built, and the old locust beams making up the frame were still in good shape, but some of the tin roofing had rusted through and a few of the wooden planks on the sides had rotted.

Dave had been stubborn about getting the barn in shape. He brought in roofers to repair the topside while he and Sarah spent several days working to repair rotted out portions of the exterior walls. Sarah took a few days and cleaned out the interior of the structure as well while Dave was on shift.

Why was he so focused on this project? There are still more important things to do like fencing the yard for the dogs! She knew it made Dave happy to spend time working on the barn and the weather had been cooperative, so she did her part to help the progress move along. Still, it puzzled her. Sweating, Sarah pulled weathered wood boxes from an old room inside the barn, where tools and equipment had been stored from a bygone era. She piled rusting, hand-forged horseshoes, milk crates, and butchering equipment in the aisle outside the room.

Mice scrambled in all directions as their havens were rearranged. *We need a cat,* she thought in disgust after removing several additional, old junk items and spying more mice and their pinkies. She had been so focused on her task, she didn't hear the vehicles pull up.

She was in the middle of sweeping the old stone floor and pulling down cobwebs when she heard Gunner and Sam. Their barks brought her awareness to whatever had caught their attention. She stepped out of the room and heard Dave outside speaking to someone.

Walking out into the bright sunlight, she squinted, allowing her eyes to adjust. Dave stood in the barn's driveway with an older gentleman beside a heavy duty pickup truck. Hooked to the truck bed was a large, gooseneck livestock trailer.

A tall wispy man, with a deep chiseled jaw, in a worn cowboy hat stood leaning against the truck. Spurs hung off the heel of his boots. The man tipped his hat in her direction, then walked to the side of the trailer to peer in, checking on whatever was inside. His spurs clanked with every movement. "Morning, ma'am."

Sarah returned a warm smile and said hello. The trailer moved slightly as its contents shifted. A high-pitched whinny pierced the air. Large, soft brown eyes gazed out through the slats of the trailer. *What the hell?*

Sarah walked over to the rustic cowboy. "Hi, I'm Sarah. Pleased to meet you."

"Pleased to meet you as well, Sarah." The rugged old man offered his hand, and Sarah shook it. Although he grasped tenderly, she felt the strength within his leathery hands. She skimmed over his withered face that boasted a huge mustache hiding his top lip.

"Name's Jack Canton, but most folks in the area call me J.C. on good days. Not sure what they call me on a bad day." Smiling, he leaned back and took in the view of the barn and surrounding pastures. "Looks like you're fixing the old place up mighty fine," he said with deep sincerity as he scanned the cabin as well.

"Thank you. It's been a lot of muscle and elbow grease, but it's coming along," Sarah said with a hint of pride. "So, what do you have there in the trailer?" Sarah moved closer to investigate.

"Got you a surprise," Dave quipped. A wide smile swept across his face.

Sarah could tell he was trying to contain his excitement.

"What d'ya mean, you got me a surprise?"

"Seems your young man here thought horseback riding might be good for you. Gotcha a couple real nice, easy-going mounts here," J.C. announced.

"Horses? Dave? For us?" Sarah wasn't sure what to think. It had never crossed her mind to have a horse of her own. This was never on the radar. She had never ridden until the therapeutic riding she had done in the rehab program with the state. She was speechless. Sarah took a step back. It was a lot of responsibility taking care of a horse.

"I don't know the first thing about caring for horses or what to do with them. What to feed them? How to put a saddle or bridle on?" Her head was spinning.

"Ah, they're easy keepers, these guys here. Not much to it. Don't worry, I'll help you out and give you some riding lessons," J.C. replied. "I can give you some hinters on their care. Well, let's get 'em unloaded and see what you think."

Dave and J.C. went around to the back of the stock trailer and lifted the gate hitch just enough for J.C. to slip through. Dave held the door closed and waited until J.C. had both horses untied and turned around, ready to unload.

"Okay," J.C. called the go ahead, and Dave swung the gate all the way open, exposing the horses completely.

J.C. led two beautiful geldings off the trailer. Both animals stood about fifteen hands with heavy builds. The one gelding had a light, golden coat that reflected in the sun. His mate was almost black with specks of frosting across his hind end. The golden-colored horse had an overflowing mane that fell to an upright shoulder.

"Well, here ya go," J.C. called to Sarah as he handed her the lead to the golden horse.

Taking the rope, she stood back gazing at him. "He's the most beautiful creature I've ever seen!" A white blaze was painted across the front of his face, and each leg had a white stocking covering from the top of his hooves all the way up past the horse's knees. "I just don't know what to say. He's gorgeous. I'm at a loss for words."

Dave took the lead rope to the darker gelding. That horse was slightly thicker built, more muscled than the lighter colored one. The horse dropped his head nudging Dave hard in the stomach, pushing him backwards and almost knocking him down.

"Make him back up and behave. He needs to respect you and listen," J.C. firmly told Dave. "Snatch on his lead rope a little and step toward him, telling him to move away from you. He can be a little pushy and determined occasionally, but he's goodhearted and a kind mount." Dave did as he was told, and the gelding immediately backed up and stopped with all four feet square. He lowered his head and stood quietly for Dave. At least for the moment.

The horse in Sarah's care stood regally against the skyline. He held his head up as he eyed her, inspecting her in return. Sarah spoke softly, "What a good boy." She raised an open hand to his muzzle and slowly ran it across his nose and chin. "It's like velvet. What's his name?" she asked J.C.

"Oh, that one there, we just call him Sunny. He's a palomino walking horse."

"A what? I know palomino is a color, but I'm not sure what a walking horse is."

"He's what we call 'gaited.' He's real smooth to ride. Good footed and solid on the mountain trails around here. This other handsome looking gelding is what's known as a blue roan quarter horse. He's built like a truck and can handle carrying Dave on the trails. We just call him Tank." J.C. gently laid his hand along the big gelding's neck giving him a light pat.

She could tell he genuinely cared for these animals and respected them.

Sarah looked at Dave with a big grin. No wonder he was in such a hurry to clean out the barn and fix the stalls and pasture fences. She still wasn't sure about horse keeping—something completely out of her wheelhouse—but she was touched by such an extravagant gift.

"I don't know what to say. They're beautiful." With Sunny in tow, Sarah walked over to Dave and gave him a big hug. "Thank you, I love him," she whispered into Dave's neck.

"You don't need to say anything. I thought riding might help you continue healing. Thought maybe, once you know the horse and how to ride better, you might be able to train the dogs to work from horseback."

"Like search work for Gunner and Sam from the back of a horse?"

"Yeah, I've heard of it being done out west. Thought maybe we could try it."

Sarah looked over at her two large dogs. They had stayed on the fringe of where the horses and people stood discussing them.

"I'm not sure. There are mounted teams they are familiar with, but I don't know enough about riding a horse and working a dog at the same time."

"We can work on it together once you get some riding time in on Sunny. We're in no hurry. We'll get to know the horses first and build a relationship. We can go from there."

Sarah was still a little skeptical, but at the same time, she was excited about the possibility of riding the trails around their farm, further than she could hike.

"I'm sure they're in great hands." J.C. helped lead the horses to the barn with Gunner and Sam in tow.

Sarah beamed but was still having concerns she would be able to care for the horses appropriately. A small twinge of guilt pricked her as well. Was Dave just doing this out of remorse for shooting her?

CHAPTER 17

DAVE

"Graves, pick up on Line 3," crackled over the PA as Dave entered the building. *Really?* He passed by two older deputies sitting at their desks, reading newspapers. Dispatch had patched a non-emergency call straight through. He didn't care that they'd seen him coming and given him the call. What bothered him was the idea of his two co-workers sitting on their fat asses.

Weekdays were normally slow, but today was proving to be a busy one—a few domestic calls, a missing cow, and now this. He took down the caller's concerns and hung up. Grabbing his hat, he headed out to the front parking lot and climbed into his cruiser.

Dave could hear the urgency in the man's voice as they'd discussed directions. He'd wanted someone to come right away. Without a fixed address, Dave sped along the country roads to a crossroad where the caller had agreed to meet him.

He turned down a wide gravel road that eventually veered off onto a single lane dirt road. Dust flew up in a smoky plume behind his vehicle, causing a huge cloud to hang in the already warm morning air. Spotting a man sitting on a tailgate of a pickup truck, he slowed and came to a stop. He rolled down his window as the man approached the cruiser.

"Hey there, deputy. Glad you could make it out here quick."

"I'm assuming you're the gentleman I spoke to earlier?" Dave inquired. "You sure about what you're seeing?"

"Not positive," the older man replied, taking off a dirty baseball cap, "but I'm pretty darn sure it's a body down in the gorge area along the river bank."

"What makes you think so?" Dave asked.

"Well, I know the area, and something just doesn't look right. It's too far down for me to make out completely from the ridgeline. But the coloring is off. It doesn't fit in with the surroundings. I noticed it this morning when I was working along the edge of the pastures, fixing fence lines."

"How far is it from here?"

"It's across the pasture." The man turned and pointed toward the scrub brush that lined the ridge. "We can drive my truck most of the way, but then we're gonna have to walk just a bit."

"Let me change into my boots and lock up my vehicle."

The man nodded and headed back to his truck. He put up the tailgate and climbed in the truck cab to wait.

Dave exited his cruiser and headed to the trunk to retrieve his hiking boots. Radioing the station, he let dispatch know he had parked his vehicle and would be out of range for a while. He checked his gun belt then fished for the binoculars from the floor of his backseat.

Once in the pickup, they headed across the bumpy pasture dotted with boulders and black Angus with their calves. The cows lifted their heads away from the supple grass to check out the truck invading their field, then went back to grazing.

"So, you're new to the area," the man said. "What'd you think so far?"

Dave grinned. Word had spread through the community about a new deputy. "Pretty invigorating, and the people a hard-working, tight-knit group. Everyone seems pretty friendly in the south."

The old man laughed and then replied, "Well, you got it almost half right. Hard-working, tight-knit, yes, but we can be a gossipy bunch as well. Rumors have been flying about that girl you got living up there with you."

Slightly alarmed, Dave tried not to react. "Oh yeah? What are people saying?"

"That she's a murderer, and we need to make sure we keep our doors locked and keep our distance."

"Well, I wouldn't worry. She was never convicted. Sarah's a good person, and she's harmless." Dave wasn't going to play into the gossip or give any added explanation. "Can't believe everything you hear." The man just shrugged his shoulders, not convinced.

The farmer drove to the far side of the pasture, stopping at the fence line. The high tensile wire was several strands tall and ran close together to keep the cattle in. The fence line ran along the ridge and looked like it went on for several miles. With no gate on this side, it was as far as they could drive.

"We need to park here and climb through the fence. It's a short walk to the edge of ridge from this point."

Dave followed the rancher's lead. Pulling the wires back, he stepped through, trying to keep his grip tight. When he released his hold, the wires snapped back, stinging his hand. "Son of a bitch!" Dave yelled.

The old man laughed.

"Lucky you didn't end up with a shock as well. I cut the power to the fence this morning," he chuckled.

Dave took in the surroundings—large lush pasture, the mountains in the backdrop, the hues this part of Virginia was blessed with. Some of the curious cows had made their way over to the truck to see if it held anything appetizing.

Dave caught up with the rancher. "What brought you over this way this morning anyhow?"

"It's calving time, and I was counting head. I was also checking my fence line along here." The man pointed to a deer path running along the outside of the high-tensile wire. "As I neared this open area, I was watching the sun rise over the gorge and saw some birds circling. Something didn't look right down there on the other side of the rocky wall." He continued to talk as the pair made it to the edge of a cliff. "So, I came here, as far as I could to get a better look."

At first, Dave was in awe of the colors Mother Nature had painted along the ridgeline. He looked down toward the rapid river and couldn't spot anything remotely out of place.

"There. Right there." The man pointed almost straight down to an area near the shoreline on the opposite side of the swift moving water. Scanning with his naked eye, Dave still couldn't make out anything but the flowing water, rocks, and boulders and limbs that had piled up.

Tugging binoculars from his pocket, he glassed the area, adjusting the sights as he scanned the terrain deep below. Finally, his eyes caught a color that didn't fit. A weird configuration broke the natural pattern of the land. Quickly making more adjustments, he scrutinized the area closer. *There!* He could see what the rancher had called the sheriff's department about.

Tangled in a pile of driftwood along the opposite edge, bright red cloth reflected a color scheme that didn't fit. The cliffs were steep and sheer on both sides of the river in this area. *Huh. Where did the body come from in the first place? If that's what's really down there.*

"Is there any way from here to access the area?" Dave asked.

"Not from here anyway. Kayakers come through on occasion. You know, the real thrill seekers. But there are no trails or paths. It's too steep with no banks right here."

"I need to mark this spot. Not sure what we have down there, but we need to investigate."

"Well, I'll be whatever help I can. The sheriff's department can have total access to my fields just as long as no one lets my cattle loose. Make sure the gates are closed behind ya. I'd appreciate that much."

Dave pulled flagging tape from the leather pouch on his police-issued belt. He tied three lengths of orange fluorescent strips to a tree and marked the entrance to the path. He pulled out his phone and used a GPS to mark the location as well.

They climbed into the pickup truck and headed back across the pasture toward Dave's parked cruiser. He was quiet for a moment, pondering a way to access the area.

"You know any locals who kayak?" Dave asked before they reached his cruiser.

"A couple closer in toward town kayak this way occasionally. You know, one of them guy couples. Or you could try the swift water rescue team the next county over. I'm sure your department has all of their information."

Once they reached Dave's vehicle, he climbed down from the truck. "Many thanks. We have your contact information. I'm sure we'll be back here as soon as we figure out a plan. Make sure you call me if you find anything else out of the ordinary."

"Sure thing," the farmer replied in his slow drawl.

Dave gave the rancher his personal cell phone number and slowly pulled away, trying not to kick up another cloud of dust.

As he drove off, Dave could just make out a few lone dark birds circling high in the sky. *I hope we can get to the body before they destroy it.* He wasn't sure how quickly the buzzards were able to pick up the scent of death or when the body produced the gases the birds found so attractive. *Something to research.*

Dave called in immediately to his superior, Sheriff Kasey, and was told to report back to the station to fill out a full report before they would decide what to do, and how they would handle it.

Used to working in a whole other type of environment where everything was done quickly, Dave needed to learn to adjust to the slower pace. He needed to learn how to slow down. There was never a true emergency here unless it involved a farm accident or a missing child.

Dave scanned the mobile computer in his vehicle for any recent missing persons. Nothing. Nothing came up for the area or the surrounding counties either. He expected to find a report of a missing kayaker or hiker, but found nothing. *Well, if it is a body down there, it's odd we don't have a missing person's report. I wonder how far up river the body might've come.*

CHAPTER 18

SARAH

Stepping out into the early morning darkness, Sarah smiled as a high-pitched whinny broke the stillness. Gunner and Sam bolted up the driveway to the barn. The horses brought new anticipation to her day. It was challenging to learn all she needed to know about them. They were a prey animal, and she worked with dogs who were predators. The psychology alone was at opposite ends of the spectrum.

The horses met her at the paddock fence. "Well, hey there, guys."

The palomino lowered his head. Sarah reached up to pat Sunny lightly on his forehead and scratched Tank behind the ear. She haltered both horses. Making a clucking sound, she stepped toward them and made them back up. Walking a few steps forward, she stopped and repeated the process to make sure they didn't crowd her body. J.C. had taught her not to "baby" the horses, but to demand they listen and be mindful. Once you had ground rules established, it was safer and easier to know what was expected of each other.

Sarah still spoiled the horses a bit with the occasional sliced apple or cut-up carrots. They grew accustomed to her and whinnied each morning when they heard her or caught her scent as she made her way from the house to feed them.

J.C. came out to the farm a few days a week. He showed Sarah how to groom and tack them. She watched how gentle he was with the horses, but how he was also firm and exercised safety and leadership. J.C. never struck the horses, but he made them respect his space. He showed her how to be a good leader like she was with her dogs. Basic riding lessons were helping Sarah become more confident in the saddle. She in turn helped Dave with Tank when he would return from his long days at work.

Keeping Dave's suggestion to work the dogs from horseback in mind, she put a lot of thought into how it could be done. She still had reservations. Although it seemed a big issue to handle, she was sure it was possible, but didn't know if she could do it. *But maybe if it works, I'll be able to extend the dogs' working time, to help keep them up with their endurance levels. Can't hurt to try.*

Sarah had been working with Gunner and Sam, maintaining their scent work strictly using human remains—cadaver problems. But she still had trouble keeping up physically. The dog's scent problems needed to be longer than the twenty to thirty minutes she set up for them.

Occasionally, Dave would hide sources for scent problems before he left for work and gave her scenarios in an area to work the search task. This way, the scent problems were blind to both her and the dogs. When Dave had down time and was home, he even hid for the dogs, rewarding them with a big party when they located him. It kept the dogs excited in their work and helped keep up their work ethic and motivation.

Sarah headed to the barn to pull out a few training sources. In what was now the new tack room, she kept her special supplies for canine cadaver training. Sarah unlocked the door and flipped the light switch on. Standing still for a moment, she let her eyes adjust to the dimly lit room.

Finding the key to her storage cabinet, she released the lock and pulled out an old military ammunition canister. With a little muscle, she flipped the lock mechanism free and popped the container open. Before reaching in to find what she was after, she slipped on a pair of nitrile gloves. Rummaging through the contents of the container, she found the training source she was after. She pulled out a few sections of human vertebra. *Perfect.* She needed a smaller source, or really, petite sized bones for what she had in mind for this training session.

Laying the bones on a table by the far wall that was only used to handle cadaver training material, she stepped back to look for a container. Locating a new metal suet cage, she pulled it down, took it out of the plastic packaging, and went to work fitting the bones into the container and wiring it closed. Training sources were hard to come by, and they needed to last as long as they could in their natural state.

They needed to stay secure not only to keep them away from wild animals, but to keep the source safe from Gunner damaging them. Although Sam would make the find and do his re-call/re-find as more of a gentleman, Gunner became obsessed. If Sarah didn't get to the source to reward him as soon as possible, the dog had the habit of mouthing the source or scratching at it aggressively, which destroyed the source's integrity. Some of it came down to their training foundations, but most was just the dog's personality.

Once Sarah had her training materials readied, she brought Sunny into the barn, tied him to the wall in the open aisle, and saddled him. She felt confident enough to ride him out alone along the wooded tree line of their property. She placed the suet container in a plastic, sealable baggie and put it in one of the saddle bags. In the other side she placed the dog's rewards—a soft Frisbee for Sam and a ball on a string for Sam.

She had been riding through the pastures each day with the dogs in tow, practicing giving them commands from her mounted position. She'd put the dogs through obedience moves, asking them to lay down or sit and sending them out in directions away from the her and the horse and calling them back. She'd rewarded the dogs with pieces of hot dogs or throwing them a tennis ball at the end of each training session. Sunny, the ever-patient soul, had become comfortable with Sarah working the dogs from his back. He stayed at a steady walking pace on a loose rein allowing her to concentrate on Gunner and Sam. But this would be the first time she'd try to run a training problem from the saddle. "Okay, let's do this."

The dogs eventually found a "space bubble" where they felt secure moving alongside the horse. Sunny ultimately trusted the dogs and became aware and relaxed with them flanking him. After a few weeks, Sarah observed Sunny keeping track of where each dog was in proximity. It was as if they were a strike force working together and keeping in-tune of one another.

If one of the dogs ran off into the underbrush or into the woods, Sunny would stop and raise his nose. Sometimes he would wait until the dog reentered his sights before moving on.

All of this was new to Sarah. She had no idea the horse would be that concerned or observant of what was now his norm. She was in awe of her animals. She'd known horses were social, herd type animals, but she thought that only accounted for their own kind. She was quickly learning how intuitive Sunny really was.

Sarah put the other horse out into one of the adjoining pastures prior to heading out. Horses were social and bound to their pasture mates, and if there were only two, their bonds were stronger. If he could see where Sunny, Sarah, and the dogs were, he wouldn't stress as much being left behind in a paddock. Tank would eat grass contentedly while they were out, but he would also keep an eye, ear, and nose toward their direction.

Sarah locked up the dogs while she set up the training problem. She untied Sunny, and slipped a bit in his mouth and the bridle over his ears with care. She rode out the long driveway, testing the air current on the way. The light wind was blowing in a westerly direction away from the barn. She continued down the road past her front pastures and turned north toward the tree lined boundary.

Nearing the corner of her farm, she and Sunny turned and rode along the space between the pasture fence and trees. Finding a lull in the overgrown vegetation, Sarah located a large, draping pine where she could hang the source. Sunny obliged her request to ride up close to the thick evergreen.

"Whoa there, Sunny," she said, draping reins across the horse's neck. She trusted him to stand while she leaned into the tree and hung the container. Speaking softly to the horse, she twisted her body in the saddle to get the job done.

Once the source was placed, she picked up the reins.

"Good boy, Sunny." She gently patted the horse's neck, directing him back toward the barn.

Checking her watch, she noted the time. She still had to ride back to the barn, so there was plenty of time for the source to "percolate" and give off some odor.

As she came to the barn, she could hear the dogs protesting their confinement. "Settle, guys!"

Sarah eased the horse to a stop and dismounted in front of the barn. Leading the horse inside, she reached the stall and released the dogs. "Platz!" she commanded as they bolted from within the stall. Both dogs dropped into a sphinx position in the dirt aisle.

Sarah remounted Sunny and started to ride him out of the barn. Once she reached the other side of the barn door, she called, "Free," to the dogs to release them.

Gunner and Sam jumped up from their downed position, running to Sarah and the horse. They loped a large circle around her and Sunny, tipping their snouts skyward. *They already know. Can they smell the source on me?* Sarah shook her head.

Sending Sunny out toward the pasture on the western side of the barn, Sarah kept the horse at a slow walk. She wanted to enter the search area from a different path and direction than she had ridden out to plant it. The dogs immediately went to work without Sarah giving their normal cadaver command—"Seek." Working with their snouts closed, both dogs started to check out the area. Sarah looked at her watch again, making sure enough time had passed. Satisfied, she continued to move Sunny along.

Sam's nose went to the ground and he checked along the gate and fence line and did a zig-zag pattern across the dirt road that led around the other end of the pasture. Sarah watched as Gunner opened his mouth occasionally, but mainly worked with it closed. He went back and forth from checking the ground to checking the air, inhaling deeply as he loped along at a steady pace.

After close to thirty minutes of gridding the length of the field, the foursome came to the far end of the pasture. The source was about thirty meters on the other side of the fence. Sarah dismounted and tied Sunny to a post. She called the dogs and climbed through the board fence. The dogs followed through an opening toward the bottom.

"Seek," Sarah commanded in a fun, high-pitched tone. "Get to work," she pushed a little harder with motivation in her voice to keep the dogs focused. While she walked as straight as she could to stay on the same grid line as before, she waved her hands in the air for the dogs to move out in a broader area away from her.

From the corner of her eye, she watched Gunner run directly west, then stop and turn back. He ran a north-south path as he entered the scent cone, a zig-zag pattern about twenty meters on the other side of where she had hung the training source.

Sam caught her eye to the south of where she was standing. She watched as the dog caught Sunny's trail from earlier and followed the track to where she had hung the source. *Smart one. I'll have to change my training protocols, at least how I set up Sam's problems.*

When Sam was under the tree, he circled it a few times, found the strongest scent picture, and stood on his hind legs. Gunner followed the scent cone into the same spot and almost ran blindly into Sam. Sam did his re-call/re-find indication and left to head toward Sarah. Gunner, in the meantime, started to jump as high as he could when he figured out exactly where the source was. *Good thing it's out of his reach!*

Once Gunner realized he couldn't get to the source, he interrupted the serene quiet of the woods with his deep, booming barks. By this time, Sam had reached Sarah and jumped at her, then took off back toward the tree. Sarah followed the dogs as quickly as she could on her injured hip. Catching up , she let them continue with the indications for several more seconds as she lavished verbal rewards of "good boys."

Reaching into one of the saddle bags, she fished out each dog's reward. She sent the Frisbee sailing through the woods for Sam then chucked Gunner's ball. After a few minutes of intense play, Sarah's leg pained her. She told the dogs, "All done." She let them keep their toys as she pulled a nitrile glove from her pack. She reached up to grab the branch where the source hung and pulled it down closer to her, so she could remove it.

After she had her source, the trio headed to where she had left Sunny tied. Checking her watch once again, she made a mental note to write down forty minutes of total training time in her log. It was important to keep notes on each dog not only to keep track of how they progressed, but in case they were ever called to court to testify in a case. *Ha,* the last consideration brought dark thoughts about her past year and made her laugh.

As Sarah rode back to the barn with two satisfied dogs in tow, she reflected on the problem and how each dog had worked. She had to figure out a better way to place sources in the field—a way Sam wouldn't be able to follow tracks. *I'll have to brainstorm about this.*

Then she thought about the whole process of working the dogs from horseback. She believed it was totally feasible. *I could make this work if I ever get a chance to deploy my dogs again.* But do *I have the guts to see this through?*

CHAPTER 19

DAVE

With his thoughts running amuck while driving back to the Sheriff's station, Dave barely noticed the countryside this time around. Over and over, he played different scenarios through his head. *So, if this is a body at the bottom of the gorge, how'd it wind up there? Where'd it come from? How long has it been there? Will the buzzards destroy any evidence?*

With a mystery on his hands, he contemplated ways to research for missing persons from the immediate region as well as bordering states, how to extricate the body, what might've happened. Dave couldn't turn his investigative nature off once he became involved. He was driven to solve a mystery.

At the station, Dave ran into another deputy who was on his way out. "Hey there, Brooks. Got a minute?"

"Kind of in a hurry, heading out on a call," Brooks replied. "Is it something quick?"

"Got a possible body at the bottom of a gorge—you know, by the Tucker farm. Got any ideas on how to extract a body from there?"

Brooks' eyes lit up, and he pulled his hat from his head. He smiled like he remembered something. Dave grinned as he watched his co-worker's thought process unfold.

"Well, there is that swift water recovery team over in the next county. In Albemarle. Maybe you can try them," Brooks suggested.

"Thanks buddy, appreciate it." Dave gave Brooks a slap on the shoulder as he filed past to his office.

Sitting down at his desk, he turned his computer on and spent a few moments surfing for the rescue organization. Finding their webpage, he pulled up the information and read through the team's capabilities and parameters for call-outs. Using the non-emergency number listed on the home page, Dave put in a call to the team. *Probably the safest way to access a body since I have no experience in white water.*

He left a message hoping to get someone in for a sit down, face to face to discuss how to go about extracting the body. It would give Dave a better understanding of the area, how the team works, the whole process in general.

"What're ya getting so riled up about?" Sheriff Kasey questioned. "You need to slow down. You're not even sure it's really a body down there and no one's been reported missing yet, anyhow."

"Sure," was all Dave could think to respond. He was put off by the sheriff's response. Dave decided to move ahead with his plans nevertheless. It wasn't like he'd put the plan in action yet, he was just researching options. Less than a half hour later, Dave received a response from the water team. He secured a meeting with a couple of senior members to go over a tentative strategy later in the evening after they got off work. Since Sheriff Kasey never stayed past his shift, it also worked better for Dave.

While he busied himself with paperwork that afternoon, a confidential package arrived by courier from the Virginia's Department of Forensic Science lab in Richmond. Sheriff Kasey signed for it.

"Well, it's about time," Kasey remarked with a smirk. He handed the sealed package off to Dave.

"What's this?" Dave asked.

"Could be one of your new cases," Kasey replied with an obnoxious chuckle. "Go ahead. Open it."

"Okay," Dave replied, accepting the package.

"Hiker and his dog found it in the woods when they were hunting for sheds back in March. He came in here all excited, thought he was doing the right thing by turning it in," Kasey went on.

Dave carefully opened an end of the package exposing the paperwork and contents. He pulled out several documents that included computer generated reports and several pictures at various angles of what looked like a large bone.

"What's the report say?" the sheriff asked. "I'm sure it was just a deer legbone. Everyone gets so worked up around here when it's nothing. Happens all the time." Slamming down into his office seat, Kasey pulled out some leftovers from lunch and spoke between mouthfuls of sandwich and soda. Flecks of food stuck in the corners of his mouth. "Come on, come on. The mystery's killing me," Kasey laughed sarcastically.

"Hang on, give me a minute." Dave pulled several more papers from the envelope. He scanned through, reading over the documents quickly. "Says here, it's a child's left femur."

"A what?" Kasey swallowed hard, choking on his food. Taking a few huge draws on his soda, he tried to speak in-between clearing his throat.

"The long leg bone connecting from the hip to the knee." Dave knew that bone too well after the incident with Sarah.

"I know that, dammit." Kasey gave Dave a hard look. "But I really thought it belonged to an animal, like a deer," Kasey repeated. "What else does the report have to say?"

"There wasn't any cell tissue left or viable marrow they could use to test due to the bone being left out in the elements, receiving animal activity and being submerged in the creek. They couldn't pull DNA. But they could tell it appears to be from a male subject between the ages of five to seven due to the growth plates."

"Does it list any reason or cause to what may have happened to the child?"

"Inconclusive." Dave continued to read through the information. "There aren't any tool marks or disease the lab could identify which would have shown the cause of the subject's demise. Do we have any cases of missing children locally from the last year or so, unsolved cases? A child that might fit these parameters?"

"Well, I don't think there were any recent missing people in our area, especially not a child. I would know about it. But this one would have been from some time ago. Still, we haven't had any local children who have gone missing or any in the neighboring counties. Does the report give any indication of race or height?"

Dave scrutinized the document for more details, but he couldn't find the answers to the sheriff's questions.

"Well, you've got other cases to work on. This bone can wait until we have some down time. I wouldn't fool with it for now." Kasey swiveled his chair around to face Dave as he spoke. "Just leave the report on my desk. I want to look at it later. Maybe I'll just handle it myself. It's not something we should waste a lot of time on." The stern expression written across Kasey's face indicated he was waiting for Dave to acknowledge.

"Sure thing," Dave responded.

"I'll get to it when I get back. Understood?"

Dave nodded in response.

Kasey ran a uniformed forearm across his mouth. "Time to get packing," he announced as he looked up at the clock on the wall. Kasey stood, brushing the crumbs onto the floor and left the office.

Dave found Kasey's attitude about the child's femur strange—it sent up a red flag in his mind. *Kasey doesn't think it's a priority? There may be a body at the bottom of the gorge and no one gets excited?*

Dave had a hard time putting the paperwork down from the lab. He found the information intriguing, but he also found it disturbing. It reminded him of a case he had learned of in college about a young boy's remains found in a box, discarded along a lonely road in the south. The body was never identified. The person who murdered the boy never faced justice. Dave had hoped it wouldn't be the same with this case, but they didn't have a lot to go on and there were other priorities to contend with.

Dave made a copy of the lab report and filed it away in the back of his desk drawer. He laid the original report on Kasey's desk and sat down at his own workstation, pulling out a standardized form to start his report regarding the body at the bottom of the gorge.

Refocusing on the prior call from this morning, Dave had a difficult time concentrating, his mind wandering back to the conversation between him and Kasey. *What the hell is going on? Shouldn't this child's femur be a top priority? Shouldn't the sheriff be more interested in retrieving a body found by the river?*

CHAPTER 20

SARAH

Planting her feet squarely on the barn's dirt floor, Sarah balanced herself and reached up, lifting the saddle clear from Sunny's back. She took a step away from the horse and a sharp pain shot through her hip. She stumbled backward with the heavy saddle, falling on her ass. "Well, that was graceful." Sunny bent his neck around in the cross ties to get a better look at his rider sitting in the middle of the barn aisle. The horse curled his lip up in response, making Sarah laugh.

Using a curry comb, she rubbed the sweat marks from the horse's back, cleaned his feet with a metal pick, and walked him out to the paddock. Tank greeted them at the gate with a short, low-pitched whinny. The roan was excited to have his buddy back. "We weren't gone more than an hour there, Tank," Sarah spoke softly to the other gelding. "You can come out for a ride next time." Sarah patted the horse on the neck as she pulled treats from her pocket. Checking to make sure all the gates were closed, she called for the dogs, told the horses goodbye for now, and headed toward the cabin.

A wave of fatigue flooded over her as she and the dogs walked up the dirt lane. She had done more than she should've. Caring for the horses, training the dogs, doing odd jobs around the barn, she suddenly felt depleted. *I just need to slow down, take a short break.*

Dave sent her a text stating he would be home later this evening after he finished working on a pile of paperwork. She didn't care. Sarah couldn't shake the feeling of complete exhaustion. Her left leg was throbbing, her thoughts scattered.

Overdoing herself. She had pushed her body too much today—saddling, mounting, walking, twisting in the saddle—torqueing her body too soon. The pain brought back dark memories.

Sarah downed a couple anti-inflammatories. Stretching out on the couch for a well-deserved break, she had time to relax before Dave arrived home. A quick nap before figuring out dinner.

Trying to keep the dark thoughts at bay, she closed her eyes. She couldn't rid past images. She opened her eyes and stared out the front window. Her back and leg injury brought a chronic and dull constant pain, but it still didn't compare to the pain of her tortured past.

Ominous thoughts crowded her mind, clouded her vision. She had been fighting to keep her views positive, buoyant and focused on the moment. She had everything to be happy about. But shadowy reflections continued to haunt her. Lately, there were some days she found it difficult not to go there.

Pondering her past, she considered where she was in life and tried to turn her thinking to the future. Lately, it was getting harder to do. She was spending too much time alone. It gave her too much time to think, dwelling on long ago experiences. Allowing what had transpired in her past to tarnish her future. She had unanswered questions regarding the murders which still haunted her. She never figured out why Eva had come back all those years later. *What triggered her to return in the first place? And is she really gone for good? Dead? What if she does show up again? How will I know? Will Dave be okay?*

Sarah remembered years back when she lived alone in her house by the lake. Waking up to the subtle scent of cigarettes on her clothes after a blackout. A light soot smell on her hands. She would find cigarette butts in the backyard and ashes along the deck railing. Every now and again, Eva would record messages on her phone for her to randomly find. Items in the house always seemed to be misplaced. Sarah shuddered. She'd never told anyone about the cigarettes or the messages. *I would've been locked away in the psych ward forever.*

Fractured feelings were never far from her emotionally as well. She thought of her baby—her daughter—who now would be a young girl. Nine, almost ten years old? *Where is she now? What is she doing? I wonder what she looks like.* Events from her past, and recent events, would make her wise and keep in mind, her daughter might not even be alive. But, somewhere deep in Sarah's soul, she knew her daughter was still alive. Somehow, somewhere, one day she hoped to find her. A dream, a longing she would never give up on. An emptiness in her heart, an ache that could only be filled by knowing what had happened to her baby.

Giving in finally, she fell into a fitful sleep. Her unconscious allowed demons from her past to make their appearance. She dreamt she was falling, falling deeper into a dark hole. Rising out of the ground, rotting and partially decomposed hands grabbed at her legs. They pulled her into the loose loamy soil. She was slowly losing sight of her dogs, Dave, the horses, the farm. It was as though she was falling back in time, into the grips of her foster parents and brother. She couldn't see their now rotting faces, but could feel the torment, the anguish from the pain. She kept reaching out for the shadow of a little girl, just beyond her grasp... primal screams escaped her.

Sarah woke up with a sudden start, bolting upright with a twinge from her hip. Gunner was licking her face with his scratchy tongue. Sam paced and whined. Her phone buzzed with a text, but she ignored it.

Sarah eyed Gunner and Sam as they watched her. They moved across the room from Sarah and curled up in the corner. They held their bodies tight to themselves. Sarah could tell they sensed when she was emotionally unstable. She knew it bothered them, making them fearful, anxious and untrusting. But, always in the end, they stood by her. They were faithful to their handler, their partner. They were so forgiving.

"Stop it!" she yelled more at her spinning head. The dogs stood for a moment, then moved further away. They were clearly taken off guard. They laid down, their ears lowered in submission.

Yawning several times, they attempted to diffuse what they considered a tense situation. "I'm sorry. Sorry guys, come here." Sarah leaned down, guilt ridden. She pulled the dogs close, burying her head in their sable fur and started to cry. Sometimes, she felt like she was falling apart. Losing her sanity a few shreds at a time.

Pulling herself together, she stood up and made her way to the laundry room. She pulled Gunner and Sam's kibble from the cabinet. They followed her, eyeing her movements in anticipation. The dogs continued to keep their space between her and them, still a little leery of their handler.

"Crate," she ordered.

Gunner and Sam ran in their metal wire cages, and spun around so they wouldn't lose sight of their dinner. They wagged their tails and looked up at her with anticipation. Sarah laughed. It lightened her mood for a moment.

Dogs taken care of, she started to think about dinner herself. It had been hours since she had eaten anything substantial. She checked her phone. Dave's latest text said he was working on one last report and then would be heading home. Dusk would soon settle around the farm.

She thought of Dave, then of her fearful dreams. She still fought off knowing he didn't completely understand what he'd gotten himself into and why he would want her... or why anyone would want her, for that matter. *If only they really knew. Maybe I should tell him what's going on in my head? Maybe not.* It was too risky, and she needed to keep her dismal and sinister thoughts of the past locked deep inside her.

CHAPTER 21

DAVE

Checking the clock on the wall, Dave let out a long sigh. He still had a lot he wanted to work on. His thoughts drifted to Sarah who had been home alone all day. He promised her they would ride this evening, but that wasn't going to happen. *Dammit, it's getting late. Where are these guys?* Dave's bad mood became worse. The swift water leaders were more than an hour late. He got up to make a pot of coffee in the break room when dispatch came over the PA system: "Gentlemen here to see you, Deputy Graves." *About fucking time.*

While waiting, Dave had put together an incident report and pulled up detailed topographical maps of the gorge and surrounding areas. He grabbed the paperwork from his desk and headed down the hall toward the front of the building. From the doorway window, he spotted two men standing in the lobby having a lively discussion.

They were loud, and the discussion bordered on the edge of a heated debate. He watched as the older man held his hands in front of him spread wide-apart. He could just make out the last part of the conversation which was delivered in a heavy Australian accent. "I swear to you, mate, she was this big and took me an hour to reel her in. And I ain't talking about fishing."

Dave came through the door in time to catch the younger man rolling his eyes at the ceiling. "Good afternoon, gentlemen. I assume you two are with the swift water rescue team?" The men nodded in unison. "I'm Deputy Dave Graves. I believe you are here to help me get to the bottom of a deep problem." Dave extended his hand.

"Well, aren't you a funny mate?" the older man smiled. A wide grin exposed a broken front tooth.

The younger, more serious man offered Dave his hand. "Hi, I'm Jonathan Black. This here funny guy is the captain of our swift water rescue team, Max Walker. Pleasure to meet you."

"Ah, nice to meet you as well. Jonathan here is a little too sober all in all. He needs to learn how to loosen up a bit." Max laughed, grabbing the younger man's shoulder and giving it a good shake. "He says you may have found something down in the Devil's Gorge, mate?"

Dave had to think for a second. The farmer hadn't mentioned the area had a name. But "Devil's Gorge" was fitting.

"Why don't you two follow me back to one of the interview rooms where we can sit down and discuss this? We can lay out some maps and look at what I believe may be at the bottom of the area. I took some pictures this morning as well, but it's still quite questionable."

Arriving at an unoccupied conference room, Dave motioned for the men to have a seat. He dropped the material on the table—maps, pictures, and detailed reports. He unfolded the antiquated topo map and spread it wide across the table. Using the tip of a pencil, Dave pointed to the spot where the sighting had been made by him and the old farmer.

"Right here is where we believe a body was sighted this morning. The farmer who owns the property runs cattle along this portion of the cliff. He made the discovery. I took a ride out there and used binoculars to get a better look. It appears to be a light flesh-colored object with bright red around segments, indicating clothing. But it's an odd shape and I couldn't make out accurate details from that far of a distance."

The men studied the map for a moment.

The Australian's brow furrowed as if he was in deep, serious study. He looked up at Dave. "Huh, tough area to get to, you know?"

"Yeah, reason why we called you guys in. Where it's located, we have no idea how to get to the target to find out if it is, in fact, a body. That's the part I was hoping your team could help out with."

Jonathan and Max took another moment to look at the map, trading comments regarding terrain, river current, recent weather events, and other details Dave didn't quite comprehend. The pair discussed the last time they had been in that part of the river—which happened to be to retrieve a drowned kayaker—and continued to delve into that mission for a moment. There were places upriver to put in their boats. They noted the closest bridge was well over a mile or more.

Dave sat back and let the two have their exclusive discussion. Much of the lingo was out of his area of expertise. He figured they would know best, so he let them have their time to hash out some sort of a plan.

Max continued to be the livelier one as Dave silently observed their animated conversation. Jonathan seemed to be the one who erred on the side of prudence, the more cautious teammate even though he was younger. Dave could sense Max was more experienced and had taken chances over his lifetime that had paid off and taught him life lessons and made him better skilled. Dave was completely entertained as he watched the two.

"Well, the area happens to be one of the toughest ones to access," Max said. "But it can be done—"

"Conditions need to be just right as far as the weather though," Jonathan broke in. "Wouldn't want to attempt heading into that rapid when the river is high, or the weather is rough."

"Weather and conditions are perfect right now," Max finished. "With the unusual drier spring conditions over the last few days, the river has receded a bit. I don't think there's any rain due in the forecast for several days."

"The diminishing water is something to take note of," Dave thought out loud. *Maybe the body might've been there for a while and is just now showing up.* "Could it have been under for a while?"

"Huh? Did you say something, mate?" Max asked.

"Just thinking. If it is a body, I wonder if it could've been there a while... trapped in the driftwood or trapped underwater and it's just now visible due to the water line declining."

"Well, I'm sure that's a possibility," Jonathan replied.

"Can you take us to where you spotted the body from?" Max inquired.

"Sure thing. We should have just enough time before the sun starts to set. Shadows from the gorge might make it difficult to see anything below. Give me a second to make a quick call first."

Dave texted Sarah to break plans and let her know he would be home even later. She never responded to his message.

The trio piled into Dave's cruiser and headed out to the ridgeline. He decided it would be better to park along the front gate of the pasture and walk to the gorge area. Dave didn't want to chance driving through the rough pasture and getting his vehicle stuck.

"So, how many drowned bodies have you seen now there, Dave?" Max asked as they walked across the field heading to the ridge. The cows watched with suspicious eyes as the men crossed through their grazing area, but never moved a muscle and went back to eating the early seasonal grasses. Many had calves alongside and kept a wary eye out to make sure they maintained their offspring's safety.

"Well, only one really, and that victim had only been in the water a day or two and it wasn't a moving body of water. There was an undercurrent, but it had been caught up in vegetation and held in place. Cold body of water fed by underground, natural springs. There really wasn't any environmental damage other than a little nibbling on by fish."

Making it across the pasture field, they climbed through the high-tensile wire which was still turned off. Once at the edge of the cliff, they spied a few large black birds riding air currents above.

Dave used his binoculars to focus on the object of concern. It took him a few minutes to find it, focus and zoom in. Once located, he handed the binoculars off to the Australian.

Max took a few minutes, found what he was looking for and then scanned the entire area. After he was finished he handed them off to Jonathan. "Sure looks like it's a body, mate," Max said. "Subjects who are swept down fast and hard in quick moving waters can make it difficult to discern. They don't much look like what a person is used to seeing. They can sometimes look like mounds of grey or pinkish colored flesh or, sometimes, even clear like cellophane. They are usually so distorted, destroyed, and on occasion, they ain't even a whole body no more. Between the strength of the water, rock damage, other objects Mother Nature likes to throw at 'em like logs in the water churning around, it can really do some damage."

Jonathan finished with the binoculars and handed them back to Dave. The rescue team members began to discuss a course of action, the hazards, timeframe, and parameters of how to attempt to not only get to the site, but to be able to dock in the fast-moving current and extract the body from the pile of wood where it was caught.

"Have you ever been on swift water?" Max asked.

"No, never. Haven't had the pleasure of experiencing white water rafting here in Virginia yet. So, what d'ya think? Can we do this? If so, how soon?" Dave asked intently. He was beginning to find a little excitement in the possibility of being included in the boat. "I would like to be on board during the recovery as well."

"Well, it would be an option, but we will need to go over some training first. I'm assuming you understand how dangerous this can be? We need a day or two to get another boat and team on board. Since this is a recovery and not a rescue, we have the luxury of added safety measures. Having another team and their boat will aid in the mission. I'm going to tentatively say Friday? Then it will give us a couple days to get everything together. The water level will most likely continue to recede, and it doesn't look like the body can be moved by the water. This Friday? Will that work?"

"Sure thing," Dave responded. "I'm just hoping the carrions don't do too much damage." His department would have to work around the rescue team's expertise. "Whatever works best for you. Safety is definitely the number one issue."

The three men started back across the pasture toward the parked cruiser. Dave was finding his new position a bit more exciting than he had as a Pennsylvania State trooper.

It would be a great opportunity to bring Sarah along, but the timing wasn't right. The sheriff knew about her past, as it seemed, did most of the community. Dave had been up front and informed the department prior to being hired he planned to bring Sarah with him if she was acquitted. *And of course, if she had agreed.*

Then he overheard Max and Jonathan discussing some of their teammates who had drowned while on missions. *But what if something goes wrong? What if something were to happen to me now? What would Sarah do? What would become of her?*

Chapter 22

Sarah

Sarah stood up from the kitchen table abruptly, shoving her chair. Gunner and Sam's heads shot up from where they lay curled on the kitchen floor. She had just read Dave's text, cancelling their plans once again. Eyeing the dogs' reaction to her sudden anger, she was overcome with guilt.

She knelt by them, as much as she could manage with her injured leg, petting each one with long, slow strokes. "Sorry, guys."

They beat their tails softly against the floor boards.

Accustomed to Dave's strong work ethic, Sarah hoped this wasn't how it would always be. She wanted... she needed more of him. More than she was getting. It was something she felt warranted a discussion with him, and soon.

Preparing dinner, Sarah wasn't sure how late Dave would be or if he would pick something up to eat on the way. She tried to put her negative thoughts aside. Setting out two plates, she filled them with leftover lasagna, a side salad, and a portion of garlic bread as the dogs looked on. Once made, she covered the plate for Dave and placed it in the microwave for safe keeping.

Darkness began to settle around the small farm. Sarah relaxed on the couch with her plate of food. Grabbing the remote, she flipped on the television and surfed through channels trying to find something worthwhile to watch. Nothing appealed to her.

Spending too many long days alone at the cabin was wearing on her. Sarah missed her canine search and rescue team. She craved interaction with dog handlers, just people in general. She missed the dog training, the work and helping to bring closure to families of the lost and missing. She was more than lucky, she knew, but sometimes she felt stuck. She needed something more in her life, something meaningful to occupy her time.

Everything in life is temporary, right?

CHAPTER 23

DAVE

Navigating his cruiser nearing headquarters, Dave noted the sun slowly dipping behind the mountain range. It was late evening by the time the three men returned to the station. Dave listened as Max contacted another swift water rescue crew he had worked with on past missions. Both organizations had a mutual aid agreement allowing them to work together. Max secured the team. Since it was a recovery mission and not an emergency, they had time for prep work and planning. Staying safe for all involved was the most important aspect of the undertaking.

Tentative plans were set for Dave to meet the teams Friday, 0500 hours, at the bridge underpass upriver from the sighting. Per Max, this was the best place to put the boats in. Vehicles had easy access to the pull-off area from the main road, and decent parking along the shoreline. Max and Jonathan gave Dave an overview of what to expect and what to wear, then parted ways for the time being.

With daylight fading, Dave's shift ended, but there were still mysteries in his head he couldn't lay to rest. Sarah would be home alone. He wanted to touch base on a couple things prior to leaving the office, though. He was torn between going home to her or working on compelling matters he couldn't let go. It stressed him some to leave Sarah alone for long stretches of time, but these pressing issues wouldn't let his mind rest until he did something about them. He headed to the office he shared with Sheriff Kasey near the rear of the building.

Dropping his large frame down into the chair with a thud, Dave fired up the computer as he pulled open his file drawer. The recovered bone incident required opening a new case, questioning the lab, and interviewing the hiker who had found the bone.

Kasey had made it clear he would personally take care of the case involving the child's femur, but the sheriff had been called out of town to a family emergency for at least a few days. Dave decided he would "help out" by doing the baseline research and reports. *I wonder why he didn't want me working on this? There's not much to it. What's the worst that can happen?*

Retrieving the copied report from his file drawer, Dave read each piece of paperwork in its entirety this time. He deciphered what testing had been completed and what information was gathered from the single, weathered bone. Most of the reports were technical, above his level of medical comprehension. Many were inconclusive.

Pulling up mapping software, Dave located a full color satellite view of the area where the bone was found. He studied the mountainous region and the major roadways that wound through its peaks and valleys.

He studied how far the location was from the roadway. *Huh?* Dave rubbed his forehead. Usually human predators dumped bodies within fifty feet of the road. Easy. Convenient. Just far enough off the road that no one would notice, but close enough to get the job done quickly. This bone had been unearthed at least a few hundred meters from the road—at least 600 feet or more into the woods.

Deeper into the area where the find was made, there were thousands of wooded acres stretching up the mountainside and over the top before it hit another blacktop road or privately-owned property. Most of the area was in forest preservation or state-owned. Where the bone was found, was state lands. Hunters had access only with special permits during certain times of the year. From what the hiker had stated on the original report, he hunted in woods near there, but never in that exact area.

The hiker had been told by friends about several buck sightings there. They believed it would be a lucrative place for him to look for antler sheds.

Continuing to study the area map, Dave noticed old, improved trails. "But they might not even be there anymore," he stated out loud. They could've been logging trails. Sometimes a skeleton of a logging trail stayed cut into the ground years later. Trees and foliage could grow up there, but they might still be followed to some extent by foot or horse, or even an ATV or motorcycle.

Things change. New roads go in. Old roads and buildings fade. Maps weren't always up to date or accurate. But usually major terrain features stay the same such as drainages, creeks, and ridgelines. Having someone with a general knowledge of the area, and an understanding of a map and how to use it could make a big difference for such a search.

Looking out the window to complete darkness, Dave checked the time on his phone. Plans for the retrieval of the suspicious item along the gorge area wouldn't start until early Friday morning. That gave him a few days to check out where the hiker had found the bone.

Dave wrote up his report tying all the information together, and decided to call the hiker. After a quick discussion, arrangements were set to meet the next morning. Dave cleared his work space and sent Sarah a text letting her know he had one more report to work on and then would be heading home. He decided to ask her if she would like to come along tomorrow. He wanted to include her where he could. But he still wasn't sure she could handle navigating steep terrain with her injury, or if she would even want to come.

"Sure," came a prompt, short response from Sarah.

He found the more time she spent alone, the more depressed and quieter she seemed to be. He knew she needed more to do, more to keep her socially engaged... but it was also going to take time. He just hadn't thought it would be this hard and sometimes it escaped him what she'd been through.

Dave started contemplating another agenda. *It would be nice to see if there were any more bones near where the hiker found the femur. Maybe we should bring the dogs as well.* Dave knew he couldn't "deploy" Sarah and her dogs officially. But what would it hurt? *No intent, really.* Dave had decided not to mention his plan to anyone else though, including Sarah.

There was much to do for both the bone case and the recovery mission, but he also had another research project he had opened on his own—a more personal project.

It was a private matter. A special undertaking in which he hadn't told anyone about. He had started working on it as soon as Sarah had been indicted. His investigative nature and curiosity compelled him so much that he had to find out what he could. It was his own private investigation into her background—the foster family, the children who had gone missing, the story of her infant who had been taken from her—all of it had piqued his interest on a deep, dark level.

Dave hadn't mentioned the investigation to anyone because it had been difficult to communicate with Sarah while she was incarcerated. Between her being a ward of the state in the psych unit and the doctors not allowing many visitors, face to face meetings were short, monitored, and few and far between. He mostly had kept her updated with short letters which he penned with upbeat messages and light notes that never really spoke of what was going on in his life. Dave was also leery any mail sent to the prison might be read before it was given to her. He knew the drill when it came to inmates receiving outside mail.

It wasn't that he didn't want to let on to Sarah what he was working on, he just didn't know how to tell her. Dave had started his investigation—unofficially—with Sarah herself, researching into her background which was a short, but unique history. He wanted to know why she ended up in foster care, why she had been raised in the system. Working his way through what had been sealed files for years and fell under the 'Title Five Rules', Dave had been able to garner access to Sarah's records—sealed state records she probably wasn't aware were opened on her and other children in the Pennsylvania foster care system.

From what he could find, her young parents were originally from Ireland and had fled to the states to escape both sets of their parents who didn't approve of their romantic involvement. Families from two different regions, two different religions.

Sarah had been two years old when the small family had been involved in a serious car accident involving a tractor trailer along I-83 in the Harrisburg area. Both of her parents had perished in the accident. Although Sarah had sustained minor injuries, the car seat she was confined in had saved her life, and the life of a sibling.

Dave discovered she had a younger brother who had been an infant at the time. *A biological family member*. Dave couldn't find any information on him, whether he had been hurt or survived the accident. There was no trace of info regarding him. Sarah had never mentioned a brother. *Did she even know he existed?* Then Sarah had been taken in as a ward of the state. The state had tried to locate immediate family members in the area, then within the states, and then finally located her extended family in Ireland.

According to the reports, both sets of Sarah's grandparents had been in Northern Ireland. The one set wanted nothing to do with what they had called an abomination. Evidently, this family was blue blood, royalty among the Irish, and they blamed losing their son on the other family that was considered low class, even by Irish standards. The other set of grandparents had no means to retrieve their grandchildren or any financial stability to help raise them. But it was actually the difference between the families' religion that had torn them apart—one was Roman Catholic, the other Protestant. Wars had been waged over less from where these families hailed.

By the time all this communication had transpired, Sarah had been in foster care long enough she was passed over by prospective adoptive parents. Her curly red hair and fiery personality set her apart from the other children. It was so noted that potential adoptive parents didn't find these as good qualities.

No one wanted a "ginger." Everyone was looking for a blonde haired, blue eyed fair skin, "perfect wrapping on the outside" child. Sarah had also formed what reports called a bad attitude and had been labeled as a troublemaker. Due to outbursts, physical self-abuse, and outward destructive tendencies she was branded a "disturbed child." *Because she was most likely already being sexually molested.*

Digging deep into the foster parents' background, Dave was able to find a long trail of information. He had unearthed some interesting clues that might one day help them locate Sarah's daughter. Dave's thoughts drifted. *But what kind of person will she be? If she is still even alive?*

Dave had access to many databases and he was able to run background checks on both the foster mother and her family. He found information on the foster father, but it ended there. From police reports he gathered on both of them, neither should ever have been allowed in the foster care program. Both had alcohol and drug problems, numerous DWIs, domestic abuse reports, retail theft, and the list went on and on. *Interesting.* The foster father even had charges for sexual molestation and rape of a minor—a relative—but had been dropped for some reason. The foster mother had charges for taking a minor across state lines into Virginia. *Both had been worthless pieces of shit.*

Apparently, the state had been in such a need of housing and care for foster kids at the time, they allowed anyone and everyone who applied to be accepted. Sarah's foster parents had been approved quickly and they learned early on how much money they could garner from the state. Each child came with a monthly allowance which could be anywhere from a few hundred dollars to close to a thousand dollars apiece.

From several years of records, there appeared to be hundreds of children who had been wards of this foster family. Most were accounted for, but there were still many who were not. Some of the information he recovered involved children who had gone missing for months and the foster parents had never reported them missing. And they continued to collect the children's monthly allowance. *What a fucking racket! How many other foster families had been up to no good as well?*

Dave had known several foster families who were decent, law abiding citizens. He had been called out to their homes on occasion when he was a Pennsylvania State Trooper. A lot of the children forced into foster care carried stormy backgrounds before they ever entered the system. Others happened into foster care due to their parents' problems or an event in their life such as Sarah's. The children had nowhere else to go.

He knew he needed to tell Sarah. Dave wanted the timing to be right. He figured she might blow up. She might think he was being sneaky going behind her back, when in fact that wasn't the case at all. He needed to figure out how to tell her and at some point, soon. Dave couldn't help his deep, inquisitive nature. It always had him thinking and searching for answers—however unwelcomed they might be.

But he uncovered something which he believed to be a true concern. Something that might help them locate information on where Sarah's child may have ended up or at least information on what had happened to her. The foster mother had family in the Charlottesville area at one time. In fact, she was originally from Nelson County—the same county in which he worked, and he and Sarah now resided—southwest of Charlottesville where her roots appeared to be deep.

Dave remembered the note Eva held in her hand the day she had been shot. The paper only had read: "Charlottesville." He had taken it from the scene and pocketed it. If it had been seen by others, it must have been written off as a tissue or trash.

Dave worked on trying to locate as much information as he could on the foster mother. She seemed to be the link in the whole equation. There was more to that woman. He had an intuition about her that told him this was the route he should take. His instinctive investigative nature had proved him right in the past.

Following several attempts to track down family history, he was able to find a lead. *Bingo!* His research led him to an older brother of the foster mother and more of her family who resided in Albemarle County. He found other relatives in adjoining counties and a tie to an old family name of wealth and power—the Madisons. Apparently, they had owned large parcels of land in the mountains at one time. After checking several databases, he realized the family still owned several large tracts of land. *Huh, interesting.*

Next, Dave decided to put his energies and efforts into finding the older sibling, this brother of the foster mother. He would have to be in his late sixties at least because the foster mom had been in her mid-sixties. From the information he could conjure up, the man appeared on and off the grid. He was currently wanted by the IRS for tax evasion, had a warrant, but it seemed it wasn't on a grand scale, so he wasn't being actively pursued.

Dave pulled up a picture of the man from the DMV. It was old, but showed a tall, thin man with reddish, almost chestnut brown tinted hair. He sported a wiry beard with mustache and sideburns as well. His eyes struck Dave the most—they reminded him of a wild animal's. *Not what I was expecting.*

Well, at least the current warrant would give Dave a reason to come calling if he was able to track him down to speak with him. There were numerous other charges on his rap sheet as well, but they were all minor infractions. Dave printed off several reports and added them to a file in his desk drawer.

The area where this brother was supposedly located was in a heavily forested place of Nelson County. Not a densely populated area, but it seemed only hunters and hermits, people who wanted to live off the grid tended to live there... making it even more difficult to track someone down.

Dave's intuition told him this brother was one of the keys to not just information regarding leads or the whereabouts of Sarah's daughter, but to details in what happened to the missing foster care children as well.

Soon, he would have to confront Sarah about the research he had been doing without her knowledge. He hoped she would welcome it, be okay with it, but he knew she would be defensive at first. He knew she would feel suspicious and exposed. But he wanted to find something of concrete value first, before bringing her into the fold. He could only hope she would be okay with that and forgive him.

He entered his findings in a file he kept on his work computer and sent a copy to his home email address as a backup. His mind kept wandering, going over the information, trying to sort facts. There was something he was missing, that he wasn't putting together. He knew there was a piece of the puzzle right here among the information he'd just sorted through. It was late as he signed off his desktop and packed up.

Passing the few deputies who were on for the night shift, he headed out the front door to his patrol vehicle. He texted Sarah saying he was on his way home and asking her if she needed anything. She didn't respond. He hoped she wasn't mad at him for another long day in the office. Pointing his vehicle toward home, he only half listened to dispatch as they issued calls to deputies, sending them to various locations around the county. Hearing a certain address suddenly made Dave realize what he had struggled to put together earlier in his office.

That's it, that's it! All of sudden, he put the piece to the puzzle together that had been laid out in front of him. The child's femur had been found on state game lands which were adjoined to the foster family's property.

CHAPTER 24

SARAH

Eager to take the dogs out for a hike in the woods, Sarah jumped at Dave's offer to accompany him and a hiker, even though the summer had brought hot temperatures.

Dave had been so busy lately, they hadn't done much outside of the farm. They rode horses some evenings after work, or if he was scheduled for second shift, they might ride the trails around their farm prior to him going to the station. Sarah enjoyed their time together, and the occasional horse lessons with J.C., but she still felt so isolated, cut off from the rest of the world.

They met up with the hiker along the highway at a pull-off area. A split in the guardrail allowed a vehicle to pull through, down a small decline which leveled with enough space for a few cars to turn and park. Once accessed, it was difficult for passersby to see the parked vehicles. It was well protected from view.

"Pretty much hidden," Dave commented.

Sarah knew his investigative nature was always turned on and he was thinking along the same lines as a predator.

"You take your time, Sarah," Dave said as he put the SUV in park. "We're gonna be a minute looking at the map. Take your time with the dogs," he reiterated.

"Okay, I won't be long." She silently wished he would quit coddling her. Sarah waited in her seat until Dave and the hiker made introductions and spread a map out over the hiker's Jeep Cherokee hood.

Pulling on the door handle, she flinched when Sam and Gunner began to bark. "Settle," she firmly told them as she stepped out of the vehicle.

Sarah walked around to the back end of the SUV and popped the hatch. Gunner and Sam spun in the crates to face her, whining incessantly. She wondered if this had been a mistake. The dogs would think they were heading out on a search problem, when they were only going for an outing in the woods.

There was no real agenda. She had no plans to walk with Dave or the hiker. There really was no reason. She would take it slow and easy. She wanted to work on her physical endurance and slowly traverse difficult terrain.

"Easy, guys," Sarah calmed the dogs. Taking a deep breath, Sarah realized she needed to relax as well. She smiled at the dogs' comical antics as they pressed up against their crates vying for her attention. "Give me a minute to get ready."

She pulled out brown leather collars which carried their rabies tags, county licenses, and owner information—*the jingle from the tags should be enough to hear where they are. On second thought, it would probably be a good idea to attach bells to the collars as well.* No need for search vests. She pulled the dogs' brass bells from the bottom drawer of the crates and attached one to each collar. Grabbing two well-worn tennis balls, she mashed them into the back pockets of her jeans.

Readying herself, Sarah grabbed a can of bug spray. She applied the repellent to her clothing then carried it to the two men studying the map. Gunner and Sam watched as she walked to the other vehicle. They weren't barking, but they weren't taking their eyes from Sarah either. "It's okay, guys, I'll be right back," Sarah promised.

"Bug spray?" she offered. The hiker waved his hand indicating he was good. *Probably already used repellent before leaving the house.* Dave took the can from Sarah, starting at his shoes, and covered himself in the acrid smelling spray.

"Thanks," Dave said as he handed the can back. "You ready?"

"Yep. I'm going to carry a small backpack with a couple water bottles and bowls for us and the dogs. Let me just grab them."

"We're going to head out in a northwestern direction," Dave pointed. "If you need to rest, just yell and we'll stop and take a break."

"Sure thing," Sarah answered, not bothering to say she really didn't care if she kept up with them. She would keep them in her sights, but she wanted to go at her own pace, allowing Dave to carry on a conversation with the hiker—a conversation she really didn't care to be involved with.

She thought of her hip and how the injury continued to heal and how her endurance improved a little each day. Wincing at a twinge of pain, she knew she had overdone it the day before. She thought of how Sunny and the dogs had worked so well together yesterday. *Soon, maybe, I can work Gunner and Sam from the saddle on a deployment... that is, if I'm ever asked to work on a search again.*

Pushing the negative thoughts from her mind, she turned to the dogs in their confines. "Wait," Sarah told them while she popped the latch on each crate. Although they were parked near a road, she didn't worry about traffic. She hadn't heard a single car pass in the half hour they had been parked. Still for safety's sake, she attached a leash to each dog before releasing them. "Off," she commanded. Both dogs jumped down from the SUV's tailgate and immediately began pulling on her, straining at the end of their leashes.

"Hang on, guys! Down!" Both dogs whipped around to look at her and dropped into a downed position in the gravel lot. *Maybe I should bring the GPS?* She reached in the truck and grabbed her Garmin Rino, switching it on before shoving it in the pack. Sarah closed the truck up and locked it.

Ready to head out, she picked up the dog's leashes and released them from their down. "Free."

Gunner and Sam jumped up running and hit the end of their leads hard. She braced her body for the impact, then headed over to the incline where Dave and the hiker had gone into the woods. She leaned down to unhook the leashes. Sam and Gunner took off in a race toward the men. They barked and snapped at each other competing to be in front.

"Dave! They're heading your way," Sarah yelled. She really wanted to warn the hiker as well. Gunner could be a little boisterous during introductions.

She watched the men turn and greet the dogs. Sam and Gunner ran around the two men and then headed back in Sarah's direction.

Sarah took her time getting down to where the ground leveled off, following several meters behind the guys' path of least resistance through the initial underbrush. She was worried she might hurt herself if she wasn't conscientious, and planted each foot with care. She had lost a kidney and sustained substantial damage to her left hip, but she was young and healing well. *More of a mental block.*

The recovery process had been painful. While incarcerated, she'd spent numerous hours working on building her body back up. Fortunately she had been in good physical shape when the injury happened, which helped her heal faster.

Declining down the path into the woods, she walked at an angle. Sarah kept an eye on the ground. Dave and the hiker were engaged in an animated conversation several meters away. They weren't moving very fast. She figured Dave was stalling, allowing her to catch up.

Gunner and Sam hesitated as well. She watched them run off into the distance, then circle back behind her before heading forward into the woods again. Sarah didn't say anything. She allowed them full freedom; it was their decision to stay close to their handler. Sarah smiled. *They always have my back.*

Sarah saw Dave peer over his shoulder. The hiker pointed toward the northwest and moved his arms and hands as he spoke. They stopped for a minute and were deep in discussion when Sarah caught up.

"Doing okay?" Dave asked.

Sarah nodded her head and smiled. "Have you noticed the dogs? Their circle and distance from me has changed."

"Obviously noticeable. I think after being separated from you for months, it's made them more concerned about you and your whereabouts. They noticed your gait and speed have changed. They're not about to take their eyes from you."

"Well, I was afraid of that. I hope if we start working searches again, they'll move out and do their jobs first and worry about me second."

"I'm sure they will. It'll just take time," Dave responded. "We're going to head this way," he pointed. "Evan here says he was searching around for sheds when his dog headed down over this ravine, into the creek and found the bone. Think you can keep up?"

"Don't worry about me. I'm going to hang back a little. When the ground levels off a bit more, I'll catch up."

"We'll wait for you at the bottom."

Sarah made her way to the edge of the ravine. She stopped and studied the degree of the incline, the ground cover, and how the trees were spaced apart. With an inconsistent pace, she started to make her way down toward the intermittent creek which flowed at the bottom.

All was silent except for the babble of the creek. Sarah wondered where the dogs had gotten off to. Pausing for a moment to observe her surroundings, she looked back up at the rim of the ravine and spotted Gunner who had stopped. He was watching her. Turning downhill she spied Sam waiting for her to finish her descent. "It's okay, guys. Go do your thing. I'm fine."

Finally reaching the bottom safely, Sarah called, "Come on, guys, there's a cool creek to swim in." She watched as both dogs ran to the wide bank. *Shallow. Not much rain this past week.*

The creek was about twenty feet wide and clear water flowed. With high banks, there were areas cut deep under trees along the sides in tunnel-like formations. Obvious signs the creek handled flash floods occasionally included dried muddied leaves and old broken branches forcefully pressed into the earth.

The dogs didn't hesitate to jump in with full intensity. It was game on as usual between the two Shepherds. Gunner ran as fast as he could with Sam at his hip trying to vie for the front. It brightened Sarah's mood, causing her to laugh hard enough to lose her balance.

She grabbed a low tree branch for support. Dave looked back and smiled. He and the hiker continued downstream along the jagged embankment. The hiker liked to talk. A lot. Sarah could see in Dave's pained expression he was growing wearing of the man's constant drone.

It wasn't hard to tell Dave was getting tired of being polite. The man appeared to enjoy being the center of attention, feeling like "the key" to their investigation. Sarah smiled, knowing she would tease Dave about it later.

Dave saw it first. He must have recognized the dogs' abrupt change of behavior. "Sarah," he called in a firm but flat tone, then a second time louder and more direct. Sarah caught Dave's stare and followed his line of vision. Sam was standing in the stream with his tail straight up, stiff over his back. The dog's hackles along his spine had risen. He was trying to sniff as close to the water as he could without sucking it into his nose. Sam bit at the water—a few short, frustrated nips. The dog continued to be concerned with a scent which didn't belong. He looked perplexed, confused.

What the hell? Sarah recognize this behavior, what his body language meant. Sam had found something of deadly interest.

CHAPTER 25

SARAH

"Oh, shit," Sarah muttered, realizing what her dogs' body language signified.

The trio watched the German Shepherd, Sam, standing rigid and alert in the stream reading his surroundings. Gunner bounded toward where Sam stood in the water. Initially with playful intentions, his mind quickly set on something else. Within a few feet of Sam, he abruptly stopped and snapped his head to the left. It looked like the dog had run into an invisible wall.

"What's going on?" the hiker questioned. A look of confusion crossed his face.

Dave put his hand up and quietly said, "The dogs have picked up a scent they're not sure of. We need to stay quiet, and stand here to see what they do."

"Scent?" the hiker asked.

"These are air-scenting dogs. Sniffer dogs," Dave rephrased, annoyance in his voice.

Comprehension finally registered on the hiker's face.

Sarah inched closer to the dogs from the creek bank. "Whatcha got there, buddy?"

Sam ignored her. He continued to check the water. He was locked on a specific scent picture, honing his focus and intent in that direction. The dog stuck his head, up to his ears, under the water, lifting his snout out, barking, then becoming more frustrated at the situation. Shaking the water vigorously, he pawed aggressively where he stood in the stream.

Gunner swept past Sam, leaping onto the bank where Sarah stood. The dog didn't even stop to shake the excess water from his wet coat. *Something's really caught his attention.* She watched as

Dave bent down to pick up a handful of dirt, letting it disperse through his fingers to see which direction the air was blowing. "Dave? Can you stay here and watch Sam? I'm going to follow close to Gunner to see what he's interested in."

"Are you sure you don't want to stay here? I can go after Gunner."

"No, I'll be fine," Sarah answered, then turned and stepped off. She could hear Gunner's bell and dog tags jingling. Adrenaline replaced her pain. Picking up her pace as best she could, she headed toward the chime of his movement.

Gaining visibility of Gunner, Sarah stopped and watched him continue to air-scent as he worked to pinpoint the location of the scent source. She didn't want to get in his way. He seemed as perplexed as Sam. *It has to be more than just a few mere aged bones.*

Sarah had witnessed many dogs over years of training. Different sources and varying quantities at different stages of decomposition would elicit different levels of excitement or indications from the dogs. An older dry human bone might only produce a simple trained indication, while a larger portion of fresher human body source would elicit an excited and animated response. Each dog was different, and it was the job of the handler to understand their dog's body language intimately.

Sarah leaned against a large mature oak tree for support. Pain began to course through her hip and back. *Put it out of our mind.* Mystified at her dog's behavior, she stood back to see what would come from the dogs as they continued to search with great intensity.

She didn't have long to wait.

Gunner gave the impression he was going to attempt to lay down in one spot—which was his trained final response, his indication. But at the last minute, his nose went up into the air again, then back down to the ground, then to the tree branches. He followed the outline of the tree to its roots and sniffed at them with intense focused concentration.

Gunner started to perform his indication again but was compelled to continue sniffing. Baffled. It was as if scent was coming from every pore of the earth. *What the hell is going on?*

"This is the weirdest behavior!" Sarah yelled back to Dave, who was still standing watch over Sam. "I've never seen Gunner act so frustrated."

"Yeah, Sam is still acting interested and frustrated over here."

Sarah continued to survey Gunner's actions. He lifted his head upward toward a different tree. A lip curled, exposing large white canines, emitting a deep, low guttural growl.

"What is it, Gunner?" A rush of panic swept through her. She suddenly felt exposed. Spinning in a full circle, she studied the immediate area. Her breath quickened. A dark feeling flooded her senses. Something awful had happened here. Gunner and Sam's peculiar behaviors were telling the story. An evil story. Sarah felt vulnerable and unprotected. Thoughts of years past came rushing back. Claustrophobia overwhelmed her. *Stop it!* she commanded herself. Lost in a mental tangent, Gunner's activity brought her back to the situation.

The dog started barking and began digging insistently. Leaves, sticks, and dirt flew through the air. The soft loamy soil gave up its contents willingly. Sarah rushed to his side. Dave also came running toward the commotion. Sarah watched as debris scattered through the air. *That looked like bone! What the fuck is going on?*

"Settle, Gunner!" Sarah yelled loudly, her voice cracking. The dog stopped for a quick moment and looked in her direction, then moved several feet to his left and started digging in a new area. In the soft soil, Gunner was able to dig deep fast. Within a few seconds, he was down into the ground several inches. Sarah could see what looked to be dark plastic and pieces of clothing evident as she grabbed him by the collar. A dank, dark unwielding stench reached up and assaulted her nose. *Oh my god.* Sarah knew the smell.

Sam came running toward them and shot past her. He put his nose to the ground, inhaling deeply, his jaw closed tight. Then Sam also began to tear at the earth several feet away from where Sarah and Gunner stood.

"Dave! Sammy! Grab him, hurry!" was all Sarah could get out as she used all of her energy to hold Gunner's collar with both hands and drag him away from the disturbed earth.

The dog was zoned out. Sarah used her forearm to cover her nose and sucked in air through her mouth.

At last able to wrestle the dog into a sit and get his attention, Sarah leashed Gunner. Dave had Sam by the collar, holding his front feet off the ground as Sam tried to slip his collar. Reaching Sarah, Dave connected the leash, but ran it under and around his chest, behind the dog's front legs and then back up through the collar, fashioning a quick, make-shift harness for more control.

Remembering the tennis balls, she struggled to pull them out of her back pockets. Although, what the dogs found wasn't confirmed human remains, she trusted them and rewarded the dogs with the balls. They snatched them excitedly and continuously mashed them in their strong jowls, centering their agitated energy on their toy.

"What the hell is going on?" Sarah asked, locking eyes with Dave. He shrugged his shoulders at first.

She had a sudden feeling Dave had an ulterior motive for bringing her and the dogs today.

CHAPTER 26

DAVE

Once Dave was convinced Sarah had control over both dogs, he moved closer to where Gunner had become overwhelmed in scent, and where Sam had followed.

Surveying the scene, he took note where he walked and what the dogs had disturbed. Overturned dirt, debris and what appeared to be bone, were scattered everywhere. He needed to document every detail of where they had traversed, where the dogs had trekked, what transpired during their "hike" in the woods. The entire incident. Everything the dogs had touched, *destroyed.* Everything. *Not what I expected.*

A horrendous smell permeated. A thick, heavy odor, it stuck to the entire surroundings. Dave had been exposed to the foul odor before. *Death.*

The soil around the hole Gunner had dug appeared "fresh," like the dirt had been turned over recently. The leaves surrounding the location seemed out of the norm, as if they had been placed instead of falling naturally onto the ground.

Dave leaned in for a closer inspection. There was some type of liquid putrefaction oozing from a black plastic trash bag the dog had torn open. He covered his mouth with his shirt to try to lessen the smell. Still it burned his nose and stung his eyes. Swallowing hard, he tried to quell the bile rising in the back of his throat. He didn't want to spit or compromise the scene any more than they already had.

Could possibly be deer remains, he tried to tell himself. *No, no one would bother to "hide" deer remains this far into the woods or that deep underground.* He used the toe of his boot to push around what looked to be a rib bone. He knew the shape. Slightly smaller than the ones he had studied, there was no denying it was human.

As he scrutinized the piles of dirt, he could tell there were several more, large, intact bones and small bone fragments. He saw what he thought was a leather sole—maybe the bottom of a shoe or boot—partially decayed. *Small sized, whatever it is. Where have I seen something like that before?*

Pushing the thought to the back burner, he continued to check for more details. There were several signs pointing toward human remains.

Then, recognition of the sole. *A toddler shoe! That's what the leather shape came from!*

Finally dawning on Dave, he mouthed the words without speaking. "This is a goddamn dumping ground."

He spun around taking in the whole scene once again. One of the first rules he learned as a state trooper was the acronym STOP—*Stop, Think, Observe, Plan.* Don't rush in. Be prepared.

His thoughts started to run crazy. The distance from the road wasn't great, but it was still far for one person to haul a body. But someone could possibly drag a body downhill. The soil was soft which made digging a grave less difficult. It was almost a perfect spot. Hidden. Down an incline. *Out of sight.*

Dave noticed a few well-worn trails nearby, suggesting more than just wild game used them. The trails headed deeper into the mountain away from the highway. They looked wide enough to accommodate an ATV. *I wonder if hunters use these trails?* He hadn't noticed any deer stands since they entered the woods.

Feeling his blood pressure rise, Dave realized the situation he was in. Sarah and her dogs had made the discovery. He had been so lost in what was going on, he forgot the implications. This was going to cause major problems. He hoped it wouldn't jeopardize the circumstances of their discovery. *Maybe I could say Sarah wasn't involved.* But there was a witness—the hiker. *No, I need to be straight up on this deal.*

He hadn't cleared any of his plans with the department prior to meeting up with the hiker. Not only was he out here unauthorized, he had brought a person of great interest and her dogs into the fold. A murder defendant. Although Sarah had only been indicted, he knew how his supervisors felt about her and the fact that she'd stood trial for three murders.

Think, dammit, think. What do I need to do? With no search supplies, Dave needed to use what he had on hand to secure the scene. He grabbed a couple good sized dead branches and stuck them in the ground. He laid a couple more across the bottom of the others. It gave a "T" effect that was distinctly different than the surroundings.

He asked Sarah for the red bandana she had tied her pony tail up with. Taking the cloth, he secured the bright material around a small tree near the putrid smell.

"By the way, I brought the GPS," Sarah told him. "It's in the backpack if you want to grab it and mark the points. I used it to mark our trail."

"Perfect. That will help when I detail the map and report," Dave responded. "Okay, scene secured as much as I can for the moment. I want you two to just stay put for a little while longer until I can get this all figured out and called in."

"Sure thing," the hiker replied. "Can I do anything to help?"

"Not just yet. Hold tight," Dave replied.

Moving to higher ground for better reception, Dave pulled his cell phone from his pocket. He held his breath as he waited for his supervisor to come on the line. He was pretty sure Sheriff Kasey was still out of town, so he needed to deal with the next in line, Deputy Sheriff Felding.

With growing impatience, Dave waited to be put through. He slowly let the air escape between pursed lips. He knew he was going to get reprimanded for bringing Sarah into the woods with her dogs, even if it was completely innocent. *Or was it?*

He'd known the extent of the dogs' abilities, but he had no idea this was what they would find. Maybe he'd thought the dogs would be able to locate more bones that belonged with the femur that had been found in the stream bed several weeks earlier. With all the animal activity, the bones could have been dragged off several hundred feet in all directions.

But he never expected this. Apparent grave sites—not just partial remains, but a decomposing body as well? This was much more than he had been prepared to deal with.

"Hallow?" An older man's voice came across the phone line interrupting Dave's mental tangent. His drawl left no doubt he was a southerner.

"Hey there, Felding. It's Graves," The deputy sheriff reminded Dave a bit of the character Archie Bunker from 1970's show, *All in the Family.*

"Yeah, what's up? Whatcha need?"

"Well, I'm out at the site with the hiker who found the femur off State Route 634 near Deer Run. You know where I'm talking about?"

"Not exactly. Fill me in, will ya? What bone?" Felding questioned.

Dave gave Felding a quick rundown and requested a crime scene unit to be sent ASAP. "We've uncovered something of significance. I think you're going to want to get down here right away."

Dave could hear Felding's exasperation clearly through the phone. His supervisor didn't need to say how he felt about getting up out of his comfortable chair and huffing out to some desolate area of the woods.

"What's going on? Did you find more bones?"

"Yeah and it appears there may be a body as well. I think there's more to this area than even what I've discovered."

"What d'ya mean, more to the area?"

"Well, we've found several bones in a couple different areas and the dogs are still interested in spots even further away than normal animal activity would drag a bone. I'm thinking this may be a dump site."

"What do you mean, dogs? What dogs?" Felding's voice deepened. "Whose dogs are you using?"

Dave got quiet for a moment. He knew he had to spill the information. He knew it could compromise the finds having her on site, but he didn't care.

"Sarah and her dogs are here."

"Goddammit, Graves. You know you shouldn't have allowed her to come onto a potential crime site. You know how everyone feels about her even being in our county. Don't make the agency sorry you got hired. Kasey is going to have a field day with you when he gets back in town."

"No one ever said anything definitive about her, Felding. We were just taking the dogs for a walk in the woods with the hiker."

"Yeah, sure Graves, sure you were." Dead air came across the line. Then Felding let out a long, exasperated sigh. "Don't you go anywhere, you hear me? You stay right where you are. I'll be out there in thirty minutes."

"Okay. I'll send the hiker up to meet you along the road. He can bring you back to the site and help direct the crime scene investigators."

"Sure, we'll head out in a minute," Felding growled. Dave could hear him cussing and yelling for one of the deputies as he terminated the conversation.

Relieved the call was out of the way, Dave shut off his phone and stood there for a moment. He had thought about telling his boss not to run hot to the site. He didn't want to advertise their presence to whomever was dumping bodies. You never could tell who was around, who might drive by. But he knew better than to say that. It would just piss Felding off, being told what to do by his subordinate. The deputy sheriff acted and looked like a dumb, redneck country boy, but he was quite smart and very savvy.

Dave let out a long, deep breath. *Let's hope this isn't the end of my career with the county.*

Next, Dave kept his phone out and started taking pictures. He also pulled the GPS from Sarah's pack and saved the coordinates to his phone, and added notes about where they had stepped, where the dogs had gone, and what the dogs had done.

Dave looked around the area once more, taking note on the direction of the trails, the distance from the road, even the direction the stream ran. *Just beautiful here in the mountains.* The colors varied—shades of greens from fluorescent budding leaves, to deep, already mature foliage—and purples, yellow, red and brown tones accented nicely in small measures. Dave didn't want to believe this place might hold a dark, sinister secret underneath its fertile soil.

CHAPTER 27

SARAH

Sarah trudged from the site leaving Dave and the hiker behind. With the dogs leashed, she allowed them to pull her back toward the parking area. She didn't envy Dave. She almost felt sorry for him.

Arriving at the point where the steep incline led up to the parking area, she told the dogs to "climb." Advancing uphill with both dogs leashed, they helped pull her forward, up the grade. She was glad they didn't mind the pressure of her weight dragging on them.

Sam and Gunner continued to carry a tennis ball in their mouths. The balls weren't either dog's normal reward after a find, but they were the type of dogs who would play with anything, anywhere, at any time, and with anyone—a key component in a search dog.

Sarah's mind wandered back to the remains and the totally unexpected craziness. She wasn't entirely sure what had just happened. Adrenaline pumped through her body keeping the pain at bay.

Finally, she climbed over the guardrail that separated the steep drop off and the shoulder of the parking area. The dogs panted, their tongues hanging out, but they still held onto their rewards. They only opened their jaws wide enough to take in air. The balls stayed locked between their molars. Sarah smiled at them. No matter what, they were not dropping their well-earned prizes.

"Down," she commanded Gunner and Sam as they made it to level ground. The dogs dropped to a sphinx-like position. She needed to rest, catch her breath, and give her leg a moment before walking to the vehicle. She leaned against the guard rail for support. Although they were far from the site, she could still smell more than just a trace of the remains over the fresh country air. It clung to her hair, her clothes, and the dogs' wet coats. She wrinkled her nose. She tried to spit what she could to rid her mouth of the taste.

The dogs kept a watchful eye on Sarah as they lay on the ground waiting for her to tell them what to do next.

"We need to get you guys some water," she said, just to say something, anything. Sometimes their intensity made her feel as though she owed them some sort of response.

Gathering her strength, Sarah released the dogs from their downed position and headed to the SUV. Opening the hatch, she dropped the tailgate and made sure both crate doors were wide open before telling the dogs to jump up. Once crated, she refreshed their water buckets, then closed and locked the crate doors, securing them.

Now that Gunner and Sam were in their space, they finally let go of their toys, holding the balls between their front paws, keeping ownership. Both dogs drank deeply, devouring the fresh water. "How about we trade the toys for a treat?" Sarah chided.

She pulled out a few pieces of beef jerky from a container in the back. Laughing as she watched the dogs pick up on the scent, their interest changed from their toy to the treat. Opening one crate at a time, she traded the jerky for the ball. Each received a large rubber Kong to chew for the trip home. Tennis balls were notorious for choking unsupervised dogs.

Satisfied the dogs were taken care of and secured, she made her way to the driver's side and collapsed into the bucket seat. After closing and locking the door, she remembered she was in the country and most folks didn't lock their doors. *Old habits are hard to break.* But on the other hand, she'd just come from a mass burial site. It seemed so surreal.

Leaning back in the leather seat, she closed her eyes, taking a moment to let her nerves settle, relax. Her mind and body were exhausted. After a few deep breaths, Sarah downed half a bottle of water and ran everything through her mind from start to finish. Her thoughts remained on the point at which the dogs finally made the connection and how they had been trying to tell her something more.

While Gunner had run from area to area digging frantically and barking, Sammy had made his way into the middle with just his nose to the sky scenting, his whole body shaking. Sammy's raised hair had emitted an eerie looking display. Then he had started to growl as well. It just didn't make any sense. It had given Sarah the creeps.

The dogs were trying to convey a message of deep importance. Sarah had gotten the feeling something awful had happened there, something sinister and spine-chilling. She had to get out. She felt as though she would suffocate.

Dave had wanted her to leave the area ASAP anyway. She could tell by his exasperated looks. He didn't have to say anything to her. She shouldn't be there. He shouldn't have brought her and the dogs out with him.

At first, she felt a slight hint of disdain—Dave knew what could happen by bringing Sam and Gunner with them. He had used her, used the dogs.

But then she also realized this could jeopardize his job, his future. Their future. She could once again compromise his life. But they might not have unearthed what they did without the dogs. *But what did we find, anyway?*

Readjusting the driver's seat to her shorter stature, she adjusted the mirrors as well. Sarah carefully maneuvered the SUV around in the small parking area and drove up to the lip of the entrance where it met the roadway. She stopped to check for traffic before pulling out. A vehicle was heading in her direction, so she turned on the radio and surfed through the channels for a music station that would come in clearly as she waited for the vehicle to pass. She looked up from the dashboard as it—a van—made its way toward hers from the direction she needed to head.

It was an older model Dodge, well-worn, and showing years of neglect. It slowed down as it passed Sarah. The side and back windows were covered from the inside with old newspaper and peeling cardboard. The side mirrors were loose and held together with duct tape. The faded paint had oxidized and partially eroded. Surface rust dotted the quarter panels and parts of the lower door and bumpers. *POS,* Sarah thought.

The Explorer Sarah was driving had dark tinted windows, making it difficult for the van's driver to see into hers, but she could see him fine. *I know I've seen him somewhere before, but where?* It felt like déjà vu. She racked her brain but just couldn't remember. *Probably hit me later.* Sarah wasn't concerned.

"Ugh, you guys stink!" Sarah voiced as the SUV filled with the odor of hot, damp dogs. Rolling the driver's side window down partway, the van's driver locked eyes with her and then quickly sped up and took off. The van coughed forward, smoke billowing from its tailpipes. *Suspicious. Recluse country folk.*

Sarah turned on the rear A/C and blasted the dogs with cool air. She checked in her mirror to make sure they were laying down and settled, then pulled onto the highway and took off toward home. She wanted to make sure she was long gone before the deputy sheriff and crime scene techs showed up. She also hoped her being involved didn't cause a big problem for Dave. She knew one day soon, everyone around them would have to come to terms with her as a Nelson County deputy's live-in girlfriend.

Chapter 28

Dave

Deputy Sheriff Felding showed up without lights and sirens running. At least Dave didn't hear Felding's vehicle, but from where he stood, deep in the woods, he would have a difficult time hearing. The crime scene investigation technicians arrived within the hour. A handful of Nelson County deputies, Dave's co-workers, made it out to the site as well. It was no longer a private party.

The crime scene techs weren't pleased about trudging deep into the woods carrying equipment. Felding ordered another deputy to make some calls to round up an ATV with a wagon. Skeptical about bringing in heavier equipment, Dave wanted to make sure the woods from the remains site to the road were thoroughly checked for clues prior to destroying any evidence with a heavy piece of equipment. But he wasn't running the show.

Several vehicles were parked along the highway's shoulder. The small pull-off parking area was jammed full. Marked vehicles showed up as well. Anyone passing by would be able to associate agency vehicles parked in the middle of nowhere as meaning something out of the norm was going on. Someone who might have had something to do with what lay buried in the woods, would know they'd been found out.

Since Dave's call to the sheriff's department was made privately and hadn't gone through the 911 system, at least reporters wouldn't have been alerted right away. But it would only be a matter of time... It was protocol for news reporters to call the EMS—emergency management system—to ask if there were any police incidents or events happening. If there was a major accident, EMS would contact local stations to alert the public. The news hounds would soon get wind of something major going on. Dave was hoping to keep this find under wraps as long as possible. He knew it could get out of control quickly.

Deputy Sheriff Felding made it down the embankment without mishap—physically. But Dave could hear him cussing and making a fuss long before he saw him. Dave laughed to himself. Felding liked to complain, but it was just his way. He really wasn't a bad guy. Just older, heavier and not as agile as in his younger days.

Sarah had gone back to the SUV with Gunner and Sam of her own accord. He hoped she had made it without any issues. Dave hadn't had to say anything to her. She'd left without words, automatically understanding it would be best if she wasn't on scene when Dave's boss showed up. He knew she was trying to make it easier for him, but now he really didn't care what Felding thought. Sarah's dogs had made a tremendous discovery and he would have to deal with the fall-out later.

"So, what have we got going on here, Graves?" Felding asked in his slow enduring drawl. The deputy sheriff pulled his cowboy hat from his head, beads of sweat covering his bald skin and reddened face. He used a handkerchief to wipe the dampness from the top of his scalp and forehead as he waited for Dave to elaborate on the details.

Dave began by going over the background information, showing Felding firsthand where the original remains find was made by the hiker. "Over there is the creek," Dave pointed in the direction, "where the hiker found the child's femur. The water level was a bit lower in March when his dog dug it up from the creek bed. Now the water level is about a half-foot deeper but still low for this time of year."

"Okay, got it," Felding said nodding his head, but confusion still loomed over his thick, furrowed brows.

"So, we made our way down here to the location to scout the area out some. Sarah's dogs were off lead, we were just letting them range and go for a walk with us. When we neared the creek however, one of the dogs showed interest in the water and surrounding bank area, while the other dog took off past him and became very interested in the trees and ground on the opposing side of the creek."

Felding continued to look confused, appearing as if he didn't understand how dogs could pick up on scent from several feet away and covered in dirt. But he nodded his head, so Dave continued.

"Are you with me on all this so far?" Dave asked.

"What do you mean by 'the dogs showed interest'? Explain this, will ya, please?"

"Sure. As the one dog entered the creek, his body language changed." Dave pointed out maybe an animal had dragged the bone to the creek. He clarified how the water tunneled under the bank and perhaps an animal could have dragged more bones under the area or the first scents the dogs had picked up were from remains that had permeated the dirt and aired out along the banks. The dogs might have picked up on them because they were standing in the water, or the dogs' bodies may have been directly at the same height of the banks.

Felding nodded again. He looked like a bobble head sitting on someone's car dash.

"Changed? What do you mean, his body language changed? What the hell do you mean?"

At least he's asking the right questions. Dave needed to slow his thought process down, so he could explain in a way that would make sense to Felding.

"It means he gave natural alerts he had located human scent. Both of Sarah's dogs are air-scenting search and rescue dogs. They are also recovery dogs. That means they've been trained to locate missing live human subjects... or human remains as well. They give off not-so-subtle clues when they get interested in an area, in a certain scent. Both dogs gave these clues, then the one dog gave his trained indication telling us he had picked up on human scent not belonging to any of us." Dave pointed to himself and the hiker.

"What did these clues look like that first made you aware of what the dogs were on to?"

Dave took a step back. He paused a moment to figure out how he was going to respond. "The first dog to show signs was Sam. He was standing in the middle of the creek when I noticed his stance. His tail was flagged, standing straight up and his hackles were up along his back. He had closed his mouth and was sucking in the air deep. He started nipping and barking at the water."

"You get all this information from her dog acting like this way? How the hell do you know what that behavior even means? He's a dog, for god's sake!"

Dave knew it was more than just the dogs Felding was alluding to. His problem was that these dogs belonged to Sarah... had been trained by Sarah.

"Each dog has different behaviors. I know these two dogs well. I've worked with them, cared for them, trained with them. I know what their body language means. Whether you like the idea about Gunner and Sam being Sarah's canines, these are good, proven search dogs with documented finds from past searches." Dave knew this information could prove debatable on a few of the searches, but he was trying to push a point home.

Felding cleared his throat. Dave could tell he was beginning to lose patience.

"So, go on, what else did you find?" Felding asked.

"The other dog—Gunner—he caught a big whiff of scent and ran past Sam, hopped back up on the bank, and headed over to this area." Dave pointed to a big oak and some pines standing about twenty meters from the creek. "We couldn't get to him soon enough. The dog was perplexed, like there was scent coming from every direction, everywhere. By the time we climbed up the bank to where he was, Gunner was already digging up bones. He also dug down to what appears to be a body wrapped in plastic."

Felding's whole facial expression changed, his cheeks grew redder and he let out a huff of air. "You went and let the dogs disturb what could possibly be crime scenes! What the hell were you thinking?" The deputy sheriff threw his hands up in disbelief.

Dave knew agencies who had never worked with dogs—or the people who may work in an agency, but weren't dog people themselves—had a difficult time understanding exactly how canines performed. It was a learning process. There were some issues which were just unavoidable at times. Handlers tried to train their canines not to touch remains or any item they may find, but usually, the dogs with the best work ethic are also the ones who are edgy and become overexcited when they make a find.

Sometimes they do more than just a "touch," dig or lick. On occasion, some dogs have done much worse. Normally, once an agency understands how dogs work though—and how much they enhance an officer's job—whatever way the dog works best becomes accepted.

"My thought is this, Felding. We would never have found the bodies without the dogs. We might never have known this site fully existed. If you look around, there really aren't many clues showing people have even been out here. I doubt seriously, even with a tight grid search, we could have located anymore of the first child's remains."

"I don't know about this. Make sure you document everything well. This might come back to bite us in the ass somehow. Sarah's dogs making this find, her being on scene, who the hell knows? So, show me where they are and what you got." Spit flew from Felding's flustered face. He was sweating from more than just the hike into the woods.

Walking Felding over to the edge of the creek bank, Dave pointed to the other side again toward the large oak tree. "Over there is where Gunner indicated and dug up several bones appearing to be human. Just to the left side about twenty feet is where he started to dig deeper down and uncovered a plastic bag with decomp. I believe there is much more to be found in this surrounding area." Dave spread his arms and pointed, encompassing everything that could be seen. "I think we need to do a very involved, detailed search of this whole mountainside."

Once Dave and Felding had gone over what had transpired, the crime scene technicians moved in.

Felding asked where Sarah and the dogs were. "We will probably need to interview her at some point and take her statement."

"It won't be a problem. Let me know and I'll bring her to the station or you can meet her at the cabin. I'm sure she'll completely cooperate in the investigation."

Dave texted Sarah to say he would call her when he needed to be picked up. He also sent the hiker on his way, explaining not to speak to anyone regarding what he had seen or heard that day. Another deputy had taken the hiker's statement about what he had witnessed so it would be impartial if they ended up in court for some reason.

Dave knew Felding was angry with him, but he also figured the man would get over it once they realized the enormity of the situation—a mystery possibly beginning years ago in South Central Pennsylvania. He had an odd feeling that it was all somehow connected.

CHAPTER 29

SARAH

Driving back to the farm, Sarah switched on the police scanner. Chatter broke the silence, crackling across the air waves from local police and fire agencies. She paid attention to the abbreviated language of acronyms and codes dispatch used for staff responding to the situation she'd just emerged from.

She recognized many of the cryptic terms, but didn't believe it would be difficult for an untrained person to comprehend what was going on. That raised a hint of concern.

Caught up in the exchanges, a slight twinge of disappointment swept through her as she reminisced her previous life, her previous career. It made her homesick thinking of her old co-workers. She missed the tightknit group, the camaraderie she once shared with them. *Stop it!* She wanted to stay positive, but for some reason, it had been more difficult over the last several weeks. She seemed to be an emotional train wreck and she didn't understand why. Her thoughts spiraled downhill thinking how much she missed the former life she had struggled so hard to build. Now it was gone, no returning. Ever.

Pulling up to the cabin, Sarah stopped abruptly. "Sorry, guys," she spoke to Gunner and Sam as they slid in the crates. Sarah's mood turned black. The darkness loomed over her. She couldn't seem to shake it. Taking a deep breath, she unbuckled, then berated herself for feeling sorry for her situation. *I should be thankful for everything I have: Dave, the dogs, a new start. Get over it!*

Sarah sat in the SUV a few more minutes. Exhausted. Her mood swung. Overcome with guilt, she thought she was going to cry. One minute she was mad as hell and the next, she was ready to tear up. *What is wrong with me?*

Needing to deal with the dogs, Sarah didn't want to convey her bad mood to them. It would only make them question her and stress out about something they couldn't do anything about. She wanted to remain calm and balanced, if not for her sake, for theirs. The dogs had just made a huge find and they deserved better.

She closed her eyes and meditated for a moment, letting her mind settle down and rest. Taking a deep breath, she held it before slowly letting it go. They all had just been through a rollercoaster ride. Gunner and Sam had exposed something significant. She needed to make sure she let them know they had done an exceptional job as she cared for them. Attitude in check, it was time to get out of the confines of the stinky vehicle reeking of wet dogs, sweat and human remains.

Once out of the Explorer, Sarah rounded the back and opened the hatch. Two damp, foul-smelling dogs greeted her. They hung onto their rubber Kongs with clenched jaws. Sarah laughed. The sight of Gunner and Sam were enough to lighten anyone's awful mood.

"Hey, guys!" Sarah disguised her voice in a high-pitched greeting. Tails thumped in their crates. She held up her hand. "Wait," she commanded. They stood quietly, locking eyes with her. She opened their crate doors and released the exuberant dogs into the front yard still holding onto their prized toys. "Go do your business, guys. When you're done, you're both getting a bath!" Both dogs' ears perked up at the four-letter word.

Sarah leaned against the side of the vehicle as she watched them sniff around the yard. Each one took a moment to find a perfect and appropriate place to hike a leg. She felt her dark mood continue to ease, evaporate. *I do have a lot to be thankful for.* She smiled. Just watching her dogs' antics put her in a better mood.

Still, Sarah couldn't seem to shake the anxiety building deep within—a feeling something bad was going to happen—which she couldn't completely clear from her senses. She hoped the foreboding was due to the activities today and she was just tired.

Sam dropped his slobber-covered Kong, but Gunner wouldn't let his go and continued to chomp and squish the toy between strong jaws. "No wonder your teeth are getting worn down," she spoke to Gunner as she watched him mash the rubber toy.

Walking over to pick up the one Sam had dropped, Sarah noticed something peculiar. As she leaned down, she saw what looked like a fresh set of footprints by the house. On closer inspection, she found tracks in the dark soil surrounding the newly planted bushes near the cabin's front windows. *Perfect area for a track trap.* She thought about how certain areas collect prints easier and preserve them better than others... something she had learned in one of the man-tracking classes she had taken at a search and rescue conference.

There are natural *track traps* found in the environment, like wet soil protected by a canopy of trees which cover and preserve a track for a long period of time. Loose soil can catch and keep a footprint as well. It's also not unheard of for a search and rescue team on a mission to bring in sand and lay it out in places they believe the lost person could possibly walk through to try and catch a track or sign of the missing subject.

Sarah studied the impressions. The footprints appeared to be different from any of the boots she or Dave wore. They were larger with deeper welts like a construction worker's boot. There were lighter soil chunks pressed deep into the dark soil—maybe dried mud or dirt that came off the boots. And the tracks appeared recent.

"What the hell?" Sarah instinctively went into a protective, survival frame. She stood still for a moment. Her leg muscles tightened. *Maybe someone is still here?* She tried to listen, but all she could hear was blood pounding in her ears. A shiver ran through her body.

Sarah walked around to inspect the area closer, staying bent low to the ground. This angle allowed the sun to reflect in just the right way so she could see the tracks clearly and in what direction they led. They had come up from the creek bank, crossed through her side yard, around the cabin, and then right up to the front windows behind the newly planted bushes.

Standing up straight, she watched the dogs closely as they found the tracks and followed them. Both canines went back and forth, circled, and then followed the suspicious trail again. They stopped occasionally at an imprint in the grass, sniffing deeply and touching it ever so gently with the tip of a tongue. Gunner's tail flagged stiffly over his back. Sam's hair raised along his spine. He stood with his tail straight out and looked back to study Sarah's face in question. *Great, what now?*

"Whatcha got there, boys?" Sarah queried in a melodic sing-song tone. Gunner looked up for a quick second, holding Sarah's gaze, then went back to his serious inquisition. Sam didn't hesitate in his quest and followed scent off toward the barn. Gunner moved off quick on the same "hot" trail. They were locked in now, and both ran in what looked like a stiff lope, lifting their head every so many strides to check their surroundings. It was their way of being on-guard, alert, in protection mode as they worked the scent.

Sarah could tell they were tracking something or someone who didn't belong. She knew the dogs were suspicious—their body language clearly expressed it. They communicated through subtle and not so subtle movements. Every now and again, one of the dogs would look back at her as if asking, "Do you smell this? Do you understand what's going on here?" Sarah was always in awe of how they switched from working a scenario, to knowing when they should be protecting their property.

There was a greasy spot on one of the window panes in addition to the tracks. She wasn't sure if it was someone's handprint or if someone had smeared their face or nose on the pane as they tried to peer into the house. The smear was up high, on the top window. It was clearly at a level higher than she or Dave's stature. Between what looked to be sizeable, heavy boot tracks in the dirt and the smear on the glass, the trespasser had to be quite tall.

Sarah backtracked from around the cabin. She wanted to keep the tracks as "fresh" as possible so she could show them to Dave when he returned home. She grabbed a plastic trash bag from her SUV and laid it over the deepest print beside the house. "That should it keep it somewhat protected from the elements," she spoke out loud.

Stepping back to look at the cabin and the yard, she tried to think who would possibly want to come onto their property and peek into the house? Deep in thought, she temporarily lost track of the dogs. She walked around the cabin to the backyard and could see they were halfway across the pasture toward the barn. Sam had his nose to the ground following the track while Gunner had his nose to the sky checking the wind.

"*Stop!*" Sarah yelled at the top of her lungs. The dogs were about fifty meters from where she stood. Both paused in their movement forward. They stood in place looking back toward her. "*Wait!*" she yelled the second command. Sam dropped into a down position, but Gunner just stood frozen in place.

Looking across the field to where the dogs were, Sarah could barely make out where someone or something had forged a trail through the tall hay. She nor Dave would've cut across the pasture to the barn. Their habits were to walk up the gravel or drive a vehicle. No doubt the hay had been walked through recently and had just sprung back into place. There were tips and strands of grass blades that appeared broken or bent, giving away where someone had trampled across it. The color looked *different*, slightly darker green where blades had been crushed.

She could easily recognize a shadow of the trail if she didn't look at it directly, just out of the corner of her eye. Since it didn't appear to be too many hours old, she knew someone had come to the cabin and snooped around while they were gone.

Initially, she was angry. But then panic set in. It was only her and the dogs here. *Why would someone come snooping around when no one's home? Could they still be here?* Dave was on the remains crime scene and would be there several more hours, possibly into the night. She didn't want to bother him with something she should be able to handle herself. With two large, male sable Shepherds at her side resembling wolf hybrids, an intruder would think twice before approaching her.

Heading toward the waiting dogs, Sarah picked up her pace the best she could without running. Her gait replicated a stiff three-beat canter. Pain shot up from her hip. She sucked in a quick breath and tried to push the throbbing aside. Drawing strength as she neared Sam and Gunner, she shouted, "Free," and then tried to keep up with the dogs. Between the pain and short strides, she followed them as they continued toward the barn.

Sarah didn't want them to enter the barn without her. Worried whoever had come onto the farm unwelcomed and unannounced might still be lurking there or hiding somewhere, Sarah wanted to make sure they were together. She mentally belittled herself for yelling at the dogs and giving herself away, but thought if someone was on the farm, they would have already heard the sound of the tires hitting the gravel driveway.

Remembering she still had one more mode of protection, Sarah thought this was an appropriate time to employ it. She pulled a small revolver from the fitted holster snug in the waistline in the back of her pants. *Last resort.* She carefully drew her weapon, raising it in front of her. "Anyone here?" she called out. As she got closer to the barn doors, she could see someone had left the latch unhooked. *Also unusual.*

Sunny and Tank were still out in the side pasture. Both were standing near the barn with their back ends up against the fence as they watched the dogs work. They kept their heads raised, nostrils flared as they tried to identify Sarah and the dogs.

"It's okay," she called to the horses. Sunny returned her greeting with a soft nicker. Sarah and the dogs were downwind of the pair, so they couldn't catch their scent, but they would recognize her voice. Their eyesight was not the most reliable when they looked directly at something.

The horses appear to be on the alert more than usual. Maybe someone approached them and was in the barn who didn't belong?

Gunner and Sam circled the barn once. Before Sarah could say anything, they slipped under the door between the dirt floor and the boards. Sarah pushed the barn door in and entered the building in a slow manner, gun raised.

Allowing her vision to acclimate to the lower light, she stood for a moment. Slits of dusty daylight spilled through barn slats. She observed the dogs still in their guardian protection mode on a mission.

Keeping their noses close to the ground, they continued to follow an unidentified track. They sneezed occasionally as dust filled their nostrils. Gunner stopped at the vertical ladder that ascended to the hayloft. He looked up into the darkened abyss. The lower illumination made it difficult to see into the loft from the ground. There were no electrical lights hooked up in this area of the old barn yet. *Just keeps getting better.* Fear replaced a little of the confidence the gun had initially brought Sarah.

She was still in awe someone had the audacity to come onto their farm uninvited, look in their cabin window and enter their barn. But now, looking up into the space she couldn't see clearly, she didn't think it would be wise to climb up an old wooden ladder with a loaded gun looking for danger. But she didn't know what else she could do.

Standing at the bottom with both dogs at her side now, their heads snapped up. A small noise dragged across the floor above, distinctly coming from the loft.

Sarah knew she wasn't mistaken... the dogs heard it as well. A faint scraping along the hayloft floor sounded again. A puff of dust shot out from the loft and sprinkled down on the trio. Sarah sucked in a quick breath and held it. Her pulse raced. Her survival alarms were going haywire. Blood pounded in her ears. Hackles raised on Gunner and Sam. With lips raised exposing their canines, both dogs emitted a long, low guttural growl. *What the hell is that?* Sarah mustered up her determination and called out to the unknown, "Hey! Who the hell is up there?"

CHAPTER 30

SARAH

Clouds of dust exploded from the hayloft as several bats swooped into the aisle. Sarah stumbled backwards. A feral cat barreled down from the platform to a lower board above a stall. Reaching the floor, it sprinted away hissing.

The dogs froze as they eyed the cat, but kicked into prey drive when it shot out of the barn.

Sarah ducked. Covering her head with her arms, she shouted, "Sam! Gunner! Here! Come on!"

The dogs were excited. She had to call them several times before they gave up on the chase. Both possessed a keen prey drive and Sarah didn't want them locking in on a wild cat since they might end up on the losing end.

Outside the barn, she opened the large wooden doors all the way and a few more bats flew from the loft to the wooded area across the pasture. *Something stirred them up.* She made the dogs lay down in a grassy patch beside the barn where she could keep an eye on them. She needed a moment to contemplate what to do next.

Think, Sarah, think! She didn't want to call the police. Most of the units would be on-scene with Dave. The deputies would be stretched thin taking calls coming in for Nelson County. Besides, she wasn't sure how the police would respond to her and her situation.

Coming up with a game plan, she decided to keep her gun drawn and go through the entire barn, check the horses, and then look for any other trails or tracks outside. Next, she would go to the cabin and do a thorough sweep of that structure as well, then take notes, snap some pictures, and draw a map of where she had seen the tracks. She would create her own incident report.

"Free!" Sarah released the dogs. Gunner and Sam took off back inside the barn, their bodies animated with the excitement of what they considered a scenting game. Between tracking the uninvited human, the feral cat's trail, and other unknown animals who may have visited the barn—and may be still here—the dogs' noses were right back in the game going non-stop.

"Okay, guys," Sarah said to them as she started to climb the ladder. Sam sat on his haunches looking up to where she was heading. Gunner tried a few rungs then decided he wasn't agile enough to climb the difficult obstacle. The old ladder ran vertically up the wall. There were handholds along the sides, but the rungs themselves were slick and well-worn. "You guys just wait, I'll be right back."

Sarah holstered her gun as she climbed. Between the angle of the ladder, the small rungs and their awkward spacing, there was no way she could safely handle a gun and traverse to the top.

Finally, she crawled onto the loft's platform, stood up, and drew her pistol. She gave herself a second to allow her eyes to adjust to the lower light. She could see recent prints in the dust on the floor and where webs had been broken. Some bales of hay had been pushed away from the main stack and busted open.

Walking over to inspect the bales, Sarah's foot stepped onto a hard, misshapen item. She looked down to see an opened pocket knife. Pulling a tissue from her pocket, she picked it up. It wasn't one she owned and didn't look like anything Dave had. *Doesn't make sense. Who was up here, and why? Why would they move and open bales of hay?*

She closed the knife, pocketed it, and finished checking the rest of the loft. Hearing a soft mewing sound from the back of the stacked hay, she decided to investigate. Her mood softened at the sight of four scraggly kittens. "They must belong to the feral cat that came flying out of the loft with the bats," she said out loud. All the kittens' eyes were still closed. Sarah made a mental note to make sure she visited daily to socialize them. She didn't want them to be feral and fearful like their mother.

Sarah re-stacked the hay bales then climbed back down the ladder, wincing in pain as she lowered herself from rung to rung. She needed to finish investigating the barn, check the horses, then see if the dogs could find and follow any tracks or trails leading from the barn. She was confident whomever had been trespassing had left—and left in a hurry. Most likely when she had pulled up, she had surprised them, or they somehow knew she had been on her way home. *But she needed to be sure.*

Once she had cleared each area in the barn, she and the dogs headed back outside. Sarah checked on Sunny and Tank, still standing with their backends up against the fence line near the barn. Their heads were raised and focused across the pasture, at an area near the creek. *Hmm.* Sarah noted the horses' body language, paying attention to it just like she had learned to do with the dogs.

Behind the main barn, the canines picked up a trail again. It wound around the barn and the horses' run-in shed, then went straight through the pasture and to the creek. Sarah made out what materialized as a path in the tall grass where the dogs concentrated.

They lost the trail at the water's edge. Gunner and Sam jumped in and tried to cross the creek and continue their search, still interested in the trail of the stranger. Sarah called them off. The pain in her hip was radiating and she needed to clear the house before dusk which was beginning to close in.

She slowed her gait as she and the dogs started toward the cabin. Sam slowed his tempo as well to stay within several feet of Sarah while Gunner ran up ahead to check things out. Although the dogs should be tired from the day's events, they still seemed to be keyed up. She knew the vibe of this trespasser had made them uneasy. She also knew they were her guardians as well as her partners, and taking care of her was their number one responsibility. This quality seemed to come naturally to the

German Shepherd breed. But she continued to keep her weapon drawn.

The trio circled the small cabin. Sarah unlocked the door and the dogs pushed their way past her into the house. They ran from each bedroom to the bathroom, through the kitchen and living area without sniffing the air or tracking a trail. Sarah finally felt a little more at ease but wasn't about to let her guard down. With her gun still drawn, she went from room to room checking under beds and in closets.

Finally, putting the safety on, she laid her weapon on the counter. She locked the front door and checked every window to make sure they were secured as well. She turned on all the lights in the house. She knew Dave would be late, and she would be alone in a rural cabin far away from the general population. Gunner and Sam brought her some peace of mind. They would alert her if there was a problem and protect her if they needed to. She relaxed slightly.

Sarah put on coffee and rustled through the fridge trying to find something to eat. She was beyond starved. She finally settled on bacon and eggs—her go-to meal. While the coffee was brewing and the food was frying, she pulled out the dogs' bowls and made their meals. Both animals laid down on the cool hardwood floor in the kitchen watching and waiting. She gave them dinner in their crates and then sat down at the small table beside the kitchen window.

Peering out at the dwindling sunset, she watched the sun dip behind a spur of the Blue Ridge Mountains. The deep greens and purples resonated in the lowering light. *There can't be a more beautiful place on earth. I really do feel fortunate to be here.*

Deep in thought as she downed more coffee with her dinner, she reflected on the day's events—the hike, finding the remains, coming home to find someone had trespassed on the farm. It was unnerving to think an uninvited guest had peered into their house and went through their barn. She felt so exposed. *And why did they split open the bales of hay? What were they in the middle of when she pulled up and scared them off?*

Her thoughts turned to Dave and what he must be going through. She hadn't heard from him which gave concern for worry as well. Sarah felt they were forming a good relationship, but sometimes agonized it would fray. Even though Dave had told her time and time again he accepted her and everything that came with her, she wondered if he would tire of putting up with her and her past. Her history had to be a constant disturbance in his life as well as it was in hers. And in his line of work, it was in complete conflict.

Sarah finished up with her meal, put the plates away, and let the dogs loose from their crates. She sat down at the computer and fired it up. She wanted to type a few notes and a log of the trespass incident to show Dave. Afterwards, she wanted nothing more than to sink into a nice hot bath to help relieve the pain in her hip and muscles. She had done more today than she had planned on and much more than she had done in months.

Finally, the computer screen log-on appeared. Sarah opened a new document and started typing everything that had transpired from the moment she came home and noticed the dogs' activity, finding the tracks, the smudge, etc. She saved and closed the file and was about to get up when she realized she had forgotten to mention the kittens. No big deal. But she thought if she put it in the document, it wouldn't be forgotten.

Sarah clicked open the document folder and went in search of her new file entitled "Trespasser Incident." As she scanned down the list, she saw one she didn't recognize. It was titled "S.G. Background." *That's weird. Wonder what's in it.* It wasn't a "locked" document, but she noted the file had been started the same date she was incarcerated.

Sarah opened the document and began reading.

CHAPTER 31

DAVE

No surprise, Dave thought shoving his dead phone back in his pocket. *Need to find a ride home.* It was late, early actually. Well versed in police protocols, he knew from past experiences, there were no time parameters on incidents. He was spent by the time he was relieved from his duties.

Looking up to survey the forest, he spied the crime scene technicians scattered throughout the woods. Generators rallied the portable lights keeping the areas illuminated, allowing the techs to do an initial assessment of the scene. Fumes of decomposing remains graced the night air. Dave turned to face upwind.

Stress and tension were replaced by physical fatigue and mental exhaustion. Dave was put off by the tone of the incident. He felt the cold stares from his co-workers. The deputies resented him for presenting them not just with more work, but what looked like a very physical, in-depth case for weeks—possibly months to come.

Several officers had made comments stating death seemed to follow him, or maybe it had something to do with his girlfriend. Not thinking straight, he believed whatever he replied would be taken as a threat, and since he didn't need to lose his position over something stupid, Dave let the comments go.

Thoughts of Sarah flooded his mind. Guilt plagued him. He wasn't quite sure what he was feeling and tried to process it. But he didn't want to risk disturbing her at this hour for a ride from the scene. She would be asleep. *Maybe I don't want to face her?* He decided instead to opt for another deputy to give him a ride home. Using his radio, he called dispatch to put him through to the station. Desperately wanting to get home, clean up and get something to eat, he still felt unsure what to expect once he got there.

Food had been brought in earlier, but he'd been in no mood to eat between the excavation of bodies and the stench that covered everything.

Working his way back to the road, Dave found Deputy Brooks waiting for him. They rode in silence to Dave's farm. Pulling up to the cabin, they could see every light on, including the ones in the barn. *What's up with that?*

"You good?" Brooks asked as Dave climbed out of the cruiser.

Two dogs sounded as they heard the men out front. Ferocious barks and growls were non-stop.

Closing the vehicle's door, Dave leaned into the open window of the cruiser. "Looks like Sarah has the place lit up. Maybe today just spooked her. Thanks again. See you tomorrow."

Brooks tipped his hat at Dave and pulled away.

Dave turned toward the front of the cabin. Both dogs were now propped up in the front bay window looking out at him, tongues hanging, tails wagging. And whining. *At least someone's glad to see me.*

CHAPTER 32

SARAH

Startled by the dogs' explosive barking, Sarah bolted from the couch to peer out the front window. Rubbing her eyes, she felt the burn from mascara that seeped into them. It was well after three in the morning as she watched Dave climb out of the county cruiser and slam the car door.

Sarah hadn't been able to sleep. Congested, her eyes were red and swollen from sobbing. After finding the remains, the close encounter with an intruder, and then finding the document on the computer, she felt like she was losing any mental stability she had gained.

An exhausted Dave came in the side door through the tiled mud room. Dirt and debris covered his boots and lower portions of his pants. His uniform was stained with sweat and it reeked with the scent of decomposition. Unlacing his boots, he kicked them off, dropped his pants and slid out of his shirt before noticing her.

"Hey Sarah, what are you still doing up? Why are all the lights on?" he asked on his way to the shower. When she didn't respond, he turned to look at her and stopped in his tracks. "What's going on? What's wrong?"

Sarah began to unravel. She drew in a long, shaky breath and tried to pull herself together.

"What is it, Sarah?" Dave asked again.

"Everything, just everything!" she yelled, biting her quivering bottom lip. Tears flowed.

Dave stood, looking at her questioningly, still in his underwear, smelling acrid.

"I don't understand." He started to approach Sarah where she was curled up on the sofa with the dogs, but stopped several feet away. "You need to tell me what's going on. Does it have anything to do with what was found in the woods today?"

"No. Yes, and everything!" she blurted, snorting between sobs. "I found the file and there was someone on our farm! They looked in our house. They were in the barn. And the file... Why didn't you tell me?"

"Hang on, woman. What are you talking about? There was someone on our farm?"

"When I got home and let Gunner and Sam out of the truck, they started tracking around the yard and I found footprints, and there's a greasy smudge on the front window."

"You think the dogs found a human track?"

"I don't *think*, I know!" she yelled in an unsteady voice.

"How are you sure?" Dave questioned, giving her his full attention.

Sarah took a deep breath to regain her composure. With more control, she answered, "I followed the dogs scenting outside the house. There were large boot tracks in the soil and a handprint or something on the window. You can see where whoever it was went from the house to the barn through the paddock. The grass is broken, and there's a shadow trail. They were in the barn!" Sarah began to shake.

"What trace did you find in the barn?

"More tracks, the dogs followed. The trespasser had been up in the loft. Hay bales have been moved and some were broken open. And I found a pocket knife." She pulled the small item wrapped in tissue from her pocket and handed it to Dave. He stepped back to examine it in better lighting.

Sarah watched as he opened the tissue and turned it over and over in his hand. It was an older army knife with inlaid initials. It looked worn and must have been someone's prized possession at one time. Well-made and other than years of use, it was still in great condition.

"Did you call it in to the station? Did you let someone else know?"

"Call it in?" Sarah said between short breaths. "No."

"Why not?"

"Because I didn't think I should." Sarah looked away. "I didn't think they would bother with me."

"Quit thinking that way, Sarah. It's their job. It was worth calling in. I'll put in a report about it tomorrow when I get to work."

There was no transition in conversation, she just blurted it out. "Why didn't you tell me about the file you were working on? The one about me?"

Dave stood planted, silent for a moment. Crossing his arms over his chest, his forehead wrinkled. "I didn't think you were ready," he replied.

"Ready?" she shouted in anger. "I will never be ready. How did you get this information? I'm not sure I believe any of it. Why did you keep this from me?" Sarah's temper was full blown. She felt betrayed by Dave, inundated by all the things he had kept secret from her.

"Calm down, Sarah." Dave moved closer to where she sat on the couch.

She put up her hand. "Don't come near me!"

"It wasn't a secret. I left the file right there where you would find it. It's been there since we've been in this cabin."

"But how did you find that stuff? How do you know it's even true?" Her voice still quaked.

"Sarah, it's late. I'm tired. I need a shower. I'm hungry. Can't we talk about this when we've both had a good night's sleep?"

"Maybe you'd just be better off..." Sarah trailed, leaving the thought unspoken, but implied.

"Enough. I don't want to hear you say that ever again," Dave stated in a deep, serious voice.

He was beside her now. In her space. She knew he meant it in more ways than one. She knew he didn't want her feeling sorry for herself and wanted her to 'man-up' and quit the pity party. He leaned down and took her in his arms. Sarah started to cry again.

Regaining composure, she knew Dave was right. It would be better to talk about everything she had discovered after a good night's sleep. When they both were in a better frame of mind.

She slowly gained control and mumbled, "I'm not sure I can sleep." He just held her for a moment until she added, "I'm okay. You can let go now."

"You sure?"

"Yes, you really reek."

Dave loosened his grip and drew back far enough to look at her. A hint of a smile curled at one corner of her lips.

"Yes, I'm sure." She smiled. And with that she pushed his handsome but sour chest away from her.

Dave stood up. "Can you make me something to eat while I shower? Since you can't sleep?" he asked sheepishly, displaying a coy smile.

Sarah wiped her eyes and nose on her shirt.

Dave laughed. Her mascara must certainly have smeared in every direction. "You are a sight."

"Thanks," she mumbled and headed to the kitchen. "Can you please get in the shower? You're stinking up the joint."

"Why, of course."

Sarah pulled the eggs and bacon out for the second time since she got home. She felt a little better but was far from recovered from the information Dave had stored on the computer. *What if it's all true? Where did it come from? Do I really have a brother?*

CHAPTER 33

DAVE

Leaning against the wall of the shower stall, Dave tried to relax under the hot water. He worked to let go of the day's events, let go of the tension... the full realization of what they had stumbled upon. Closing his eyes, he inhaled the steamy air. The water soothed his well-defined muscles, the heat eased the soreness throughout his body.

Lathering up, he worked at scrubbing the smell of death from his body. The scent adhered to every pore. Washing his hands and face several times, he sucked in deep breaths of the heavy steam to clear his nose, but he couldn't rid himself of the acrid smell of decomp.

An exhausting twenty-four hours, and he had come home to another draining situation with Sarah. Mentally depleted. At least the information he had found on her was finally out in the open. He hadn't had any plans on when he was going to tell her about his research, yet he definitely planned on telling her... at some point.

Sometimes he found their whole situation challenging, but he knew eventually, their life together would continue to move forward and work out for the best.

At least he prayed it would.

CHAPTER 34

SARAH

Dave crept up behind her as Sarah finished buttering his toast. Wearing only a towel, she felt him lean his body in, wrapping his arms around her. "I've got one more thing for you to butter," he whispered.

A wry grin spread across her face. She wriggled from him, pulling the towel away, and used it to playfully smack him on the ass. He grabbed her by her forearms and pulled her gently back into his arms.

She relented, melting into his embrace. "I thought you were tired and hungry," she whispered flustered.

He had caught her off guard. She wasn't even thinking about sex. But it seemed sex was something men thought of on a continuous loop. Part of their genetic make-up. "Your food will get cold."

She breathed heavily into his chest, her body responding to his nakedness, his caresses. He ran his hands over her body, slowly undressing her. Clothes fell to the kitchen floor. Food forgotten.

***

The following morning, they slept in. Sarah no longer stayed in her own bedroom. She had given it up to the dogs a few months after moving in with Dave. When she had gotten to a point where she completely trusted him, their relationship took on a more loving and sexual degree. Their intimacy grew deeper.

She allowed Dave to explore her body—the good and the bad—though emotional about the scars he could see. She knew he was just as aware of the ones he couldn't see.

It had been several weeks before they made love. He didn't want to hurt her in any way—a hurdle he had to mentally get past. She had to let him know over and over it was okay and that she was ready for this point in their relationship.

It had taken time for her to feel completely comfortable when openly naked in front of Dave. As well as her to be just as comfortable looking at his naked body. She viewed his strong physique in a sideways glimpse, blushing when he caught her. Many nights, Dave would just hold her and talk. Calm her, let her know what she had experienced in her youth was not normal, that he would never hurt her in any way—physically or emotionally.

Nakedness, the human body, sex had always been associated with shame, humiliation and abuse. It took time to allow her primitive and natural feelings, her body's sexual cravings to flow... to allow them to emerge. After a few months of relationship building—and a bottle of wine—she finally quit fighting her sexual desires and gave in.

Dave was a few years older and more experienced when it came to making love. He was tender with his hands, caressing her gently in just the right spots. He smothered her with soft kisses. She let him take her body over. He learned what turned her on, pushing her to the edge some nights. She'd let him lead in the beginning.

Becoming comfortable engaging in sex, she became braver. She found it was a turn-on for Dave when she took control and steered their lovemaking in a direction of her choice. For her to reach out and touch him and take him in her hands would make him writhe and moan. She felt empowered she could do this to a man and enjoy what she was doing... a place she thought out of reach forever. It had only taken the right man to walk into her life. One that understood what she had gone through and who was willing to put the effort into her and their relationship.

It was as if she was letting go of baggage that had kept holding her against the pain of the past. She realized she could really love this man and be with him forever. But this thought, for some reason, scared her more than anything. *Maybe it's normal.* To be afraid of loving someone so much, you give the rest of your life to them... the commitment itself was scary.

She knew if she fully submitted and allowed her feelings to flow for Dave, if she let her guard down all the way, that would make her totally vulnerable. She wanted to be able do this, to make the commitment, but a small piece of her stood in the way. She couldn't bring herself to tell him she loved him. She held onto that corner of her heart for her stolen daughter whom she hoped to one day locate. Until then, she wouldn't feel complete.

Their late morning was interrupted by Dave's cell phone buzzing.

"Yeah," he answered groggily.

Though they had slept in, they hadn't gone to bed until the early morning and only gotten a few hours of sleep. Sarah lay half-awake listening to Dave's part of the conversation.

"So, you do believe there is more to this area? Yes, my sentiments exactly," Dave nodded as he replied.

He looked over at Sarah. She could tell there was a long pause. She looked at him and shrugged her shoulders questionably.

"Are you sure about this?" Dave continued, interrupted by short pauses. "I'm not even sure she'll want to bring the dogs back. No, they only work live-find for me. She's the only one that's worked them on human remains. Not sure, not sure. I'll have to check with her."

Sarah sat up in the bed. Her interest was piqued. Uncertain she was hearing what she thought they were conversing about, she had a clue. She continued to try and listen in. Dave kept looking at her. Gunner and Sam had heard the pair stir and now pushed the door open to their bedroom. The dogs needed to be let out and fed breakfast. Gunner bounced around the room. Sam whined.

"Okay, sure. I'll talk to her about it. Call you right back. Okay, yeah, got it."

With that, Dave hung up and looked at Sarah. A lopsided grin on his sleepy face smiled at her. He sat up and threw his feet over the side of the bed.

"No way," Sarah expressed, not believing what she thought she just overheard.

"Yep, they want you and your dogs on scene. Sheriff Kasey is back in town and all fired up. For some reason, he's trying to play all this down, but Felding is in charge and holding firm. Felding wants you to explain to him how the dogs work and what would be the best way to handle this site. There seems to be several areas in the bottom where the dirt and fauna look a little different, messed with in some way. Felding had a couple deputies scour the area but they didn't notice any more burial sites. What d'ya think? You up for this?"

They both knew she had overdone it the last few days. Sarah was stiff and sore, but she was addicted to searches and wasn't about to give up a chance to take her dogs on a mission. Especially, one that could be this significant of a find. This could be the opportunity she'd been waiting on—to redeem herself.

Sarah's mind went into overdrive. Her thoughts went directly to gearing up for a search. Her head in a frenzy, she needed to prioritize her thoughts and figure out a game plan and how she needed to execute it.

With her mind spooling for the search, there would be no going back to sleep.

"Yes, I'll do it. But I need to do one thing first before you call the deputy sheriff back. Can you give me another fifteen minutes first?"

"Sure, no problem," he replied, though Dave looked puzzled.

Picking up her cell from the night stand, she slipped on a pair of moccasins and headed for the front porch. Gunner and Sam padded after her.

Sarah pushed the front door of the cabin open and let the dogs run through before she stepped outside. She didn't care the dogs were pushy; she didn't believe in all that nonsense about the 'pack leader' going out the door first. She knew they had relieving themselves on their mind and were making a beeline to the yard. She thought anyone who made it a big deal that dogs could reason in such a way to understand their handler or leader should be the first through an open door was full of shit.

Sarah watched the animals sniff around for a moment. She wanted to make sure they didn't take off to follow the track they had discovered yesterday. Sitting on the top porch step, she continued to keep an eye on them then pulled up the contacts in her phone and placed her call.

"Oh, hey there!" Kellee answered on the first ring. "We really miss you here. How are Gunner and Sam?"

Sarah hadn't called Kellee in several weeks, but they exchanged emails weekly. It wasn't difficult to fall back into conversation, picking right back up from where they left off with ease.

"Good for the most part. The guys are good, including Dave," Sarah added. Canine handlers sometime forget about their people. "Some weird stuff going on, but I'm calling for search strategy advice for an HRD search right now that's high priority."

"Search advice? Did you find a team that would let you work with them?"

"Well, uh, not exactly. I don't have time to explain the situation surrounding me working the dogs or why. I'll have to call you back later for that. It's involved. Complicated."

"Are you okay, Sarah? You're not in any kind of trouble? You and Dave good?"

"Well, yeah, like I said, for the most part. We're good." Sarah knew Kellee was concerned.

"So, what's going on?"

"We have a site to search later today that may prove to be a very large area. It might involve discussion of search-strategy later with the agency, more than dog work. I think the work will be more than just my two, or Dave and I can handle by ourselves."

"Like how large? Can you give me more info?"

"Not sure, but maybe as large as a football field or more, and over some difficult terrain which is mountainous, some level areas, a ravine. It varies, but it will likely involve several burial sites..." Sarah trailed off, then added, "...and the victims may have been there from anytime recently, to several years. I think they're children, Kellee. So far, the clues we've found point to young subjects."

There wasn't an answer on the other end.

"Kellee?"

"Hang on, I'm trying to digest all you're telling me."

"I know, this is a major undertaking and I don't think Dave and I and the dogs can handle this alone," Sarah repeated. "What do you think I should do? The deputy sheriff is waiting on an answer. Dave needs to call him back ASAP."

"Tell me quickly what's been done and a little more detail."

Sarah gave Kellee a quick overview of the day prior. How Gunner and Sammy had reacted to the finds and the whole area in general, the eerie feeling which had overcome Sarah herself, how the area could be the perfect location for a dumping ground... reiterating the point it was probably children who were buried there.

"Sounds like this might be the opportunity for you to get back out there and make a difference, Sarah. At least, if you are feeling up to it. Don't overdo yourself or the dogs."

"Do you think this is something Gunner and Sam will be able to handle? They were out of control yesterday. I think the scent was overwhelming for them. It seemed to come from everywhere," Sarah voiced.

"I would tell the sheriff how you plan to work your dogs. Be clear and concise. If there are bodies buried near each other and if the soil is soft and super loose, I would work your dogs on lead, on a long line, if the foliage allows for it. Find out what more you can, but don't wear Gunner and Sam out. Give them several breaks. Make sure you have a strategy— split the area into large grids. If it's several burial sites in that kind of terrain, you're going to need more canine teams. If it's as big a case as it sounds, you may want to go up the chain to a bigger agency. Just make sure you record everything," Kellee stressed.

"I'm pretty sure it's state-owned property for the most part, so I know the state police will be involved soon, at some point. Maybe they will even bring in the bureau."

"Well, if there are children—and possibly children who were brought across state lines—the FBI will come knocking no matter what," Kellee interjected. "Nelson County won't have a say in the matter."

Dave stuck his head out the front door and looked at Sarah. She knew he needed to call Kasey back. "Okay Kellee, appreciate it. Gotta run. I promise to call you as soon as I can." With that, Sarah ended the call and turned to Dave. "Guess we're a go," she smiled.

She couldn't believe she was going on an official call-out. She knew she would have to watch herself carefully. She was excited and scared at the same time. Her adrenaline kicked in and the dogs caught her energy.

Gunner and Sam bounced and jumped up on her. "Okay guys, settle down. We need to get ready."

Dave stepped into the hall to contact the deputy sheriff on his cell phone. "We'll be there shortly."

Dressing appropriately for the warmer weather, Sarah also made sure she had cooling pads in the dogs' crates to help keep them from overheating. Dave loaded containers of water and Gatorade into the SUV.

Going over her supplies one more time, she grabbed a clipboard and notepad from the hall cabinet and threw them on the front seat. Scrunching up her nose, she pulled on the dirty hiking boots she had worn the prior day, a foul smell still attached to them.

Dogs were loaded, ready to head out. Sarah stood up straight, to get herself in the right frame of mind. She wanted to appear confident in this undertaking. She needed to portray a mindset to the sheriff, the deputy sheriff, and the officers working the scene.

Scared shitless about working with cops who she knew already judged and condemned her, she wanted to make sure she came off as a seasoned professional who worked and trained successful HRD canines. Not as the defendant from a multiple murder case.

"You good to go?" Dave asked, hands on his hips.

Sarah hesitated. The dogs were barking wildly, excited and ready. Lingering on the porch, she worried about leaving the house and farm completely unattended. A foreboding hung over her. She wasn't sure if it was the details surrounding the search and what might be uncovered, or leaving the horses alone, with no people or dogs on the farm.

"What's wrong, Sarah?"

"I'm just a little leery leaving the farm after what I found yesterday. Sunny and Tank will be all alone."

"If it makes you feel better, I'll have an officer do a drive-by later."

That alleviated her concern slightly. *I just hope all is well and safe here.* Intuition? Or did she have real foresight?

CHAPTER 35

DAVE

Loaded up and heading out, Dave concentrated on where they were going. Less than a half hour from the scene, he asked, "Do you have any sort of game plan for today with the dogs, Sarah?"

"Depends somewhat on what transpired last night. What all was done?" Sarah inquired in a serious tone.

"Well, after you left, the hiker was told to leave. Another deputy interviewed him and took his statement. They had to file an incident report about why he was there to cover the department's ass."

"Really? They were concerned with a statement and account from him?" Sarah asked suspiciously.

"Yeah, this is a *murder scene,* a dumping ground, Sarah," Dave emphasized. "Either way, it's a very serious case and will be given top priority. You never know who is involved," Dave said, insinuating everyone was a suspect. "After the hiker left, I walked Felding through everything that transpired. He wanted to know how the dogs acted, how we knew they were on to something. And how we knew it looked like human bones the dogs had uncovered. It was like an inquisition."

"Wow. Sorry I missed it," Sarah said with a cynical smile. She looked out the window, following the shadows of the clouds passing over the mountains.

The day was becoming humid. A light breeze blew through the tree line. It would be decent conditions for scent to pool and condense, making it easier for the dogs to get a good whiff if they encountered the cadaver scent. But the humidity could make it tougher to keep the animals cool. Humidity could zap a dog and a human's energy quickly.

"I saw that," Dave sparred back. "Once the crime scene technicians made the site, the areas Gunner dug up were roped off and they spent hours uncovering bones bit by bit. They found two almost complete skeletons."

"What do you mean by 'almost complete'?"

"There looks to be some animal activity. Some of the bones were disturbed. Strewn about, missing." Dave motioned with one hand outstretched as he drove. "One of the reasons the dogs may have been overloaded. There were bones all over, just from those two bodies. There are teams on scene now working on the buried body in the bag. It's definitely a recent burial."

"The strewn bones would explain some of the dogs' frantic behavior. Gunner can be easily overloaded. He may have had a hard time deciding where to lie down for his indication and just gave into foundation behaviors from his original training where he had a more aggressive indication," Sarah added. "Plus, when you add in a body in a stage of major decomp and putrefaction close to the other remains... it's kind of like system overkill."

"Yeah, I tried to explain all of that. Felding was none too happy to learn the dogs had disturbed the scene. I told him it was better they had found it and disturbed it than not. It could've had much more animal activity than it did." Dave's brow furrowed, continuing with the point. "Which is kind of weird, right? Wouldn't you think between all the bones and the decomposing body, there'd be more damage to the remains?"

"Yes, I find it odd as well. I would think there had to be enough human activity in the area to make it difficult for normal wild animal behavior... so, animals wouldn't have disturbed the burial sites that much," Sarah added.

"Well, you have a point there. If people were in and out enough, animals wouldn't feel safe to spend time digging up or hanging out for long periods."

"In the meantime, we need to get a strategy together," Sarah said. "I know you've only trained and worked them for live-finds, but I think you'll do fine handling Gunner. He's a thick-skinned dog and there's not much you can do that'll distract him from his job."

"So how do you want to approach working this?" Dave questioned.

"We have to take this slow. We need to partition off the area first, then break it down into smaller sections so we can cover with the dogs on long lines in their harnesses. Use the creek as the baseline and move out from there. Go east and north of the creek. From there we can eventually move out from the west side of the creek to see if there are any remains in that direction. But if this search does turn up more finds, we're going to have to tell Kasey and Felding to go up the chain and ask for help to bring in more dog teams... unless I can find teams who won't have an issue working with me."

"Sounds like a plan. But just remember, *suggesting* things to Kasey and Felding works better than telling them how it's going to be. Kasey can be put off easy and I'm not sure what his deal is right now. Felding is a very savvy Southerner and if he believes you're genuine and you know your shit, he'll give you the lead and the go-ahead. I think I should still do most of the talking. Sorry."

Sarah continued to stare out the vehicle window as they neared the site.

"You okay, Sarah?" Dave laid his hand on her shoulder as he drove.

Sarah stiffened against his touch. She was outside her comfort zone.

"It's all about the dogs, remember. You and your dogs. Don't think about everyone else," Dave offered.

"I know," Sarah replied with a smile. She took a deep breath.

They pulled up behind white vans covered in advertisements for the local news channel. Sarah rolled her eyes mockingly at Dave and laughed. "I'll be sure to pawn these guys off on you!"

Somehow, the news crew always had a way of tracking down a hot story. "Their noses must be as good as Gunner and Sam's." Sarah let out another laugh that sounded nervous this time.

"Everything will work out, okay?" Dave stated in a firm voice.

"I sure hope so."

"Okay. Wait here until I can clear this news team from the area."

Dave stepped out of the Explorer and walked up to the van in front of them. He was still groggy from lack of sleep. With a gruff tone, he told the media to vacate the area. His patience waned. His main concern was the media finding out Sarah Gavin, murder suspect, was on scene—*The* Sarah Gavin—working dogs in a human remains case. It would bring excessive and unwanted attention to the sheriff's department and to this case. It would explode. Dave wasn't taking any chances.

The media van pulled away from the shoulder and sped off, kicking gravel up on Dave's Explorer.

Sarah jumped in her seat when flying stones hit the windshield. "Son of a bitch!" she spat out.

Dave leaned into the SUV. "You okay," he smiled.

"I'm fine," Sarah responded rolling her eyes at the fleeing van. "But, it's also... it's just that..." she trailed off.

"What, Sarah? What's wrong?" Dave asked.

"I dunno, not sure. I still can't shake this uneasy feeling about leaving the farm. It's making me feel out of sorts."

"I'll make sure a deputy runs by a couple times today. Come on, woman, you've got work to do." Dave hoped Sarah was just jittery about the search. He walked to the back of the Explorer and raised the hatch to two German Shepherds barking obnoxiously. "I guess everyone knows were here now."

CHAPTER 36

SARAH

Back at the incident site, Dave and Sarah finished packing their gear. Sarah wore a fishing vest with several zippered pockets, loops, and open pouches. Dave preferred an over the shoulder pack consisting of deep compartments he could access supplies quickly.

Both handlers carried a toy reward for their dog, water, maps of the area, a GPS, handheld radio, compass, and first-aid supplies for humans and canines.

Confident they had all their provisions organized, Sarah and Dave harnessed the dogs with their recovery vests. The specialized vest was a cue to the dogs as to what type of scent they would be hunting for. This vest had a handle with a heavy-duty D ring sewn into the top portion where a long line could attach. This way, it helped keep the handler from interfering with the dog's work.

Gunner exhibited his normal, boisterous behavior. The dog recognized the area where he'd made a find the day before. It added to his excitement level. Sam, the opposite, became fixed and serious. He locked on to Sarah and held his pose, keeping his eyes turned up to hers. Sam's quiet, but intense energy was powerful. Sarah leaned down and gave him a light stroke along his ribs.

"You sure you want me to work this beast?" Dave asked in a questioning tone, cocking one eyebrow. Dave could barely contain Gunner at the end of the leash.

"He'll be fine once we get moving. You won't have to worry about anything with him. There's no gray area when he works. When he has a hit, it's obvious. The same as when you've worked him in the past for live-find wilderness search. And you know, he'll work for just about anyone who has his toy. Gunner will make you look like a rock star."

Sarah smiled at the dog, then at Dave.

"Now Sam, on the other hand, is more serious, a little quirky in a different way and I think he prefers to work only for me. Especially since we've been reunited, he always keeps an eye on me."

"Okay, sounds good. How's your leg and hip holding up?" Dave asked.

Sarah could see the shadow of a grimace on his face. "I'm fine for now. Not sure what I'll be like after a couple hours working the dogs. Especially in the woods over uneven terrain." Sarah preferred he focus on working Gunner. "I'll be okay, don't worry about me."

"Call me if you have a problem. Don't persist in searching if you're in pain, you hear me? You've done a lot these last few days."

"Yes, boss," Sarah responded with a smile and a sassy tone. She knew she would have to work through her worries about the farm and through her pain.

Dave radioed to the officer running the tasks at the scene to alert management that they were ready to brief. Sheriff Kasey wasn't on scene. He had visited the area as soon as he had returned from his out of town emergency but left quickly. Felding continued to be the point of contact and main supervisor in charge.

The incident site was set up as a recovery scene with CSI technicians scattered throughout the forest. The techs' main task involved removing the two sets of skeletal remains and the decomposing body in the bag. They took pictures, sketched maps, and scribbled notes, documenting everything. One technician was occupied with the task of taking soil samples of the surrounding area and from the trees beside the remains. She carefully chose the specimens, enclosing them in containers and labeling each one aptly.

Today's main objective for the canines would be a fact-finding mission. Gunner and Sam would be utilized to locate more clues and perhaps discover additional remains in the area or anything else that might prove to be a hint to the case. Between what Dave and Sarah and the crime scene technicians had observed, there was a definite belief there were more remains.

Observation was a good skill to learn, and could be a powerful tool. Learning to stand still and take in your surroundings—to look around with what's called a 'soft eye'—enhanced your ability to notice the subtle changes in environment. The ground appeared to have been tampered with in the past, and in several areas. Numerous spots where vegetation appeared to be slightly different—more dirt exposed in some areas than covered with dead leaves, some animal activity, sunken and depressed places—were all evidence pointing toward additional burial sites.

The technicians methodically went through the area and poked small holes in the soil in several different locations to allow the ground to aerate. They used a thin, rounded metal stake, about three feet long and one-half inch in diameter. A small handle attached perpendicular to its end. That one piece of equipment was simple enough in its design but very efficient and easy to use.

Sarah didn't believe the apparatus really had a technical name and always referred to it as the 'poker' or 'aerator'. It would allow scent to rise through the small round openings, so the dogs could access the smell easier—every puncture in the ground was carefully marked with flagging tape and logged into the computer. It was important to keep track of what had been touched.

Dave and Sarah stepped over the guardrail that separated the shoulder from the edge of the forest. They pulled the dogs through underneath. As soon as they were on the wooded side, Sarah eyed the steep incline. She couldn't turn the dogs free this time with all the activity going on.

"Can you handle taking both dogs down, and then wait for me at the bottom?" she asked Dave. Although the rest of the terrain was varied and there were a few steep grades into the ravines, this was the hardest part to get through.

"Sure, no problem." He took Sam's leash.

The dogs tugged at Dave, pulling hard as he walked at an angle. Reaching the bottom, the terrain leveled out which would make hiking somewhat easier.

Dave handed Sam back off to Sarah.

"Thanks."

The dogs continued to pull both handlers toward the crime scene. Gunner and Sam eagerly took in all the human smells, straining toward the CSIs.

"Slow down, guys!" Sarah harshly reprimanded.

Sam and Gunner looked back at their handlers for a quick second, slowing down just a notch, then hit the end of their lines just as hard and continued pulling until they got to the first set of officers.

Reeling the dogs in, Dave and Sarah put them in a down stay. They needed to speak with the officer in charge and go over their initial search strategy.

The cold stares and hard looks were difficult to avoid. *Mental whispers,* she thought, as though she could almost read their minds. LE—law enforcement—knew Sarah's background. Feeling as though she were on display, she stood up tall and squared her shoulders.

Dave checked in with the deputy but turned the situation over to her quickly. "Sarah, can you fill in Deputy Harris on our search strategy?"

"What?" Sarah mouthed and shot Dave a look of confusion. She couldn't believe he had put her on the spot. That's not what they had discussed before disembarking from the SUV. Her temperature rose sharply. She felt her blood pressure rise. Her face flushed.

"Oh, sure." She turned to tell the dogs to stay again and stepped away from them and toward the deputy in charge.

A make-shift staging area had been set up in the woods, just outside the area where the technicians were working. It was base and staging all rolled into one.

Composing herself, she unfolded a topo map and laid it on the table. Smiling at the deputy, she began, "So here we are. This is where the remains were discovered yesterday." Sarah pointed at an area with the tip of her pencil.

She and the deputy brushed shoulders as they leaned over to study the map. It sent waves of panic through Sarah's body. *Control yourself!*

"This whole area here is where we would like to concentrate our focus today. We would like to break the area into 100-meter square sectors, working one at a time with the dogs on lead."

"How many sectors do you think the dogs can cover successfully? What's the Probability of Detection? Will the percentage decrease as the length of the dog's time in the field adds up?"

This guy seems to know and understand search and scent work. And canines. "Yes, a dog's accuracy can diminish due to fatigue, overload, unforeseen circumstances. I would say their POD would start out at about sixty-five percent and might decline to somewhere around forty. We plan on working each dog about a half-hour at a time with twenty-minute breaks in between. We'll document all the timeframes, including finds, clear areas, breaks. Anything we do will be added to our notes and records, including a hand drawn map."

"Okay, sounds like a plan. I have men ready who can flank as you work the dogs. I want to make sure you have a deputy with you every moment." The officer hesitated. "Of course, that's because if your dog discovers something..." he stumbled over his words. "Will that work?"

The words stung. She knew what he really meant.

Normally, on this type of search, a handler would always walk with a police escort anyway, but it was the way the deputy's point had come across.

"That would be great," Sarah replied, her jaw rigid. "We already entered the sectors on the map. Once we set our GPS, we should be ready to start working."

Having a difficult time staying in place, the dogs stretched their necks as far as they could, inching their way in the direction of the activity. Noses pointed skyward, Sam and Gunner tried to take in as much of the remains scent as they could as it wafted toward them. Sarah wondered what the scent picture looked like to the dogs as she watched the pair and their non-stop noses.

The deputies who were assigned to Dave and Sarah made their way over to the incident command area. Between the deputy in charge of the scene, the two deputy escorts, and Sarah and Dave, they discussed a plan of action.

Lost in the appropriate police protocol discussion, Sarah drifted. She eyed the dogs. She was slightly concerned the light breeze blowing toward them carrying the scent of the already located remains might interfere with their work. It shouldn't matter once they began their search though, when they got on the other side of the area. Once started, they would be upwind, making it easier for the dogs to concentrate on working their sectors.

The briefing finally broke up. Dave and Sarah gathered the dogs and started toward their sectors.

Dave, Gunner and their escort crossed the creek at a shallow area. "Just work Gunner in a grid pattern lengthwise across your sectors into the breeze," Sarah reminded Dave. "Be patient and watch Gunner's natural body signs closely. And whatever you do, don't turn him loose."

"Will do, Sarah. Call me if you need help or if your hip starts to bother you," Dave called back over his shoulder. "I mean it," he reiterated in a stern voice.

Sarah nodded. She felt seized up inside and needed to relax and concentrate on what lay ahead. *Pull your head out of your ass. Sam's not going to work to his best otherwise.* Her attitude sucked right now and if she wasn't careful, Sam would pick up on it.

Taking several deep breaths and stretching her back, Sarah turned and faced the deputy escorting her. "Okay," she said with a smile. "We need to get past the burial and bone remains where the crime scene techs are working so we can let Sam work without distractions."

"Fine with me. You just tell me what you need," the deputy replied, smiling and reaching out to shake her hand.

Her history didn't seem to concern him, or at least it didn't show. A man in his late forties, he looked fit and acted professional.

Just as they made their way past the previous day's discoveries, she could hear urgent chatter over the radio. She smiled. It was Dave. He and Gunner had already made a find.

For a quick moment, Sarah thought of her daughter. Her heart sank. The remains that lay in this forest all seemed to be from young subjects... like the children missing from her foster home. She remembered the note that was found the day she had been injured. Not sure why, Sarah knew all this tied into her past.

She kept hope that one day she would find the child who had been stolen from her as an infant. She just had to believe it wouldn't be in this type of situation.

***

Time consuming, each task took a certain amount of fine detailing which was more stressful on the dogs and their handlers. The dogs moved slow on lead as they thoroughly searched their sectors. Although it was only early afternoon, it was time to call it quits.

As the dogs had worked, the search area had continued to grow, looking like it might extend far up the mountainside. Both dog teams were exhausted, their finds bringing the tally up to twelve different sets of remains. Some of the sites were within feet of each other.

Additional items, clues, were located as well. The newer remains followed the same pattern as the day before—small statured skeletal remains. Between locating human remains, drug paraphernalia, clothing, and what looked like used condoms, the work had been tedious. Every item had to be tagged, photographed, and logged.

The mood surrounding the crime scene was dispiriting and it had begun to affect the dogs. Sarah realized this search was bigger than what she and her dogs alone could handle. They needed more resources.

Sure, this case would be turned over to the FBI at some point even though Sheriff Kasey seemed to be fighting the intention for now. But it was already too large and too in-depth for a county sheriff's department or the local state police team. This seemed to be the work of a serial killer or possibly even multiple killers. She couldn't understand why the sheriff was insisting his agency could handle it. *Doesn't make sense.*

CHAPTER 37

SARAH

Later that afternoon, Sheriff Kasey and Deputy Sheriff Felding stopped by the farm unannounced. Kasey had seemed agitated when he'd visited the remains site that day. Distracted. Comments he'd made while on scene were short and blunt.

Granted, Dave was his employee and involved in the investigation, but it wasn't hard to tell Kasey was more interested in speaking with Sarah.

Sheriff Kasey stood just inside the small cabin's doorframe. He was holding his weathered tan cowboy hat against his chest. Sweat stained the felt lining, small tears noticeable around the brim. He was a big man. A very big man. Not overweight, just size extra-large. At 6' 5" and wearing size fourteen cowboy boots, he was an imposing individual.

"Evening, Sarah," he called out to her as she entered the kitchen. "Did I catch ya'll at a bad time?"

"Good evening, Sheriff, not at all. Just a little surprised to see you both. Good evening, Deputy," she returned in a flat, even tone.

Kasey nodded in Dave's direction but kept his intent on Sarah while Felding remained in the small alcove, just outside the kitchen entryway.

Dave stood and nodded back in their direction.

Sarah motioned with her spatula for Kasey and Felding to sit at the kitchen bar, and then flipped burgers in her cast iron skillet.

Kasey obliged and sat down on a stool after first studying to make sure it would handle his weight. Felding remained against the wall.

"You hungry? Beer? Soda? Coffee's on as well."

"Just a coffee, straight up." Kasey pointed toward the dark brewed liquid on the opposite counter.

"You sure?" Sarah looked at the deputy sheriff as she poured a cup for Kasey. Felding just shook his head. "You're missing out," she smiled trying to be friendly.

Dave watched, making small talk while Sarah waited for Kasey to initiate the conversation regarding why he was here. The air felt heavy, tense. Could Dave feel it as well?

Finally, Kasey started to pepper Sarah with questions about dogs in general and how they worked, and how and where she trained them. Skeptical at first, Sarah only answered in short, clipped replies. She knew Kasey was after more.

Finally she realized he wasn't versed in air-scent dogs when he seemed baffled that a dog could not only be trained to locate lost persons, but deceased remains underground.

Sarah wondered if it was a good time to share all the background information with him. But she was having misgivings. The timing and the setting weren't right.

She hoped Dave would keep his mouth shut regarding what he and Sarah believed were ties from her Pennsylvania foster home to the land owned by relatives of the foster mother and the missing children. Right now, Sarah only had loose facts and a gut feeling, but this gut feeling also warned her to be careful around Kasey.

She and Dave were really the only ones who knew that where she was raised might be tied to the Charlottesville area. If Sarah were to expose the connection, she felt certain Kasey would remove her and the dogs from the search.

Dave looked at Sarah. They locked eyes. She could tell he knew what she was thinking. Breaking away, Dave looked at the floor. She eyed Felding as well and knew he had witnessed her and Dave's eye contact.

Was Dave picking up on the same vibes about Kasey as she was? Or did he know something he hadn't told her? *Wouldn't be the first time.*

Several of Kasey's questions seemed misplaced or just outlandish. Kasey had asked if the dogs could track a human remains scent to the killer. He also asked if the dogs could sniff out or tell them about other people who might have known the subjects when they were alive. Questions like that just didn't make sense, dog person or not.

"So, you know I don't think it's a good idea for you to be involved in a crime scene investigation, especially one this big, that most likely will have national coverage."

There, Sheriff Kasey had put it on the table. No sugar coating.

"I understand your concerns. I'm only here to help. Gunner and Sam are some of the best human remains detection dogs out there. I'm not trying to cause any problems for your agency." Sarah drew in a long breath contemplating the man who sat before her at the kitchen counter. She wanted to make sure he understood where she was coming from. "But I'm also not going to work with, or under, an agency who doesn't believe in what my dogs and I can do, or who doesn't want me there."

Dave listened in silence as Sarah stood her ground.

Deputy Sheriff Felding stepped from the doorway. "Some here don't understand what you've been through, Sarah. They are quick to judge as I was. These are a tightknit country folk. Not used to outsiders, especially outsiders who are tied to a murder trial. Your hide's gonna have to be a little tougher here."

"What else are you needing for me and my dogs to do?" Sarah asked.

Kasey didn't answer for a moment.

Felding, looking exhausted, gave Kasey an unpleasant sideways glance. "I... we... would like to know how you think this search should move forward. We want to know what you've experienced with other agencies you've worked for. How other searches like this have played out? What you think our next steps should be?"

"To begin with, there's never been another remains recovery incident like this one utilizing canines. Ever. There've been searches with multiples bodies, maybe three or four, and searches for scattered remains, but nothing like this." Sarah wanted to make sure Kasey and Felding understood this was bigger than their little Podunk sheriff agency could handle. But in the meantime, it could help her get her foot back in the door of the canine search world.

"I believe the search area is much larger than what we have already covered. First thing we need to do is get more canine resources. This is too big for me and my dogs. You may want to send a chopper up to take aerial photographs and have access to LIDAR—this remote sensing method has been beneficial for locating disturbed areas of the earth." As Sarah spoke, Kasey hung his hands on his hips staring at her with his jaw dangling. He seemed almost challenged. It cost her focus. She had to concentrate to stay on point. "Finding an agency who can bring in GIS—Geothermography—or ground penetrating radar. Maybe we can locate someone in the area who can help with that? Is the area secure and contained?"

"GIS? Radar?" Kasey asked. "Not sure about those fancy contraptions."

Felding took over the conversation once again. "Well, we have people on-site twenty-four hours working the scene. But the only part completely secured is the area beginning along the shoulder of the road. The sides and back are too large to contain. We're not sure how deep or wide this scene will end up going."

"You're going to need several good canine teams. Not necessarily a whole search team, but teams who are proven and professional."

"Do you know any we can call in?"

"I know a few. But they will have to travel here so they will need somewhere to sleep. They're civilian volunteers. They can't take money, but they can accept food and board in exchange for working their dogs. They're all credentialed with background checks. They can make their records and paperwork available to you."

"Well, I think we can arrange to take care of them. How many handlers and canines are you thinking?"

"I can probably get five or six handlers here by early morning ready to work tomorrow. Will you be bringing the feds in?" Sarah asked.

"Not just yet. These are state lands, so the state police will be involved beginning tomorrow. We still need to determine whether these remains are all children. You can bet your ass the Bureau will be here ASAP if they are," Felding stated.

"And I would really prefer no outside agencies if I can help it," Kasey interjected. "They will just add to the mess."

Right, try and keep the Bureau away.

There was something about Kasey's mannerisms that didn't sit right with Sarah. A small red flag rose again. But maybe she was being overly critical and suspicious.

Sarah looked away for a moment, remembering a short, bright spot in her life when she had applied to The Academy. When she knew the direction she was heading. Back before Eva had resurfaced and brought havoc into her life. *Focus.*

"I'll make some phone calls and see who can respond."

"Okay, I expect to hear from you later this evening, Sarah. And I don't want you speaking to anyone but me and Kasey regarding how the dogs will be worked or your search strategy," Felding added.

Sheriff Kasey turned his attentions to Dave who sat at the small kitchen table near the window where Sarah had found the smudge a few days earlier. The thought occurred to her that Kasey was the right size for the footprint. But he wore cowboy boots most of the time and she knew they didn't have a deep track that would match the print she had found.

"Dave, you still heading out with the swift water rescue team tomorrow?" Kasey asked.

"Yes, I'm meeting the two water teams near the overlook bridge at 0500 hours," he answered.

"Well, keep me in the loop, you hear? Call me and let me know how the day is progressing. If I don't answer, leave me a message and I'll call you back."

"Sure thing."

Panic mode set in. Sarah had forgotten about the recovery in the deep gorge. That meant she would be on her own with the sheriff's agency and state police... as well as whatever canine handlers she could get to come work with her.

In charge. She set herself straight. *So I need to get my shit together.*

She had told the sheriff a white lie. Fact was, she wasn't sure any handlers would respond to her request.

CHAPTER 38

DAVE

Dave was proud of the way Sarah handled herself with Kasey and Felding. The sheriff's size alone could intimidate the most confident individual. Watching her assert herself and take control alleviated any worries he had about sending her out on her own tomorrow.

"Are you coming back to the station with us, Dave?" Felding asked. "We have a lot of paperwork to work on, plus the staff meeting."

"Sure thing." Brows raised, Sarah looked at him questionably. "Sorry honey, save me a burger. I'll eat when I get back home."

"You'll be lucky if Gunner and Sam don't get your dinner tonight," Sarah said with a trace of fire.

Dave knew she wasn't happy, but he didn't have much choice.

"You guys can head out and I'll catch up in a few," he told Kasey and Felding.

He figured it would be better and easier if he just followed them in his own vehicle. But that would leave Sarah without a car, though he only planned to be gone a few hours. He would need to pick up his patrol cruiser at some point.

"You gonna be okay?" he asked Sarah as he grabbed his wallet, phone, and firearm.

"I'll be fine. Got these two." She eyed the resting sable colored shepherds. "At least they'll keep me company for the evening while I work on getting some canine handlers together."

"Sorry Sarah, but duty calls. I also want to find out what the deal is with Kasey. He's got me a little concerned. Something just doesn't sit right about him."

"Got the same feeling," Sarah replied and went back to preparing dinner.

Dave had an unsettled feeling. He couldn't tell why, but he felt warning signals deep within.

CHAPTER 39

SARAH

Sarah looked on as Kasey and Felding filed out of the cabin. Standing at the window, she watched the two men climb into Kasey's extra-large vehicle made for an extra-large person. The old, battered Ford Excursion had seen better days, but looked like it fit his frame just fine.

Pulling Dave to her, she gave him a quick hug and told him to stay safe as he left to follow them in his SUV. Thoughts swirled in every direction. Once again, the farm would be left unattended while she worked the search tomorrow and Dave set out to recover the body on the river. *Bad juju.* Wincing, she rubbed her temples. It was more than just a feeling; it was visceral.

Sarah knew Dave was already spent from the day's search and hoped he could hold up. There was still paperwork to finish, other resources to check on, plus giving an update on what was going on at the recovery site. The sheriff's department would be holding a staff meeting with the CSI team assigned to the recovery efforts for the evening and Felding needed Dave to brief everyone.

Turning away from the front door, her eyes cased the cabin until she located her phone. Plucking it up from the kitchen counter where she had been cooking dinner, Sarah placed a call to Kellee. She trusted her old friend and knew she was the only one who could help her navigate this situation.

"Oh, hey there, Sarah. How's everything going?" Kellee answered with enthusiasm.

"Hi Kellee," Sarah answered, exasperation in her voice.

"Are you okay? What's going on with the search? How are the dogs? You kind of left me hanging."

"I know, I'm sorry. This is so crazy," Sarah paused. She felt like a weight had been placed on her chest. "I still don't have time to explain everything, but this is big, Kellee. Really big. In every aspect."

"Okay. So, start at the beginning and just give me an overview so I can understand the situation better. How did the dogs first discover remains?"

Sarah paused as she tried to figure out how to condense everything that had happened.

Dog handlers like details... they want to know every aspect of a dog working. *Everything.* The weather, temperature, wind speed and direction, to time of day, terrain and more. And she didn't have the energy to go over all the specifics right now.

Her head was complaining, her temples still softly pounding. "Well, out on this *hike*, both dogs hit scent and uncovered several burial sites including a newly buried decomposing body in a plastic bag." Sarah emphasized the word hike. She wanted to make sure Kellee understood the depth of Dave's deception.

"Like Dave didn't know the possibilities of taking the dogs—cadaver dogs, no less—along on a hike where a human bone had been recovered? Did it not occur to him that there were 205 additional bones still missing just from that skeleton? And maybe, just maybe, Gunner and Sam might make a find? Did he understand he was putting you in a compromising position?"

Sarah was silent. Kellee's words hung dead in the air between them.

"Sorry, just stating the facts. You know he had to realize there was a possibility." Kellee had said the obvious. "Sorry, but I'm sure this is something you've already considered. I'll move on for now. I've seen a few details circulating on the internet news channels, but there really isn't much information available regarding what's going on in the mountains down there."

"I know, and I can't go into too many particulars yet. I need you to keep this confidential. The sheriff, Dave's boss, has requested I help manage the search. I don't know why, but I don't trust this man."

"Why not?" Kellee asked.

"Not sure, just a weird vibe. Seems like he's only involving me because he wants to know how much the dogs can find out, like he's watching his back. I don't think he would have brought me in if it weren't for the deputy sheriff."

"Maybe it's everything going on, Sarah. Maybe it's your history." Kellee sighed. "Well, it seems like you got your foot back in the door. The sheriff's agency has accepted you to work Gunner and Sam."

"Not exactly. It's complicated. But I need help."

"What kind of help?"

"I need to bring in some HRD canine teams—several handlers who have a history of good working dogs for Human Remains Detection. Dogs that are proven in the field, that have some endurance and work ethic. I need you to help me single out who you think can handle this type of search, who has a certified dog and is completely credentialed, including recent background checks. I prefer teams who've had confirmed finds. And I need them ASAP."

"What size is the search area?"

"Still hard to tell. It could be anywhere from forty acres to several hundred. Gunner and Sam have worked two days in a row. We're exhausted. Dave can't be on scene tomorrow either. He's going out with the swift water rescue on the other side of the county."

"Wow, sounds like there's a lot of activity going on in Nelson County, Virginia."

Sarah let out a sigh. "Morbid excitement follows me." She was trying to be funny and lighten the mood with her dark humor, but her words were awkward.

"How many canine handlers were you hoping to get? And how soon?" Kellee asked.

"Not sure exactly, but I was hoping to get at least four or five teams. Maybe more to work while others have down time. I'll have to see how Sam and Gunner bounce back this evening. We worked them on long-lines today and it stressed them not to be able to run loose, free from constraints..." Sarah trailed off as her voice weakened thinking about the whole situation. "Do you think you can help me with this, Kellee?"

"I'm positive a couple of your former teammates can make it, but I'll have to scope out a few other handlers from your area. Let me make some calls. Give me, say, a half-hour?"

Sarah held the phone with her shoulder, listening, trying to rub some anti-inflammatory gel into her hip. She didn't want to tell Kellee—or anyone how bad her hip really was. Gunner and Sam could work another day. Really, it was her and her injury causing the problem.

Then the thought hit her—the area was open enough to ride a horse through in some of the sectors. Maybe now was the time to try and work her dogs from the back of Sunny. *Why didn't I think of this earlier?* Her mood brightened immediately.

"Okay Kellee, sounds good. Just tell the handlers the search is south of the Charlottesville area. Don't give them an exact location just yet. Don't want any locals showing up self-deploying. We'll talk more when I hear back from you, okay?"

Sarah had left the information out regarding the background research Dave had done. And that her history—the history of the foster home—could somehow be tied into all of this. It was still only a theory, but it was becoming a stronger and stronger possibility.

Thinking of heading out for another day of searching in the woods with the dogs and her painful hip made her realize she wasn't up to handling this type of deployment yet. But the flicker of excitement lingered when she began strategizing the actuality of deploying and working her dog from horseback.

This tactic wasn't anything new in other disciplines like hunting, but to work a cadaver dog while astride a horse wasn't something you would normally see in the mid-Atlantic or southeastern region. She would be scrutinized. *No other way but to put the plan in action and find out.*

CHAPTER 40

SARAH

Recalling past deployments with Gunner and Sam alongside mounted responders, Sarah knew not all missions were friendly when it came to utilizing horses on a search task. It wasn't only that most search management teams were unaware of the benefits of a mounted team, but they didn't understand how horses could be best applied.

Sarah knew parking for a truck and trailer would be another key component. Luckily neither of those two factors would be an issue for this search. She knew where she could park, and had been in the forest firsthand. The trees were open enough to ride a horse safely through.

Grabbing a pen, pad and road map, she jotted down a supply list. Sarah marked on the map where a horse trailer could park and noted any other situations that would need pre-planning. She pulled out the topo map from the day before and with a yellow highlighter, she marked the sectors already searched. With pink, she marked areas she could possibly work her dogs from horseback, and red marker for sectors that wouldn't be conducive, like the rocky cliff ridges where there were sheer drop-offs. She also kept in mind expanses for access to the area.

Her next thought was to call J.C. to see if he could transport her and the horses. She would still need an officer escort and hoped one of the officers working the scene had the skills to ride a horse. She would need help to handle two dogs and two horses. It would be impossible without another person. Maybe she should only take one dog out at a time? It would be easier to keep track of one dog.

Prior to calling J.C., Sarah headed out to the barn with the dogs in tow. She found a cantle pack that fit snugly onto the back of her western saddle, replacing the bulky bags she had used for training. On each side, smaller saddle bags containing several compact compartments with Velcro and zipper closures would make organizing equipment easy.

She could use the side saddle bags for trail and horse supplies, while saving the main pack behind her saddle for search and dog supplies. She filled the one side with a few equine first-aid products and related tools like a hoof pick—a must have tool in this rocky terrain. On the side of the cantle bag, she added a Leatherman tool, a small pair of pruners, and a folding saw.

With the pack filled, she carried it back to the house and went through drawers pulling out only the supplies she thought she might need. The required human first-aid items—this was a cadaver search, but she and her partner might require first-aid at some point. At minimum, she required a powder bottle, map baggie, markers, flagging tape, first aid kit, bug spray, and a water container.

Satisfied she had inventoried her cantle pack appropriately, she placed it on the front porch. She and the dogs headed back inside where Sarah jotted down a few more notes and called J.C. "Hey handsome, it's Sarah."

They exchanged the normal pleasantries. She asked him if he might have time to trailer the two horses over to the search site tomorrow and help her tack them both up. Sarah explained her plan. J.C. thought it was a great idea.

"I'd do anything to help you. I can be out at your place by daybreak."

Sarah had just finished revising her plans and getting her supplies together when the phone buzzed. Kellee's name flashed across the screen so Sarah rushed to answer it. "Hey, what'd you find out?"

"Well, seems we do have interest. Several handlers would rather work their dogs... regardless of who they are working with.

But what I also found out… is that many are still in your court and support you."

"Well, that's nice to know," Sarah smiled. Her spirits elevated slightly. She sat down at the table where her pen and pad were waiting. "So, tell me who we have."

"Joe and Garrett can be there late tonight. Will that work?" Kellee asked.

"No problem," Sarah answered. She smiled thinking of how nice it would be to work with two of her former teammates.

"It's close to a four-hour drive for them and they plan on traveling together. They're waiting on a call from you with details of the location and lodging arrangements." Kellee gave Sarah their updated contact information. "I will also forward their credentials by email, so you can print them out to give to your commanding officer."

"Okay, perfect."

"And I have another team from Virginia who will only send what resources you require. They have a couple canines and handlers I worked with in the past, and from what I remember, they are decent dog teams."

"So, I need to call and talk to them?" At first the thought miffed Sarah. *Pull up your big girl pants, it's just a phone call.*

"Yes, the team's commander is waiting to hear from you. I paved the way. Call her and be frank. She'll appreciate you being blunt and straight to the point to your needs—whatever details you can share regarding the search."

"Okay, I really appreciate it. I'll call Joe and Garrett ASAP, so they can get a move on."

"When you slow down, call me back so we can catch up."

Sarah wished Kellee could join her with the search as well. It would be like old times. But Kellee had retired her cadaver dog and her other dog was only certified for wilderness live-find. *And it would never be like old times*, she reminded herself. Too much time had passed, too many events had elapsed. Too much jaded history.

Once she made the arrangements with her former teammates, she looked at the number on her pad of paper for the Virginia dog team Kellee had suggested. Taking a deep breath, she dialed.

"Hi, is this Jen?" Sara asked.

"Yes. How can I help you?" the woman answered.

"Hey, this is Sarah Gavin calling from Nelson County. I'm working on a high-profile case and Kellee Dunham gave me your contact information regarding acquiring additional resources for this search."

Sarah knew of Jen through other handlers but didn't know her directly. From what she'd heard, Jen was a top-notch professional, but had little time or patience for small talk.

"Kellee advised me that you may have a couple HRD teams who can respond to a search in my county."

"I may," Jen responded. "It depends on what you need and who exactly is running the search."

"What information do you need?" Sarah asked. She was polite, but could tell Jen was fishing... making sure it was an agency-run search.

"Who will be officiating? Who will be in charge of the dog teams?"

Keeping her temper in check, Sarah responded with the requested info. It made her feel like she had to prove herself.

"Can you tell me more about the search requirements?" Jen proceeded. "How large the area may be?"

Taking a deep breath, Sarah replied. "We were able to do some preliminary search work and believe the site covers several acres. This search may reach into a number of weeks as well. It will also be a highly confidential homicide investigation and will need to be kept under wraps," Sarah went into more detail to make Jen understand how involved the mission would be.

"I understand. Our team can supply two canine teams immediately who can work several days if needed. We have another two teams that can be available in a few days if more are required."

Sarah thanked Jen and gave her contact information and the address of her farm. Jen would have the team members respond with their ETA and additional info if needed.

Hanging up, Sarah closed her eyes for a moment to settle her nerves. The anxiety and excitement of bringing the horses to the search, worrying about Dave being on the river tomorrow, and the trespassing incident all caught up with her.

After several minutes of trying to meditate, she gave up. Sarah pulled out her notes and started to write down details regarding the dog handlers and what teams they were from and when they should arrive. She needed to keep track of all the information.

Finally, she felt like she had the data organized and was ready to speak to Sheriff Kasey. He picked up her call after a few rings, but didn't speak right away. Sarah could hear a lot of commotion in the background.

"Hello," he finally answered in a gruff manner.

"Hey there, Sheriff. It's Sarah."

"Yes. Whatcha got for me?"

Sarah went over the details of teams that would work the site and when they would be arriving. She discussed search strategy for the next morning, but hesitated to mention she would be working her dog from horseback. She did mention a mounted team would be there but didn't elaborate. She felt the less said, the better. After all, it was an experiment.

In a loud harsh tone, Kasey let Sarah know that he wanted to look over the search sectors first, prior to anyone getting tasked or going out in the field. He wanted to know the areas being searched and oversee where the teams would be at all times.

Hanging up, Sarah's thoughts raced. She needed to ready the house for the handler meeting, and make sure she had enough coffee and food on hand. It was going to be a late night.

She was happy to be back in the action, even though it felt like she had just jumped in with both feet and a red-hot branding iron to her ass.

CHAPTER 41

DAVE

Heading to the rendezvous point to meet the swift water teams, Dave watched soft hues spread across the sky above the jagged mountain ridges. Carefully negotiating the winding roads, he slowed up as he neared the river. He braked hard and swung his cruiser into the entrance, almost missing the small turnoff. A rough-cut gravel ramp curved its way down to the water's edge underneath hefty pylons supporting the towering metal and concrete bridge.

Dave spotted both swift water teams already on site. They had backed their trucks and trailers down to the water's edge. Half a dozen men looked over supplies, inspected the boats and checked safety equipment, thoroughly securing all the apparatus. Dave could feel a pulsating energy, an undercurrent flowing through the activity of the day's mission.

Thankful the summer rain levels were down for this time of year, Dave knew this made the river a little tamer, the rapids less fierce. But not the best when it came to a swaying and rolling vehicle, Dave popped a Dramamine and hoped it would keep him from heaving his guts overboard.

"Morning, all," Dave waved and tipped his baseball cap.

A few of the men grunted greetings or nodded, but most focused on their prep work.

Dave went through a mental checklist. In charge of the operation today, he knew he had to defer the logistics of the mission and their safety to the teams. A little apprehensive, Dave was out of his element. He hid his reservations well and maintained a stoic front.

Finally, there was a lull in activities. He called the teams over to his county-issued cruiser. "Okay, I'm sure most of you have an idea of what our mission is about today. But I still need to brief everyone prior to heading out." Dave stopped for a moment, spreading a topo map across the hood. "A few days ago, what appears to be a body was spotted in a large pile of debris near the Devil's Gorge area."

Dave used a pencil to point to the area on the map. Heads hung over the map as the men looked on.

"As you're no doubt familiar, it's pretty much sheer rock face up on both sides of the river. No shorelines or banks to beach or anchor to. We're not sure what is holding the debris in place, but it may be boulders or large rocks exposed due to the lower water levels. We need to somehow extract the body and stay in one piece. We don't want anyone taking chances or getting hurt during this recovery operation."

Dave finished going over the specifics then turned the briefing over to the team commander in charge. An in-depth discussion pursued on how to anchor, reach the body, package it for removal, and head downriver to the catch point where drivers would meet them with boat trailers. In addition to the main plan he included a few back-up scenarios as well.

Grabbing his shades from his vehicle, Dave attached a lanyard to keep them safe and slipped them on. Now that the sun was completely up, it penetrated the area. He jotted down a few notes on the topo then folded it up and stuck the map and his radio, cell phone, and GPS in a re-sealable plastic baggie to keep them from getting water damaged.

Dave turned to Max. "We're about two miles from the target area. I believe there are several rapids between here and the collection point."

Max raised an eyebrow. "The rapids are calmer than normal. There shouldn't be any issues with us getting there in one piece."

"You're forgetting I've never done this before," Dave added with a nervous chuckle.

The Australian laughed, "You okay, mate?"

"I'll be fine if you can promise you'll take it easy on me," Dave replied with a smile.

"Ahh, you'll be fine. Just do what yer told."

After going over hazards they might encounter, Dave was handed a tightfitting helmet and high-end life jacket. Black and almost flat, the compact jacket carried a CO_2 cartridge that would expand the jacket if he pulled the tab. Several pockets contained wilderness and first-aid supplies. Dave shoved a small pair of binoculars into one of the others.

The men split into two teams, climbing into inflatable Zodiac crafts. Each member had a specific job, a specialized responsibility. Dave's job was to stay out of the way and not fall overboard. He watched in awe as the men worked together without words, took their positions and began to steer toward the intended destination. *Flawless.*

Steering the boats to the middle of the river, the men worked to stay away from exposed boulders that towered up from the riverbed. It was organized chaos. Dave held tightly to the rope running along the topline of the boat as it rolled over swells, bucking and kicking. Dave couldn't wipe the excitement from his face.

Max looked back at him. "By the looks of your smile, I see you're doing fine."

Within half an hour, the boat teams made their way to the point without incident.

"Okay, we're coming up on Devil's Gorge," Max called out. "Be ready to throw the rope and anchor along the rocks. We'll drag a line along until it catches. Try and settle into the small pool over there," he pointed out as the boats floated closer to the recovery site.

"I can see the body. It's still along the pile of logs," Dave stated. He pulled out his waterproof camera and began taking pictures.

Once they got close enough to their target, they confirmed it was indeed a body—or at least what was left of one.

Max helped the team members anchor the first boat to a log secured in the debris pile. Their crew caught the second boat and tied it off to the anchored one. It allowed both boats to stay in place alongside the victim.

By the looks of the corpse, it had come from somewhere upriver, severely abused and beaten by the churning waters. Between the boulders and rocks, trees floating downriver and the currents, there wasn't much intact. Limbs were torn and barely attached. Long, blonde hair gave the first clue it was female.

Dave instructed the men in their initial attempts to extricate the body, to make sure to keep their eyes peeled for clues. There could be other items washed up along the water's edge or floating that could be pivotal in figuring out how she ended up here.

Dave's inquisitive mind raced with questions. Did she jump to her death? Was this a body dump? Was she already dead when she hit the water?

Knowing the answers would lie upriver, he understood this was going to be a difficult case to solve. When he had checked through missing person reports, he couldn't find any record regarding current subjects missing from the immediate area. Or any areas close by.

Dave stood in the boat, knees slightly bent as he labored to keep his balance. He watched the men work the grappling hook to pull the mass from the debris pile. His stomach knotted in tight cramps. The air shifted toward him, sending the stench of the remains his way. Swallowing hard, he pushed bile back down his throat. Surprised at how fast a body begins decomposing out in the elements, Dave was ready for the mission to be over.

Physically demanding, the men were silent as they strained to extricate the body. Deadweight. They tried to be as gentle as possible but the process took its toll. After several attempts, they hauled the mangled mass onto the boat and slid it into a black body bag.

"Grab the loose debris as well," Dave instructed. "Just stuff it in the body bag."

Dave took a few more pictures of the area and shoved the camera back in a pocket. Using orange flagging tape, he tied three long stripes to a log jutting out of the debris where they had recovered the body. He took one last look around, then stepped back to sit and secure himself before they headed downriver to the pre-determined pick-up location.

Suddenly, a distinct sound rang out. *What the hell?*

Splintered rock rained down on the men. Dave swung around, scanning the opposite side of the river up the high cliff. *There!* Up on the canyon's ridge—the place where Dave had stood only a few days ago—he spied a lone figure.

Dave ripped open a vest pocket and pulled out his binoculars. Glassing the ridgeline, he could make out a few features of a man raising a firearm with a scope pointing in their direction.

"Get down now!" Dave shouted. "Shooter on the ridge!"

The men reacted instantly, but not quick enough. Before Max could lean back from grabbing the anchor rope, he went limp and fell overboard.

A loud noise exploded in Dave's head as the second boat was also hit and several men tumbled into the river. Confused, the others hastily shouted back and forth.

Reacting instinctively, Dave dove in after Max. As soon as he hit the cold, fast-moving water, he was sucked under and could only hope one of the remaining swift water members was able to radio for help.

CHAPTER 42

SARAH

Sarah swung in behind J.C. as he pulled out of the farm drive with Sunny and Tank. Kicking up dust, the trailer shot gravel from the tires as they moved down the lane. Sarah slowed to put a little distance between the two vehicles. Gunner and Sam stood in their crates in the back, sensing something different was up.

Eyeing the side mirror, Sarah watched as her cabin grew smaller and eventually disappeared altogether. She continued to have uneasy feelings about leaving the farm unattended.

Shifting her thoughts toward Dave, she wondered how he was making out on his mission. Her heart beat a little quicker. *Just breathe. Concentrate on what I need to do today,* she tried to tell herself. *Maybe I'm just used to always carrying a bad vibe. No, it's more than that.*

The other handlers hooked up along the highway and followed caravan style. It would be easier all the way around if the dog teams showed up on scene together. If they signed in at the same time, got briefed on the search information and received their assignments in one segment, everything would go smoother.

Sarah trailed behind J.C. as he took his time deciding on just the right spot to pull off the shoulder. They would need enough space to unload and care for the horses as well as ample room for the canine vehicles to park nearby.

The horses were already brushed, their hooves cleaned out and saddled. Sarah and J.C. had planned to leave them in the trailer with their hay bags until Sarah had received her assignment and was ready to head out.

Gunner and Sam began barking as soon as Sarah put the SUV in park. Exiting the vehicle, she headed around back and opened the hatch, allowing air to circulate for the dogs. She waited as the other canine handlers parked, cared for their partners, and then headed her way.

"I'll wait here. Just let me know what to do when you get back," J.C. called to Sarah.

"Thanks, J.C. I couldn't do this without your help."

Sarah decided to use only one dog and had chosen Gunner for the job. If time afforded another search assignment, she would take Sam out while Gunner rested. *If everything goes well.* She kept her fingers crossed.

J.C. looked in on the horses through the slats in the stock trailer and spoke softly to them. Sarah smiled to herself. She knew he cared for the horses more than he cared for most people.

The canine handlers had gathered behind Sarah's vehicle. "Everyone ready to head over to sign-in and get briefed?" she asked. They nodded their heads. "Okay then. This way."

Joe and Garrett made small talk with Sarah as the handlers followed her to the ICC—Incident Command Center. Dogs barked furiously from their crates as they watched their handlers walk away. Sarah strode up the shoulder of the road to the small pull-off area that had been turned into a base camp area. The parking lot was at full capacity.

The state had supplied the county with a mobile command unit. Under the awning, there was a folding table set out with a deputy running check-in. The dog handlers lined up and one by one filled out the paperwork the deputy handed them. He also checked their ID and credentials. "Make sure you leave an emergency contact number as well," he stated bluntly.

Once everyone had signed in, they entered the command center as a group.

"Hey there, Sarah. It's about time you all showed up. Thought I was gonna have'ta send a search party to find you guys."

Sarah had a hard time reading Sheriff Kasey. His nervous laugh put her on edge.

"Well, it took some time to round up the big guns," Sarah responded with a head toss toward the other dog handlers. "These are some of the best civilian volunteer HRD canine teams we have in the Mid-Atlantic area." *Most are better trained and maintained than police canines,* Sarah wanted to add but didn't. *Kasey might not appreciate that.*

"HRD?" Kasey asked.

"Sorry, Human Remains Detection. Some agencies call them cadaver dogs."

"Before we get started," Kasey boomed, "I just wanna make sure all of you know that you answer to me. Don't step out of your sectors and do not speak to anyone about this search," he declared in a menacing manner, with hands on hips. "Do I make myself clear?"

The canine handlers stood blankly, as if unsure whether to respond. Kasey's attitude and mannerisms put everyone on guard. He reminded Sarah of someone suffering from bi-polar issues. She and the other handlers continued to stare at him.

"Understood," Sarah replied, breaking the silence. Gathering her wits, she introduced each dog handler to the search management team and gave a short bio of their working history, abilities and certifications. When she was done, she finally got to the point of explaining her strategy for the search work. She had thought long and hard about the approach.

Sheriff Kasey wouldn't really know the difference; he didn't understand or know much about air-scenting canines. He had only been around tracking dogs. But she still felt it would be best and fair to let him know it was unusual to work a dog from horseback, but she planned to do this to keep herself in the field.

The group crowded around the command center's table. She handed each handler a 7.5-minute topographical map. Search management distributed a GPS to each of them as well, with predetermined coordinates loaded to mark their search sectors. It would make it easy to find and stay within their task area.

Later, when they would return to base at the end of the day, management could easily download information from the handlers' GPS into the computer to see exactly what they had covered.

Another, larger topo map lay spread open on the table. "Okay, find your corresponding sectors. Keep your dogs on a line as search sectors are smaller and adjacent to another team working." She gave the wind and temperature conditions and made it a point to make sure no one discussed what they encountered outside of the immediate management team. "Any questions?" Sarah looked around as the handlers studied the larger map.

"Will we be paired with LE?" one of the female handlers asked.

"Yes, the state police are sending troopers to escort each canine handler. If your dog finds something, try not to let them disturb anything." Sarah thought back to the moment a few days ago when her two dogs got a little over enthusiastic with their finds. "Show the officer what you have, denote the find with flagging tape, and mark it on your GPS.

"Now, just so you're aware, I will be working my dog off lead, several hundred meters away from your sectors, at what we hope is the back boundary of the search area. We will have two horses— one for me and one for my escort—and Gunner on my team." Sarah braced herself. Pokerfaced, she held a firm gaze at the handlers, waiting for a response.

The handlers gave her a quizzical look. Joe, a former Pennsylvania teammate questioned, "When did you start working Gunner from horseback?"

Sarah felt the blood drain from her head. All eyes focused on her mainly out of curiosity. It wasn't every day you heard a canine handler was going to work their dog from the back of a horse.

Sarah froze. She wished he hadn't "outed" her like that, but she knew he really hadn't meant any harm. Recovering from her anxiety, she replied, "We started training early this summer. With my hip injury, it just made sense. All our dogs are well versed around horses."

"Very cool," Joe replied.

"So," Sarah looked directly at Sheriff Kasey, "Do you have any deputies who can handle trail riding through a wooded area and varied terrain?"

The sheriff thought about it for a moment. "We may have one. I'll see if we can pull him from his assignment."

"Well, the handlers will all be ready to head out in about twenty minutes. They just need to get their gear and their canines. Are the troopers here who will be escorting them?"

"Sure are. I would have preferred to have my deputies work with you, but the state decided to step in and *help.*" Kasey accented the last word. "I'll let them know to get ready."

Sarah knew the case was too large for the county sheriff's office to handle, but it wasn't her place to get involved with the drama. And not to mention the fact this was state game lands. But she had enough of her own issues to handle. She was still in awe she was in charge of the dog teams and all the planning strategy that was involved with the work in this search.

The handlers headed out with their canines and LE escorts. Sarah wanted to make sure her escort could really handle a horse so she asked the deputy to bridle Tank. J.C. handed over the bridle while Sarah watched the officer carefully maneuver the rounded leather strap over the horse's poll, then stuck his thumb in the corner of the horse's mouth and easily slipped the bit into Tank's mouth in one swift motion.

Now confident the deputy was a seasoned and compassionate horseman, Sarah noted he was self-assured as well.

Once they had their horses fully tacked up, Sarah led Sunny in one hand and Gunner in the other down the shoulder of the highway while the deputy followed with Tank. Sarah left Sam in J.C.'s care, knowing he would be safe.

They came to a small break in the guardrail where the shoulder met the forest and the ground had leveled out. They walked the animals about twenty feet into the woods before Sarah unleashed Gunner. "Platz," she commanded, and Gunner fell into his sphinx-like position on the forest floor.

Sarah found a large fallen tree and pulled Sunny up beside it. Gunner watched Sarah climb up on the trunk to mount the horse and get herself situated.

"What can I help with?" the deputy asked.

"Can you handle the radio and compass?"

"Good with the radio, not so much the compass. Pretty good with a GPS though."

"Okay, that will work," Sarah replied. "We are heading straight out to the perimeter of the search sector on these coordinates." She pointed to numbers printed on the margin of the map. "They are already loaded in the GPS—just push the 'go to' button and it should send us in the correct direction. We need to go out about 800 meters ascending somewhat up the mountainside. That should put us at the back of the whole search area."

"Got it." The deputy pulled his radio out. "Team Trot mounted and heading to the beginning of our sector. Will radio when we reach our starting point."

"Base copies. Keep us posted," base replied with the time of their transmission.

It didn't take the mounted team long to reach their assigned sector. Sarah was glad they were upwind of the already found remains.

Once they set their bearing and made a ninety degree turn to begin, their back would be to the main wind as they traversed to the furthest end of the search sector. They would head to the back boundary and work their way toward base camp, gridding their section.

Traveling lengthways in 1000-meter sweeps, they decided to repeat them about thirty meters apart. Unless the dog located more remains heading up the mountain, they would stick to that plan for now. This way, they would have a definitive border or end of the search sector.

Looking around her immediate surroundings, Sarah gave an eerie shudder. She felt like there were eyes in the woods watching them, a feeling she couldn't shake. *Quit creeping yourself out,* she reprimanded silently.

They hadn't gone very far on their first sweep when Gunner and the horses caught scent of something. Sunny stopped in his tracks, raising his head slightly. His eyes widened. Nostrils flared as he tried to identify the scent and where it was coming from. Tank reacted as well. The horses held their heads higher, their backs rose slightly. Sarah sensed the horses' reactions reflected a predator—they were trying to make their bodies appear larger. Their ears perked, turning and twisting like sonar trying to catch any sounds.

A low growl resonated deep within Gunner's chest, and his hackles rose along his spine. He looked back toward the area where they had just finished. The trees were thick with vegetation. It was hard to see clearly more than thirty meters in any direction.

Crack! A branch snapped behind them. Both horses spun around quickly, almost unseating their riders.

"Who's there?" the deputy called out, his tone deep, authoritative.

The sound of someone or an animal crashing through the trees, was barely audible to Sarah, but she could hear it, as could the animals.

"Stay here, I'll be right back," the deputy told Sarah, turning in his saddle. He took off on Tank toward the sound.

Gunner stood in front of Sunny, parallel to the horse's body as if he was their guardian.

"Good boy, Gunner. Just chill. He'll be right back." Sarah tried to sound reassuring. Sunny stood tense, alert, with his head still held high trying to see where his buddy had gone. She slid her hand along the horse's muscular neck to reassure him that everything was fine.

Sarah could hear the deputy calling, "Hey, hey you!" Then she heard silence. Finally, the whipping of tree branches alerted her that the deputy was riding back toward the little posse.

"Find anything?" she asked.

"There was someone out there, watching. I just caught a glimpse. Looked male. Tall from what I could see. No one should be here without permission at this time of year—and I'm not aware of any game lands permits being processed. I'm going to radio this in, then we can get back to our search assignment."

When the deputy finished his unsuccessful attempt to raise base, the team returned to their task. They hadn't gone far when Gunner started showing signs of interest.

"Got something there, Gunner?" Sarah asked when she saw him check the air, moving his body in a zig-zag pattern like he normally did when he was in a human scent cone.

The deputy listened to the exchange then asked, "Does the dog have something?"

Gunner stopped and looked back at the deputy for a moment.

"Yeah, quiet." In a low voice Sarah tried to explain what was going on. "He must be hitting on something that's further away, something pretty small, or remains that have been here a very long time. The scent is not as strong and it's easier for him to become distracted if he isn't locked on the source completely."

Nodding his head, the deputy let her know he understood. He kept an eye on the dog and loosened the horse's reins, letting Tank pilot.

Stopping abruptly, Gunner closed his snout and made a snuffling sound. He dropped into a down position, looked up at Sarah, his tail thumped, and then he rolled onto his side excited.

"Good boy, Gunner." Sarah poured the compliments on with enthusiasm. She pulled his tug from the saddle bag and pitched it to the dog before he decided to get up and start digging.

As the team continued to grid the sector, Gunner located more finds along what they were considering the back perimeter of the dump site. Although, none of them disturbed the soil to dig up any of the finds, Sarah reasoned that they must be older.

"Maybe they could have had animal activity years old, been in the elements, who knows? Gunner may be starting to show wear, but if these were fresh remains, it would renew his energy and he would show more excitement. It's a mystery."

"Buried human remains are always a mystery," the deputy teased.

"Copy that," Sarah laughed. She still had a dark feeling about the day, but she was enjoying riding with the deputy and working Gunner from the back of the horse.

At each point when Gunner indicated a find, Sarah rewarded him while the deputy dismounted and tied a long strip of flagging to a nearby tree, marking it with their team's call name and the date. The deputy also played a game of tug with Gunner to keep the canine happy while Sarah marked the coordinates and put any notes down in her notebook. She also took a picture with her smart phone.

After several hours of riding back and forth on their long grids, dodging obstacles like large patches of downed trees, boulders and spongy areas, they decided they hadn't found any additional clues or remains. It was time to call it quits. The radio transmissions were still spotty and the team decided to turn around and head back to base.

Even with several breaks, Sarah knew she had worked Gunner past the point she should have. The dog slowed to no more than a jog.

The deputy had tried several times to call into base to let them know they were heading back and what their ETA was, but to no avail. They tried riding up to the top of a hill, but they were just too far out. They stopped at a creek to let the horses drink and allow Gunner to swim for a minute and recharge his energy while Sarah set a bearing from her Ranger Silva compass that would take them straight back to camp, the shortest distance she could figure.

They started back up a grade and saw a small cleared out area as they headed in the direction of base. It looked like a crude path with some tracks, most likely from a four-wheeler.

"I wonder if this is still part of the state game lands? Looks like those tracks could be from hunters," the deputy said.

"Seems like this forest holds lots of secrets," Sarah replied. "Either way, we should mark the path on our maps and GPS. I'll take a picture as well." It seemed weird to find a small, crude, but calculated path in the middle of nowhere.

As they neared base, the radio began to crackle and cough out some transmissions.

"Base to Team Trot," finally came across clear.

The deputy picked up his mic that hung from the front of his vest. "Team Trot here."

"What is your status and location?"

"Team Trot heading to base with an ETA of twenty minutes."

"Copy that. ETA 1400. Head straight in, make a bee line. See you then."

"Team Trot copies. Out." The deputy re-positioned the mic on the front of his vest. He turned around in the saddle to face Sarah.

"Sounds like they want us to hurry in. I wonder what that's about?"

"Not sure. This is a big deal. There will be bigger agencies coming in soon. The FBI should be contacted as well as The Center for Missing Children. This is the biggest thing to happen in this region of the country and we still don't have any idea of the scope of what we're dealing with."

Sarah pulled a bottle of water and a granola bar out of her saddle bag as they made their way up a slope heading toward base and the trailers. Neither rider had to guide the horses exactly. Once pointed in the direction of their horse trailer, Sunny and Tank obliged and were happy to be heading back.

Gunner trailed behind, tired. Sarah had never seen him hit this close to the bottom of his energy well. The dog's tongue hung from his mouth as he padded behind them. Sarah couldn't hide the look of concern on her face.

The deputy looked over. "Everything okay?"

"Yeah, but I'm thinking Gunner will sleep well tonight. I just hope he bounces back quick and isn't sore from working so much. Maybe I pushed him a little hard today." A worried laugh escaped Sarah.

Nearing the base, the transmissions over the radio became clearer. The deputy's patrol radio crackled with police traffic. Two lines of transmission traffic were crystal clear: somewhere there was a barn fire, and there was also some interference or incident on Rockfish River... the same river Dave was on.

He's a big boy and he's with several other able-bodied men. She pushed away any worries until the next transmission came across the radio from dispatch.

"Oh no!" Sunny felt Sarah's body tense up, and he raised his head and quickened his pace in response. The deputy looked up from his mount and met Sarah's eyes. "That's my barn!" Sarah yelled.

CHAPTER 43

DAVE

Re-surfacing, Dave choked and sputtered, coughing up mouthfuls of water. He tried not to panic as the river shocked his body and stole his breath. Tossing in the rough currents, he worked to keep his head vertical. His personal flotation device had expanded when he hit the water. Careening down the river, Dave reached up to discover his helmet was still in place. Not completely comfortable in the water, his survival instinct kicked in as he took stock of the situation.

He spun around and could see one deflated boat trailing the other stable boat behind him. He saw several men floating, their heads up and assumed they were okay. Looking downriver in the direction he was headed, he spotted what appeared to be the top of a partially submerged helmet. He realized it must be Max. The helmet disappeared completely before reemerging further away. Fighting the tossing water and strong currents, Dave shot his body toward that target.

Catching up to Max, Dave reached out and grabbed the back of his life jacket. He pulled the man close to him, wrapping an arm around Max's neck, and held him in a choke hold as they entered a rough section of the river. Tossed about in the rapids, the current flung both men against rocky outcroppings. Busted up and bleeding, Dave knew he couldn't let Max go. He fought hard to keep both their heads above water while looking for a route to the river's edge. "Stay with me, Max!" Dave shouted above the roaring water, not sure if the man was even still alive.

CHAPTER 44

SARAH

Sarah listened to the news that came across the deputy's radio. Her leg muscles tensed, gripping the horse's frame tighter. Grasping the reins in her sweaty palms, she unintentionally pulled on her mount's mouth. Sunny immediately reacted. The horse raised his head. Pitching his ears forward he grabbed the bit and pulled downward on the reins, forcing Sarah to release the pressure. Picking up an unsteady trot toward base, Sarah readjusted herself in the saddle. "Easy, Sunny," she tried to assure him.

Once Sarah steadied herself, the pair fell into an extended gait that was smooth and covered a lot of ground.

"Come on, Gunner!" she called to the dog.

The deputy fell into line behind them. His mount, Tank, took up a quick-footed and uneasy trot. Tank's short, bunchy muscular body combined with shorter legs didn't allow him to extend into anything more comfortable. The deputy had to stand up in the stirrups, balancing with his knees to keep from smashing himself on the pommel.

The horses kept pace between soft ground, rock, and the changing grade from level ground to steep climbs. Sarah neck-reined Sunny with swift pulls, steering the horse from low hanging tree branches. She ducked her head occasionally, folding her body down along Sunny's neck to avoid getting clotheslined.

Panicked thoughts spread through Sarah's head. On the verge of hyperventilating, she tried to take a deep breath to calm herself. What was going on at the farm? What about the other buildings on the property? Was the house okay?

Coming to the point of the main search area, Sarah eased back in the saddle, asking her horse to slow down. Sunny was breathing hard. Gunner's tongue was dragging. Tank and the deputy were still trotting to catch up.

"Gunner, stay right with me," she commanded. The dog remained a few feet from Sarah and the horse, obeying his handler. There were other dogs finishing up sectors and Sarah didn't want him to interfere with any of their search work.

Arriving at the steep hill leading up to the shoulder of the road, Sarah gave the horse his head and let him navigate the incline. Breathing hard, rivulets of sweat streamed from underneath Sunny's saddle pads down the sides of his flanks and barrel.

Relief washed over Sarah as she eyed J.C. at the top of the incline. She hoped he had more info regarding the barn fire.

The horses, riders and dog made their way to the trailer along the shoulder of the road. Sarah quickly dismounted, grabbed her leash and collected Gunner. J.C. seized Sunny and led the horse to the side of the trailer, while the deputy radioed base to inform them he and Sarah were back and had ended their task.

Sarah overheard the exchange from where she stood behind the SUV. She could hear the deputy telling base they were caring for the horses and he would be over to debrief as soon as he finished.

Sarah would not be debriefing; she'd let the deputy handle it. She needed to leave the scene as soon as she loaded Gunner into her SUV. The deputy had also promised to help cool the horses out and rub them down. She was grateful for his help and mouthed a quick thank you.

J.C. already had a plan. "I hate to send you to your farm alone, but it's not a good idea to take the horses anywhere near a burning building or smoke. I think I know someone nearby who has a few open stalls and can care for them for a while. You can collect them later when it's determined what's going on at your homestead."

"Thanks, J.C. Please do whatever they need. I'm sure both will need a good bath when you get them situated. I let Sunny move out all the way back here—he's pretty sweaty and he'll probably be muscle sore as well."

"Okay, I'll take care of them. I promise you. Now, take a deep breath and be careful, Sarah. No need you getting yourself hurt."

Sammy was glad to see both his handler and playmate. His tail whipped the sides of his crate as he barked excitedly.

"Good to see you too," Sarah cooed as she readied Gunner's crate.

Thick strands of damp hair stuck to the sides of her face. Adrenaline kept her going. Sweat laden clothes hung on her thin frame as she hurried. She wanted to make sure that Gunner could cool down on the ride home. She knew if she felt this miserable and overheated, Gunner would be ten times worse with his double-coated shepherd hair. Not wanting to chance heat stroke, she gave him a little water and put cooling packs under the pad in his crate.

Sarah stepped back to give Gunner the command to jump into his crate, but he was already up and in before she got the word out.

Satisfied she hadn't forgotten anything, she took one last look at the dogs before closing the hatch.

Sweaty palms clenched the steering wheel, her mind in overdrive fearing what she would find at home. Her heart fell as she entered her drive, finding the barn engulfed in flames. Gunner and Sam were barking furiously. There were several large truck apparatuses parked haphazardly. It looked like not only her county's fire department had responded to the call out, but two other counties as well.

Firemen guarding the drive allowed her through in the SUV. Suddenly, she remembered the kittens! She knew it was too late. Surely, they had perished and were gone.

Standing outside the pasture beside the barn, she watched as the south wall crashed down. There would be no saving any of it. The firefighters were doing what they could, but this fire would have to burn itself out. They had lost the newly built run-in shed Dave had installed on the outside of the barn for the horses.

Tears welled in Sarah's eyes.

The fire chief came up to her as she stood alone in the driveway. She recognized him from trips she had made into town. No longer trying to hold back, Sarah let the tears flow.

"Ma'am, I'm really sorry. But I need to ask you a few questions," he spoke directly.

Sarah nodded.

"Was anyone or anything in the barn?"

"No, uh yes, some kittens in the hayloft."

"Was that all? No other animals?"

She stared at him for a moment. A blank look reflected his last statement. *Is that all?*

"Ma'am?"

Sarah shook her head.

"Was there any accelerant? Anything flammable stored in the barn?"

"No," Sarah gasped. "We keep gas cans and paint, anything flammable or toxic in the shed on the other side of the house." Sarah pointed to the small backyard shed that stood on concrete pavers, where they kept their lawn mower and other garden implements. The tractor was stored behind there as well, parked beneath an overhang.

The fire chief stood with his hands hanging loose at his sides. He looked around the farm, at the house, the fire and back at Sarah. Staring at the ground for a moment, he seemed like he was trying to figure out how and what to tell her.

She knew.

"Do you know how the fire was started?" Sarah asked through her tears and sniffles. It wasn't just the loss of the kittens or the weeks of hard work they had put into the building, or watching its complete destruction. It was knowing the fire wasn't an accident... it had been intentionally set. That someone had set foot on their land and deliberately destroyed their property. Sarah shuddered. She felt violated in a different way than she had known in the past.

"Well, it appears it was most likely set. We won't know for sure until the fire's out and it's cooled down enough so we can investigate thoroughly. We have an agent from the arson unit on the way as well. The fire appears to be burning too hot. It also moved too quick through the structure. Those couple elements make it look suspicious that someone would've used some type of accelerant. Do you know how much hay you had stored in the barn?"

"About 200 small square bales in the loft. It wasn't full. We had several bales of straw as well." It made her think about the kittens and the momma cat again. She pictured them terrified in what was probably their last moments. Closing her eyes, she said a little prayer hoping they had succumbed to the smoke before the flames reached them. She started to tear up again. She needed Dave.

"You gonna be alright? Do you have someone with you?"

She knew the fire chief was aware she and Dave were a couple and that he was a deputy. "Dave's on an assignment on the river. He'll be back later today. I don't want to let him know about the fire. I don't think that would be a good idea right now." Then she remembered. "Someone had been here—trespassing—and I never reported it. Dave got mad at me. He wrote up a report the next day and took fingerprints from the window. I'm not sure he's gotten a chance to run them yet, though. The dogs knew... I knew. I had a bad feeling." Sarah looked back toward the house and drive.

Clearing his throat, the fire chief rocked back on the heel of his boots and pushed Sarah for more info. "How do you know for sure someone had been trespassing?"

"When we came home a couple days ago, after Gunner and Sam—my dogs..." trailing off, she took a deep, choking breath. After a moment to compose herself, she got the information straight in her head. "I parked in the front lawn and let the dogs out of the SUV. One of them had dropped a toy and as I bent down to pick it up, I saw a deep track in the grass and in the soil around the plants beside the house. At the same time I noticed these fresh tracks, the dogs picked up on someone's trail who didn't belong. They started to follow it. One dog went around the house and came to the kitchen where I found a handprint on the window. The other dog followed a path through the front paddock toward the barn. I could make out a trail through the paddock that wasn't from Dave or I, and no animals are turned out there."

"You could see the path? You could actually see where someone had walked across the grass?"

"Yes, I'm certified in sign-cutting."

"Sign-cutting?" The fire chief questioned with a raised brow. Beads of sweat formed along his forehead, his uniform shirt clinging to his back and sides where patches of perspiration had soaked through. He appeared tense, tired and unfocused as he stood there with Sarah.

"Man tracking," she clarified. "Sign-cutting is just the formal term for looking for tracks or signs of where someone might have traveled. I could see where the grass had been crushed, walked on and hadn't quite bounced back all the way. It looked like someone had been here at least within a few hours of me coming home. The dogs also picked up and followed a trail to the barn from the house, followed it around the barn and then into the barn. I did a thorough search and found a knife up in the hayloft. It appeared as if someone had left in a haste. The dogs and I searched outside some more, and they picked up a trail again that took them to the creek behind the barn. They wanted to cross over, but I pulled them off the trail at the bank."

"I don't think you should stay here alone. Is there somewhere you can go until Dave gets back?"

"I'll be fine here. Dave might be back before you're done. We'll just stay in the house."

"Okay, stay put. I may need to talk to you again anyway. Let me know if you need anything."

"Likewise," Sarah told the fire chief. She walked back to the SUV. The dogs were still barking. "Sorry, guys," she spoke to them as she put leashes on each before pulling them out of their crates.

Both dogs were keyed up. They didn't understand what was going on other than there was a lot of chaos and commotion on their normally quiet farm—men cloaked in heavy duty gear, wielding axes, rolling out hoses, yelling to one another. As the light breeze changed course, it sent conflicting smells mingled within the drifting smoke, giving other unseen messages on the air currents only the dogs could decipher.

Spent diesel fuel wafted through the air, burning Sarah's nostrils. Both dogs blew hard from their nose with a heavy snuff, affirming the fumes had assaulted their senses as well.

The ground hummed, penetrated by large vehicles' engines. Gunner and Sam's lips pulled back tight from their gums, giving them a fierce, almost wicked smile. Their tongues lolled, gleaming white teeth exposed. Large pointed ears torqued and twisted, taking in the strange sounds. Soft growls and whines. This was their property to protect. They didn't understand these people were here to help. Both dogs pulled forcibly at the end of their leads, heads swiveled to take in every scent.

"Easy, guys. Settle," Sarah spoke in measured, low whispers as she slowly swept her open palm along their rib cages to calm them once they entered the cabin.

Sarah let the dogs mill about, hoping they would relax, but neither dog settled. Instead, the situation put them on high alert. She watched as Gunner went from the front door, checked along each window and then the back door. She studied him carefully to make sure he wasn't sore from the backwoods search. Satisfied he looked fine, only fatigued, she turned her attention to the other dog. Sammy sat beside her at the kitchen table. He leaned his body into her, panting.

"Everything's going to be okay, guys, just settle down." Sarah forgot her worries for the time being as she focused her concerns on them.

Suddenly came a knock at the back door. Both dogs bolted, racing to greet whomever stood on the other side. Hackles raised, they emitted loud, terrifying barks that threw Sarah off guard. Her heart skipped a beat and began to race with the dogs' new excitement.

"Settle down!" she shouted over the frenzied barking. "Hang on a minute," she yelled to whoever was waiting at her door. Grabbing both dogs by their collars and half dragging them backwards down the hall into their crates, she said, "Chill out, guys." They stopped barking once they were locked in, but they sulked and growled as she walked back to the rear door of the cabin.

She peeked through the window first to see it was only the fire chief. He must have forgotten something or had more questions. Opening the door, she could see he had removed his safety helmet and was nervously bouncing from foot to foot, running his hand through hair wet from sweat.

"I don't know how to tell you this, but another call concerning you just came over the radio. I wasn't sure if you had a police scanner."

"We do, but it's not on. What do you mean 'another call' concerning me?"

"The recovery team on the river. There's been an incident. A shooting event took place."

"What do you mean incident? Is Dave okay? Shooting? What in the hell is going on?"

"We're not exactly sure yet. We have very little information. Dave is unaccounted for and at least two of the swift water rescue team members are injured. Rescue teams are headed there now. They're putting a bird in the air as well."

The floor shifted as a wave of nausea overcame her. Her throat felt dry, restricted. She spun around trying to find her keys and headed to unlock the dogs, who were now barking from their crates. She wasn't going to leave them here.

"Wait, wait," the fire chief followed her as she headed out the door with the dogs. "I can find someone to drive you. I don't think you should go alone."

"I'll be fine," Sarah half yelled, half cried. Tears stung her eyes. All of a sudden, it seemed like her life had exploded out of control.

As Sarah re-loaded the dogs in the SUV, a media truck from one of the local stations pulled into the driveway. Sarah was sure there was nothing else going on in the area that was more newsworthy. Other than the remains search area. And the swift water shooting She jumped into the vehicle, jammed the keys in the ignition and turned the engine over.

Putting the SUV in reverse, she spun around and took off out the driveway as the newscaster and film crew were disembarking from their van. They must have realized who she was and stepped into the drive to stop her. Sarah maneuvered around them and shot off down the road toward the river.

CHAPTER 45

SARAH

"Hold on, boys," Sarah warned, steering the SUV sharply out of her driveway. The dogs scrambled then stood up within their crates. They kept their eyes glued to the back of Sarah's head. "This can't be happening," Sarah rambled on, hoping to settle her nerves.

Multiple stresses of the last few days compounded with the barn fire and Dave missing, hurt? Or worse... *Stop it!* It was more than she could bear.

Sarah finally came to the realization that she not only loved Dave, but she was hopelessly and deeply in love with him. Feelings she didn't think she was capable of. "I can't lose him now. He's my future, we've worked so hard to be together," Sarah whispered between tears. The dogs tilted their heads listening.

Speeding over the hilly roads, Sarah had a vague idea of where the pick-up drivers were supposed to collect the teams and their boats. She kept the police scanner on, listening for any transmission regarding the team. She could hear exchanges from the copter pilot and deputies on scene, but no information that meant anything to her.

The SUV bounced and jerked hard as she pulled into the rendezvous point already teaming with activity. A fire company idled with a large diesel truck. Paramedics were stationed near their ambulances. The helicopter flew at a low altitude above the river, sending rivulets of water in all directions.

She exited the SUV after rolling down the windows to allow cross-ventilation for the dogs. Releasing the hatch in the back, she raised the door. "Stay," she firmly told them. They met her eyes.

Not that they could go anywhere since they were crated, but her firm command meant for them to settle down and chill out—she might be a while. This was not their search and she needed them to recognize the situation.

When Sarah was sure the dogs were secure, she turned around to study the hastily set up base. Setting her emotional state aside, she started to think like a first responder. She scanned the lot. *There!* Eyeing the boat trailers parked along the edge of the bank, Sarah made her way over to where they were parked.

"Any word?" Sarah asked the driver as she walked up to one of the trucks hooked up to a trailer.

"They found them," the man replied.

"Everyone?" Sarah inquired.

"Yeah, sounds like they picked up the whole crew," he replied turning to face her. Chimes and dispatch noise echoed within his vehicle.

"Are they okay? Anyone injured?" she prodded.

Poker faced, the man stared at her. Sarah could tell he was studying her. She had a first responder team uniform on—one from her Pennsylvania team and one she was sure he didn't recognize. "Oh, sorry. I'm Sarah Gavin, Deputy Grave's girlfriend. I was working the human remains search when he left on the recovery mission this morning. I really need to know what's going on."

With that, the man dropped his façade. "Maybe you should talk to the team running search management," he responded pointing to an area under a blue tarp.

"Appreciate it, thanks for the help." Sarah's blood was pumping fiercely through her veins. She had a hard time keeping her breath in check. Just because they were found didn't mean they were okay, or *alive.*

She walked up to the table under the tarp surrounded by several law enforcement officers and more first responders. They were busy marking an area on the map.

"Excuse me," she said, three times without any response. At the sound of a boat motor, everyone stopped and looked toward the river.

It was the recovered swift water team. There were three boats, but one was towing a second that looked deflated, droopy. The first two boats were full of team members. Two men were laid out and didn't look so good. Her heart skipped a beat. She could see Dave sitting up holding one of the men's heads in his lap. Sarah could see fresh blood along the side of Dave's face.

She headed over to the area where the boat pulled up at the edge of the river. She stood to the side as several men helped pull the boats in and secure them.

The closer Sarah got to Dave, the more she saw how busted up he was—bruised and bleeding, clothes were shredded, his shoes missing. Sarah's heart tore at the sight.

Dave steadied the injured teammate's head as the man was packaged and lifted from the boat. Then he helped pull in the disabled boat, dragging it up on shore. The Zodiac craft had seen better days.

Sarah stared on as others pulled a zippered black body bag from the disabled boat. Standing silently, she watched Dave assist in loading the body bag into the M.E.'s van. *Chain of custody.* She watched as he did everything a cop was expected to do. He had handled the body with care and respect.

Dave's eyes found her. He made his way to where Sarah stood along the shoreline, and pulled her into him.

Sarah couldn't control her feelings any longer. She allowed the walls surrounding her heart to melt away. "What happened?" she squeaked out, sucking in her breath between sobs. "I thought I lost you."

"Someone shot at us. They punctured one of the boats. They shot a team member—Max, the commander. I went in after him. Two more team members fell into the river. One's hurt pretty bad, hit his head on a rock or log."

"Why would someone shoot at your boat? This doesn't make sense."

"No, it doesn't. Someone didn't want us retrieving the body. This is getting deeper and deeper. I think it's all tied in together to the remains. To your foster home."

"Are you okay? Are you hurt?"

"Nothing a little Advil won't take care of." He held her tight, burying his face into her feral curls. "Why does your hair smell like smoke?"

Sarah had forgotten about the barn fire. She didn't think it would be the best place or time to tell him. "Finish up here... do what you need to do. The SUV is over there," she said, pointing toward the back of the lot. "I'll wait for you."

"Okay, I might be a little while. They may want to check me out."

"That's fine. I'm just glad you're okay." Sarah left him standing there by the shore as she walked back to the dogs. It had been non-stop for the last several days. Mentally and physically. She just wanted to head home, shower and climb into bed.

Sitting down in the driver's seat, she remembered the horses. "Oh, shit." She knew J.C. would have taken care of them, but she needed to tell him what all had transpired, that Dave was okay, and there wasn't a barn for the horses to come home to. She pulled out her phone and dialed his number.

CHAPTER 46

DAVE

"What do you mean, a fire? What the hell are you talking about, Sarah?" Dave exploded as she tried to explain to him on their drive back to the farm. "What the fuck else could go wrong? Shot at and now this?"

"It's gone, Dave. The whole barn burned to the ground." Sarah trembled as the words spilled out. "All of our hard work—the hay, the kennels. It's all gone."

"Calm down. I didn't mean to yell at you. It's been a rough day all the way around."

With red-rimmed eyes Sarah continued, "The fire chief believes it was arson." She remained focused on the road ahead as she drove them home.

"Arson? Someone deliberately set it on fire? How? What?" Dave saw red. He had never been this angry and was trying to reel in his fury. "How does he know? How can they tell?"

"According to the fire chief, he said the barn burned hot and fast—too hot and too fast, even for an old building."

"Accelerants," Dave stated. He had a little background in arson training from his previous state trooper days.

He was so tired. He had left his cruiser at the original starting point. Too exhausted and sore to retrieve it, Deputy Brooks had promised to pick it up.

Right now, he and Sarah both just needed to get home, get some dinner, shower and rest. It had been a few days from hell they hadn't bargained for.

"What about the horses? Are they okay?" Dave asked.

What looked like relief registered on Sarah's face. He knew his negative attitude had scared her. He had never shown this side of himself before.

"I took Tank and Sunny to the search today. We worked Gunner along the backside of the area."

"Really? Where are they now?"

"J.C. took them. I spoke with him tonight. They are both fine. He dropped them off at an equine vet's stable who offered to keep them for a little while."

Dave inhaled sharply. His head hurt. Remembering he hadn't checked in with his boss, he decided to call Kasey to let him know he was alright. After a few moments, Kasey's voicemail came on and Dave left a message. Since he couldn't raise the sheriff, he put a call into Felding who picked up right away. They discussed the search and the fire, and Felding asked if Sarah and the dogs were okay. He also asked if Dave had spoken to Kasey, and wanted to meet at the office the next morning to go over the river incident.

The sun was low in the western sky as Sarah pulled into their drive. There was still a lone diesel pump truck, along with a couple of crew members from the local firehouse, surrounding the fallen barn. Plumes of smoke continued to billow. Smoldering embers still flickered and shined.

The dogs started to bark. "Hang on, guys, I'll get you out in a minute. Settle."

"Be careful with them around this mess," Dave hissed as they drove up the gravel lane. His attitude darkened as he viewed the ruins. "Maybe you should keep them on a leash for now."

Twisted metal, stone, and what was left of timbers sat black and crumpled. One spot stood higher in the middle of the pile where the tack room once was. The dog's new kennels had been on the other side of the tack room. All their supplies stored in the barn had been destroyed. At least the dogs, horses and humans were safe.

Dave jacked his door open even before Sarah pulled to a stop. Jumping out, he headed straight to the few firefighters still dousing the smoldering ash. Normally, he could roll with the obstacles in their life—at least, so far. But seeing the destruction in person was worse than hearing Sarah speak the words. It made him fear for Sarah. And after the shooting on the river, for himself as well.

Knowing someone had come on their farm uninvited and burned down their barn, the situation had come too close for their safety.

Dave didn't like the fact Sarah had to leave town for an important appointment the next morning and now he couldn't go with her, but maybe she would be safer if she was out of town for a few days. He would feel better knowing she was away from this mess. It was a court ordered appointment and she had to adhere to it.

For the first time in his life, Dave felt overwhelmed, almost defeated.

CHAPTER 47

SARAH

Turning north toward Pennsylvania, Sarah settled in for the long drive. "Dammit!" she mumbled at the Saturday traffic congestion. "This may take longer than expected. Good thing we got an early start," she said to the dogs.

Part of Sarah's agreement after the mistrial, was to be available for the internal investigation into the Pennsylvania foster care system. The meeting couldn't have come at a worse time, but it had been set up weeks in advance and had taken a lot of coordinating between state agencies.

Today would involve a forensic artist who would attempt to illustrate subjects from her past while she was under hypnosis. The focus was to identify the woman, and possibly the man Sarah had witnessed at the home several times over the years when her foster siblings would leave and never return.

This was the same couple who was there the night Sarah's daughter had been born. The woman took the infant into her arms and disappeared with her forever. The man usually stood in the back, in the shadow of the woman who controlled the situation. Although it was never spoken, Sarah always knew she was the smarter of the pair.

As Sarah drove, she tried to draw on past details of the two people she used to fear. But her memory was blurry, faded when it came to details. To think that these individuals were still out there scared her. That the children from her foster home who had gone missing might still be out there as well. Yet she knew they hadn't gone missing as indicated... they had been taken. And sold.

Gripping the steering wheel tightly, her anxiety escalated. She forced herself to inhale deeply and slow her breathing. *Why does the idea of hypnosis bother me?* The she realized, the hypnotist might ask questions concerning Eva and the murders. Sarah decided to call ahead and ask Elliot Roth to be present for the session. She needed someone there to protect her rights since Dave couldn't attend. Even though it was the weekend, Elliot agreed.

Finally, after several hours on the road, she pulled into the York County Courthouse parking area. Settling into a well shaded spot near the front of the lot, she lowered the windows to allow air to circulate for the dogs. Pulling each dog out separately, she gave them a quick bathroom break and filled their water buckets.

Once the dogs were taken care of, she began to get nervous. "You can do this," she told herself. "You got this. This will help others."

Maybe after ten years or so, they might be able to find some of these children that were taken... stolen... sold. Sarah still tried to wrap her mind around the words "human trafficking." Her college studies in criminology only slightly touched on the subject. But it wasn't just a foreign country problem. *It's a U.S. problem, right here in our own backyard. This is the right thing to do.*

Sarah exited her vehicle. She looked up at the imposing, gray government building. Uninviting, a few people were entering and she followed them in through the glass doors. She watched as they dropped their purses and briefcases into containers to go through the x-ray machine. When it was her turn, she slid her small purse into a bin. The officer asked her for ID. She handed him her driver's license. He looked over the plastic-covered badge with recognition. She maintained her pose.

"Second floor, room 217," he said. "They're waiting on you."

Sarah didn't have to ask where to go. She had been there for prior meetings with other officials connected to the state's investigation of the foster care system. Her name still rung easy, especially to the local officials and agencies. She wasn't anyone they were going to forget.

She quietly thanked the officer, gathered her purse and ID and entered the main hall. Without studying her surroundings, she walked to the first elevator. Relieved to see it was empty when the doors opened, Sarah stepped inside and rode up to the second floor. Exiting, she was met by her lawyer.

"Hey there, Sarah. Good to see you." Elliot patted her back, all positive and smiles.

Sarah knew he was trying to stay upbeat for her sake. Together, they entered the office. Musty carpet and the smell of stale candy hung in the air. A black leather sofa and overstuffed arm chair were situated between two mismatched end tables. Dreading these meetings, Sarah forced a smile. She always felt judged and sentenced prior to her arrival.

Each man smiled at Sarah and extended a hand in greeting.

Sarah immediately felt at ease with the forensic artist. He was a big, thick burly man who looked more like he should be carrying an ax to chop down trees than sporting a pencil to capture an image from Sarah's past.

On the other hand, the hypnotist was pale and pasty looking. A well-groomed gentleman in a three-piece suit with a bow-tie, he didn't stand much over five feet tall. His handshake was loose and limp, making Sarah shudder. It was as if he kept looking through her and not at her. *Looks like a perv,* she thought. *Can I trust this guy to hypnotize me?*

"Hi, I'm Dr. Vincent, I'll be the one hypnotizing you today," he said, finally looking her in the eyes. "Do you know anything about hypnosis? Have you ever been hypnotized in the past?"

Sarah thought about it for a moment. "Not really. I mean, I never have had the experience."

"Okay, well, let me explain a few things first. Why don't you sit here, where you can be comfortable?" Dr. Vincent pointed to the end of the black leather sofa.

Sarah sat down stiffly, finding it hard to relax while being the center of unwanted attention.

"I've already met with a police sketch artist," she said. "I know the drawings weren't that great, but I don't understand why we have to go through this again? And why do I need to be hypnotized?"

"I understand your concerns," Dr. Vincent stated. "The original sketches were done with what we call composite software. The officer you met with fed the information you gave him into a computer and the program found the most suitable match to a person's facial features. Although it's a very good program, it doesn't create the best representation."

"Maybe that's why it took hours for us to come up with a picture that still wasn't that close to what I could remember," said Sarah.

"I also recall from the report," Dr. Vincent continued, "that you were having a difficult time recalling specific details about their facial qualities."

"I seem to have blocked a lot of those memories. I mainly remember the woman. The man was always in the background, just bordering the edge." *I don't remember because I was never exactly there.* Sarah thought of Eva and her blackouts.

"Yes, yes," Dr. Vincent mumbled. "With hypnosis, we are hoping to delve into more vivid memories stored in certain areas of your brain. The process shouldn't cause you any problems and won't be painful at all. You really shouldn't remember much of the session afterward."

Once the doctor explained the technique, the forensic artist, Matt, went through his process and what he planned to capture. They hoped to get drawings of both individuals Sarah had witnessed in the past at the foster home.

"Now do you have any questions? Need anything? Something to drink? Are you comfortable?" Dr. Vincent asked.

Sarah spied her lawyer who was quietly sitting in the corner of the room observing. Sarah asked Dr. Vincent directly, "There won't be any questions concerning other personalities or anything to do with my recent court case?"

Dr. Vincent sat up straighter in his chair, facing the sofa. He adjusted his jacket and looked Sarah in the eyes. "No, of course not. We are only here to conduct this portion of the internal inquiry for the state's case regarding the foster home. This has nothing to do with your criminal case. But," he held up his hand, "you never know. This may in fact help you in your case down the road. Anything else?"

"No, I think that's all." Sarah leaned back on the leather. It was cold and smooth, and softly crackled under her movements.

Dr. Vincent removed his suit coat, loosened his tie. He asked Matt if he was ready, and the artist gave a quick nod.

"Now Sarah, take a deep breath. Let it out slowly. Close your eyes and relax. I'm going to give you some scenarios to think about." The doctor continued to talk while Sarah felt herself completely relax and let go of her anxieties about the situation. She was drifting free...

Sarah woke slowly at first. She had forgotten where she was. Suddenly, her mind jolted as she sat up. She could feel the side of her mouth where she had drooled, and quickly wiped her hand across her mouth. Embarrassed, a shy smile emerged. She looked around the room.

Matt was standing at his easel. He returned her smile.

"So?" she asked.

"Well, I think we did really, really well," Matt grinned some more.

"Can I see?" she asked. Her mouth was dry. It was taking a few minutes for her to come fully awake and get with it.

Dr. Vincent handed her a bottle of water.

Her lawyer stood up. "I want you to be prepared to see these. They may bring back some difficult memories. Are you sure you're up for this?"

"I think I can handle it. I've been through far worse." Sarah rose from the sofa and stretched her taut muscles.

Matt raised a brow. "Okay, here ya go." He swung the easel around.

A gasp escaped Sarah. She stood paralyzed.

There on the soft white palette was a beautifully crafted portrait of the woman who had taken her baby.

The quality of the artist's work was flawless. Stunned, it was as if he had even captured the woman's personality, her tone, in the drawing.

Sarah walked forward, grabbing the side of the portrait. "It's so real. That's her. It's been years since I saw her, but I remember now, like it was yesterday. I remember everything about her now." The memories flooded back. "What she wore, her voice. Even what she smelled like."

After a few moments, Sarah asked to see the other sketch. She didn't believe the other picture of the male—the woman's accomplice—would have as much impact. But when Matt flipped the canvas around to unveil the man, Sarah felt her blood drain. She stood gawking at the portrait. Taking a step back, she stumbled, and almost fell backwards against the overstuffed chair.

"Sarah? Hey? You okay?" The artist lunged toward her as Dr. Vincent and her lawyer reached to catch her.

"What is it?" Elliot asked.

She didn't speak at first. She drew closer to the drawing, staring at it in disbelief. "It's him. That's the same guy. I've seen him around."

"What, exactly do you mean, you've seen him?" Elliot puzzled.

"I knew he looked familiar, but I couldn't place him. It's been years. I never really thought of him as important. He always just followed the woman around. He did whatever she told him to do. He controlled the kids. He stayed in the background, like her shadow."

"But what do you mean you've seen him? Lately?"

"Yes."

"Where?"

"In the courtroom. At the back of the gallery, by the door. He was there, I looked away. Then I looked back and he was gone. I thought I vaguely recognized him but couldn't remember where I knew him from."

"Have you seen him other times? Recently?"

"Yes, I saw him in Virginia, or at least I think it was him. I knew he looked familiar, but older. I saw him along the road near the remains site."

"The remains site?" Elliot questioned. "What are you talking about?"

"Where they found all of the bodies." She quickly filled them in on the case which was unfolding in the mountains of Virginia. "He passed me in an older, beat up van. I was parked along the shoulder in my SUV and he slowed down to a crawl, with his eyes on me the whole time. It was like he looked right at me, through the darkened glass. Like he knew who I was."

Dr. Vincent was preoccupied with typing up a report on the computer from today's session. He didn't seem to be interested in what was happening once learning it had to do with an event in another state. But Matt and Sarah's lawyer made eye contact.

"What are you thinking?" Sarah abruptly asked.

"I'm not sure, but it sounds like whoever this guy is, he knows you and your whereabouts," Matt suggested.

"What exactly are you saying?" Sarah questioned defensively.

"Which means you could possibly be in some type of danger and not even realize it," Elliot stated.

Danger? She thought of the day before with the barn fire and the recovery team getting shot at. She knew Dave had glassed the shooter standing on the rim of the gorge wall with his binoculars, but she never asked for any details or a description. Could this be the same guy? Was this somehow all connected?

CHAPTER 48

DAVE

Battered, bruised and beaten from the previous day's mission on the river, Dave made his way to the station. Absentmindedly, he pulled his ball cap down snug, forgetting the stiches on the side of his head. He whipped the hat off muttering, "Son of a bitch!"

Entering the front office, blaring LED lights harshly offended his eyes. The hospital had ordered an MRI to check for a concussion, but he flatly refused. Two injured members of the swift water team had been hospitalized. One survived surgery from a bullet wound, the other was recovering from a head injury. Both were in serious, but stable condition. He would have to remember to call later to check on their progress.

The unidentified shooter who had caused the havoc during the recovery mission the day before was still at large. Dave only had a vague description of him based on what he had been able to observe with the binoculars. Aside from being a tall, thin male, maybe reddish gray hair and facial hair, Dave didn't have much else to go on. An APB had been issued to the surrounding agencies. Local media covering the incident had kept up a vigil, broadcasting what information they had of the subject, adding a warning to the public.

Dave wasn't supposed to be at work; he was on sick leave. Eventually, he would be put on light duty and limited to his station until he recovered and was cleared by a doctor. But his investigative nature gnawed away and wouldn't let him rest. He knew all the events were somehow tied together. He also had to stick around for questioning. The sheriff's office would be conducting an internal investigation of their own. It was routine anytime their deputies were involved in any gun-related incident.

A co-worker involved in the internal investigation was in contact with Dave. He would swing by at some point later this morning to interview him.

Finding it difficult to focus, Dave's thoughts drifted to Sarah. He wondered how she was making out during her session in Pennsylvania. Concerned about her mental status, he had wanted to be there to make sure no one took advantage of the situation, to make sure no one would push the issue regarding Sarah's other persona while she was under hypnosis. It would've also given him time to do some investigative work on her family history.

Growing tired waiting for his co-worker to show, Dave moved forward with some different investigative work. He searched the medical examiner's records looking for any info regarding the body they had pulled from the river yesterday. An autopsy was supposed to be performed by the coroner as soon as she could, but she had been so busy assisting with the woods recoveries, she probably wasn't aware she had another body to process.

Bingo. Scanning through the system, Dave located a report recorded under a Jane Doe. The intake coroner had apparently started a record and entered it into the system. Dave pulled up what they had so far.

He wasn't too concerned regarding manner of death for now. He was more fixated on trying to identify who the girl was and where she came from. He was sold on the idea she had been murdered. A gut feeling. Yet he couldn't understand why he couldn't locate a missing person's report. From what was left of her mutilated body, it was evident she was Caucasian, blonde, slender built and around 5' 4", give or take an inch. She appeared to be late teens, maybe early twenties.

Jane Doe's body also showed bruising in several areas, but Dave couldn't determine what damage was done prior to entering the river. Pre-mortem or post-mortem? Her left breast appeared to have a tattoo of a butterfly. There were a few other tattoos but the parts of the body they were on had been severely damaged in her travel down the whitewater and weren't discernable. Maybe the coroner's office could later determine what they had been.

He was anxious to use the NamUS.gov site where unidentified subjects could be entered, matching them with a missing report. He could add every identifying detail of the body—from physical make-up including body piercings and tattoos, to where they had been found and possible age, and then let the program try to match it to a missing subject.

I wonder if there is any way to determine where she originally entered the river? I doubt she jumped on her own account. Or did she? Star-crossed lover? Or did she have other major reasons for taking her own life?

He read over the initial report taken from the admitting staff last night. It was short.

Cause of Death: Undetermined.

First Observation: Partially decomposed body due to exposure and light animal activity. Body appears to have bruising over much of the trunk and upper extremities. Track marks found along major veins in arms and legs. Missing front bottom left tooth and right canine. Right humorous appears broken, both collar bones broken, fractured skull and fractured right scapula.

That's interesting, maybe she fell headfirst or was pushed. Were her injuries pre-mortem or post-mortem? He remembered the terrain being very rocky near the bridge where the swift water team had put in their boats.

Closing his eyes, Dave took a deep breath. He knew this was more than the river's damage. It never ceased to amaze him what people did to each other. Civilized people. He thought he would never get used to it.

Parched, Dave chugged a bottle of water as he pondered thoughts of finding the point where the young woman may have entered the river. An idea took form. He wondered if there was a way to figure it out by using a search dog. If, possibly, a tracking or trailing canine could pick up her scent trail. He had remembered hearing about a technique called backtracking in which only a few handlers in the nation had trained their dogs to perform. And those handlers were mostly border patrol, top notch canine trainers who had a need for that specific skill in their line of work.

Dave leaned back in his chair, stuck his head out his office door and yelled down the hall, "Hey, Brooks." No response. "Brooks," Dave yelled again, knowing the deputy was most likely doing his best at doing nothing at all.

"Yeah? What d'ya want, Graves? I'm busy!" Brooks yelled back.

"Yeah, sure you are, Brooks. Busy resting your eyes. I was wondering if you'd happen to know anyone around here who runs tracking dogs, being that you're a long time local. I'm sure you know everyone around these parts."

"You mean like hounds for hunting?" Brooks yelled in return.

"Well, kind of like, you know, for locating lost persons. Bloodhounds for human tracking," Dave responded slowly and deliberately, dragging out his reply.

"Why, Graves?"

"I have an idea about finding out where the body in the river might have come from."

"Whoa, hold tight." Brooks came down the hall and stuck his head in Dave's office.

The deputy's shaved head, pock-marked face and formerly broken nose made Dave think of him more like an MMA ring fighter or bouncer than an officer of the law. Brooks looked imposing but was far from it. *More like a stuffed teddy bear.*

"You're not supposed to do anything for a few days. Kasey said he didn't want you poking around on this case anymore. He says he's gonna handle this one personally."

"I'm not 'officially' doing anything," Dave replied, standing up from his desk which gave him a couple inches on Brooks. He stared directly into the other deputy's eyes, heavily enunciating the word *officially*.

"Well, you didn't get the information from me, but the next county over in Albemarle, there's a deputy who trains and run bloodhounds. He's supposed to be top-notch. Trains with all the big-time agencies like Border Patrol, ATF and the Bureau. I'm sure you can call the Albemarle Sheriff's department to get his name and contact info."

"Thanks, Brooks. Appreciate the info."

"Remember, I didn't tell you anything."

"No problem. My mouth is sealed." Dave pursed his lips tight.

Once Brooks went back to his office, Dave decided he would try to track down the K9 deputy. He hadn't met any of the deputies from that county yet, nor had he met any other dog handlers since he moved to Virginia. There hadn't been time and frankly, Dave wanted to have the occasion to do his research prior to getting involved with the local volunteer search groups. He wanted to figure out who was who. Who were the real, tried and true dog handlers who knew what they were doing and had well trained, good dogs. Up until the recent search where Kellee had located some well-skilled handlers to work the remains site, he hadn't been involved with any professional agencies or civilian organizations.

Dave placed a call to the Albemarle Sheriff's Department. He made notes of the handler's name and contact information. He was put through to dispatch to try and track down the deputy.

"Hey there, this is Deputy Dave Graves from Nelson County. Is Deputy Hein available?" he asked dispatch.

"Deputy Hein is on a call. Would you like me to forward a message, or I can give you his personal cell number?"

"Uh, cell number would be great." Sometimes he forgot how small the world was down here. Back in Pennsylvania, dispatch would never have offered up an officer's personal number without confirming that the caller was indeed from law enforcement.

Dave jotted down the info and hung up. He dialed the number on his cell phone and it went straight to voicemail. Dave left his contact information. He didn't leave specific details why he was calling, only who he was, his contact info and that he needed help on a case.

He turned back to the computer screen. Dave pulled up all the files he could find on the female's body they recovered, the file on the child's femur from the wooded area, and the latest reports from the excavation of what was now twenty-three sets of remains nestled in the region along State Route 151 in the Horseshoe Mountain's near Brent Gap. Pulling out a map, he made notes of where each incident was located.

Dave stared down, pondering the situation. The child's femur was most likely part of the mass burial site. There was no doubt about that. But he wondered how and if this young woman could be tied into the mystery. There were many odd occurrences happening too close together not to be connected somehow. He felt like they were on the tip of discovering something big, but just couldn't piece it together. Deep in thought, he barely heard his phone ring.

Scrambling to pick up the receiver, he abruptly answered, "Hello, Deputy Graves here."

"Hey there, Graves. This is Deputy Hein from Albemarle County. You called earlier about a case you were working on?"

"Yeah, I wanted to find out information about what your tracking canine is capable of." Dave laid the bait. He wanted to find out if this handler really had a good tracking and trailing dog or if he was just blowing smoke.

"I'm sorry, capable of? We don't specifically track, but rather we trail for lost persons and suspects. What information are you looking for?" The deputy sounded miffed, like Dave was wasting his time.

"I was wondering how old of a trail your dog could locate. What kind of terrain can he work? This is kind of a shot in the dark, so to speak."

"Well, we've followed trails in training successfully that were aged two weeks, but to be honest, that was in a pretty well-controlled situation. In regular experience in locating missing persons, we've worked tracks that were about a week old. What, exactly are you needing?"

Dave smiled to himself. This just might work. He still needed to get the deputy on board. "I have a body that was found along a gorge in the river. She's probably been there a few days at least. But the problem is, we don't know where she went in upriver. I would like to try and find where she actually entered the water."

"Does it really matter?" Deputy Hein questioned. "She's dead, ain't she?"

"Well, just going on a theory here. We haven't been able to ID her, and I believe she may be tied into all of the buried remains that were found in our county this past week."

"It'll be a long shot theory. What are you hoping to do? How would you want to try this with a trailing dog?"

"I thought we could start on the east side of the gorge at the point where she was found. I have a scent article taken from the body, but it's compromised. Even so, maybe your dog can use it if there is any scent left on it. Thought we could start from that point and head upriver to see if he can pick up any trail from this victim. I really would like to know where she entered the river. I think it could help ID her. Would this fall in the scope of something worthwhile trying with your dog?"

Dave knew there was only the slimmest chance they would be able to locate this girl's trail, but he also knew it was worth a try... and hoped this deputy would think so as well.

"You're talking about trying to backtrack. Not too many handlers train for that or are successful with the technique. But we've worked with a few handlers who have been certified in it, and I know how to work a dog using that practice. I certainly believe it fits within the scope of ole Smoke's abilities, I would just have to get the time and permission to be able to meet with you and run the dog. Let me think about this and talk to my super. I'll get back to you."

"Thanks, I'm not really advertising that I'm trying this. Big guy doesn't believe in using dogs, if you understand me."

"Sure, understand. I'll just see if I can get some training time that wasn't normally scheduled for me and the dogs."

"Great, appreciate whatever you can do." Dave hung up, hoping it would work out and he could keep it under wraps for the time being.

Less than an hour later, the Albemarle deputy rang back. Dave had already started working on Plans B, C, and D just in case. But he had a feeling that once he posed a scent problem to the canine handler, the deputy wouldn't be able to stop thinking about the many possible ways to approach it.

"Hey there, Graves. Just thinking, I'm at the end of my shift and have the next two days off. We could handle this like a training problem and I wouldn't have to get anything approved... and no one would have to know what we're up to. Scent problems like this have worked in the past, but from my knowledge, there were more known entities. It sounds like with your problem, there are a lot more variables and unknowns. You're not sure how long the body had been in river, where it went in, and if it went in on the east side or the west... or who the person even was. This will be a tough task, but I think my dog can handle working a problem like this."

Dave and the deputy from the neighboring county made plans for the following morning. He hung up knowing he was taking the right action—but once again doing so without permission. Somehow, it felt right. It wasn't personal this time.

CHAPTER 49

SARAH

Elliot followed Sarah out to the parking lot. She was still in disbelief over the sketches. Tripping up the curb, he caught her elbow to steady her.

"You okay, Sarah? Did you hear a word I said?" he asked.

"I'm sorry. I'm still in awe. Dumbfounded is more like it." She sighed. "I'll be okay."

"Are you sure? You driving back to Virginia tonight? That was a lot to go through."

Sarah could hear a note of concern in his voice. "I'll be fine," she returned. "I'm staying with Kellee tonight. The traffic was a bitch heading up here this morning and I really don't want to face that again right now if I can help it."

They arrived at Sarah's SUV. Gunner and Sam, excited to see her, began barking. Sarah breathed a sigh of relief and smiled.

"You sure you're fine?" the lawyer reiterated.

"Yes, I've got these two with me." Sarah pointed at the two shepherds. "And it'll be good to hang with Kellee tonight and catch up."

"Sure thing." He held the vehicle door for her. Sarah gave him a quick hug, something she hadn't been comfortable with in the past. "Well, I guess you know how to get ahold of me if you need anything. Anything at all." He lingered for a moment, not seeming to want to let her go just yet.

Sarah stood up straight and took a deep breath. "Don't worry about me. I've bounced back from bigger things." She almost laughed at the bold statement.

"That's what I'm worried about."

With that, Sarah climbed into the SUV and said her final goodbye. Sarah and the dogs set off for Kellee's home.

Looking in her rearview mirror, she could see both dogs sitting up, staring at her. Gunner and Sam had spent several hours crated in the vehicle. They were ready to get out to stretch and run. "I don't think I could've faced the traffic again. Too exhausted." She continued to talk to the dogs as if they understood. The interview with the hypnotist and forensic artist had drained her.

Sarah tried to relax as she drove several more miles north to Kellee's farm. Turning off the main road and onto a long, rutted gravel drive, the dogs started to whine. They recognized where they were going, whether it was by sight, or more likely, by scent.

Smiling inside, she felt like she was coming home. To be back in Pennsylvania, and for now, a free woman, she couldn't conceal her feeling of exhilaration.

A figure in the doorway caught her eye. She glimpsed Kellee standing in the threshold. Patches of sparkling sun reached through the oak trees, reflecting and dancing all around her.

Pulling up to the two-story clapboard farmhouse, Sarah put the car in park as Kellee walked out to greet her and the dogs. Kellee's two dogs pushed past her, running and trotting circles around the SUV.

Gunner and Sam exploded in barks, their tails whipping inside their crates.

"Settle," Sarah yelled. But the dogs continued their frenzied activity. "Okay, okay, give me a minute."

Sarah quickly exited the vehicle, opened the hatch and released her dogs. They took off toward Kellee first, giving her a couple sloppy, wet kisses and then took off with the other shepherds and ran around the expansive front yard.

Both tried to talk at the same time, hesitated and started to cry. "It's so good to have you back," Kellee voiced, engulfing Sarah in a whole-hearted embrace.

"I can't believe I'm here."

They looped their arms around each other's waist and started up the brick walkway to the house.

Sarah thought Kellee was the closet person to a mother or even a relative, aside from Dave, she'd ever had in her life. Even with all Kellee had been dealt over the years—losing her daughter Lindsey, her marriage dissolving—she still was positive and welcomed Sarah into her life.

"So, how was it? Were you all successful today with the forensic artist?" Kellee asked as the two made their way toward the covered front porch.

"The whole experience was consuming. We were able to get a lot accomplished. Let's sit down and I'll explain everything."

***

Later in the evening, Sarah finally called Dave to check in. Staying on the phone until late, they discussed the turn of events in Nelson County, Dave's plans to run the hound the next day, and the portraits she was able to help bring together while under hypnosis.

Sarah explained once again about the experience of being hypnotized, how the forensic artist had captured the ghosts from her past. She explained in detail what each of the portraits portrayed, then added, "I think I've seen him lately."

"What do you mean... you think you've seen him lately? Sarah? Where? When?"

"I said 'think,' Dave. I can't prove it. But I *think* I saw him, the first time, standing in the back of the courtroom. Then I saw him once more driving by the day Gunner and Sam made the discovery in the woods... as I was pulling out the little area where we had parked."

Sarah knew Dave held words, held his initial thoughts back. They both believed she could be in danger. Sarah changed the subject and asked how he was feeling after the boating incident and if he felt up to traipsing after a trailing hound. Sarah worried it was too soon after his concussion.

Dave gave her a full report on the swift water recovery team members and how they were fairing in the hospital. Then he changed the subject back to the trailing canine and his handler. He discussed the ideas he had in store for the next day's search.

Sarah wished him luck finding the subject's trail and hung up. They both were in need of a good night's sleep. Silently, she hoped Dave would be safe heading into the wooded area along the river. He was a deputy, but the man who had shot at them was still at large and knowingly shot at a search and rescue team—that worried her.

And once again, she forgot to ask Dave if he knew what the shooter had looked like.

Chapter 50

Dave

The sun peered over the jagged ridgeline of Horseshoe Mountain as the two men headed out. Dave and Deputy Hein planned to get an early start with the canine and cover at least one side of the river, starting from the point the body was recovered. They wanted to head northeast to the bridge, before the sun beat down on the trio and it became too warm.

In the early hours of the day, not only were there lower temperatures, but scent usually pooled closer to the ground.

Already promising to be a beautiful day—forecasted temperatures in the mid-eighties, a light breeze, clear skies, a touch of moisture in the air—it made for great conditions. Dave knew how to read the weather and how scent worked when it came to hunting with a canine. It would be a perfect day to be out in the woods working a dog.

Dave sized up Deputy Hein. He looked to be a handful of years older than himself. Tall, thin, and with a scant of peppered hair covering his premature balding head, he gave Dave the impression he was in great physical shape. Reminded Dave of a marathon runner.

Running scent hounds could keep you fit. It was easy to see Officer Hein trained consistently as he had stated in the previous day's conversation. Dave could quickly tell trailing dogs was the deputy's true passion in life.

The men discussed their backgrounds and experiences handling canines and what disciplines of scenting work they had both been involved in. Dave gave him an overview of his limited career as a bloodhound K9 officer and then went into detail with his experience working air-scenting dogs which was also relatively short.

Hein had years of experience running dogs of all breeds in his job and personal life in tracking and trailing. He'd trained and worked a tracking canine for Albemarle County because that was what the protocols required in his department—a canine trained in tracking meant the dog could follow fresh tracks whether for a suspect or a lost person. The dog would follow footstep to footstep, mainly over broken vegetation, or fresh tracks over tarmac or other un-natural surfaces. But tracks were easier to compromise between time and weather.

Hein's preference was to train and work with trailing dogs that followed a "trail" versus following an exact track. The dogs would follow the subject's scent which could have shifted to the side of the actual track. The dog could still be trained to scent discriminate and only follow that one subject's trail and disregard all other humans. Sometimes in the right conditions, the dog could also follow a trail that was days, if not weeks old.

Hein also taught classes at the yearly search and rescue seminar on tracking and trailing held in the area sponsored by the Virginia Department of Emergency Services. His excitement and enthusiasm were contagious and helping civilian volunteers with their dogs was something he loved to do. He even held titles and certifications from police and civilian organizations throughout the country.

Dave began to feel at ease the more he and Hein talked. He was confident he had found a good resource to help him try to locate the river victim's trail. Hein was working a male blue-tick hound, his best "go to" dog for difficult problems.

They pulled up to the cow field that ran along the ridge above the river where the farmer had first spotted the body in the gorge. Parking along the road beside the fence line, they pulled out their needed supplies and locked up the vehicle. Dave, Hein and Smoke headed across the cattle field to the ridgeline above the river. Dave explained how the body had been found, and how they had carefully extricated it.

"Yeah, I caught some of the action over the radio," Hein replied.

"I thought we could start here. Along this opening." Dave pointed to an area along the cliff. "This is also where the shots came from when recovering the body yesterday, so I'm sure it's pretty contaminated from the shooter and all of the deputies combing the area."

Bright yellow police tape still clung to trees cordoning off a small area where they had found boot tracks and spent cartridges.

"Any luck finding evidence on the shooting subject?" Hein asked as he eyed the plastic "do not cross" line.

"We were able to find a few spent rounds, but nothing else. There were fresh tire tracks along the dirt road, but seems this area is also well-known and popular with the local teens. They have a fire pit in the woods near here, so the tire tracks could belong to anyone."

"I'm gonna need to give Smoke plenty of time in the area so he can decipher the different human scents for himself before we move on. How far out from the edge of the ridge do you want to go to see if we can pick up a trail?"

"We could try a zig zag pattern from the edge to about thirty meters or so inward to see if the dog picks anything up."

Hein studied the area, looking at the vegetation they were getting ready to bushwhack through. "We can just walk a path along the edge, barring obstacles. We're going to have to go around anyway. The dog should pick up where the body went in or where she traveled if we should be lucky enough to cross her trail—but that's only if we just happen to intersect the location of where she went in."

"Okay. Sounds good. Are you ready to start?"

"Almost, do you have the scent article?"

"Yeah, in a sealed baggy in my pack." Dave had 'taken' a small swatch of the drowned subject's clothing before the coroner showed up to claim the body. He had already been forming an idea in his head.

"Okay, don't pull it out just yet. Let me get the dog together," Hein mumbled as he leaned down to check Smoke's equipment. "You know this is a shot in the dark, right?"

"Yeah, I know. But I don't know what else to try."

Dave wondered if Hein was having doubts or regretting his offer to help on his day off... or just realizing how difficult the problem Dave posed really was.

"Not discounting the idea, but I don't want you to have all of your hopes pinned on ole Smoke working this out. He's a highly skilled trailing dog, but there might not be a scent trail to find." Hein leaned back down over Smoke's equipment.

Dave nodded. He knew what Hein was saying, but silently, he more than hoped the dog would come through with something solid.

Hein gave Dave specific instructions on how he wanted to have the dog readied and how Dave should introduce the subject's article.

Smoke had a leather tracking harness fitted to him with sheepskin padding along the front panel and the sides. Hein attached a leather line about twenty feet long which had a large loop on the end. He reeled the dog in some while Dave pulled the envelope with the baggy from his pocket.

Smoke looked up at Dave with inquisitive brown eyes. He saw the package and his tail started to whip back and forth, anticipating what was next.

Hein nodded to Dave he was ready, then straddled his dog, both hands on the harness with the dog pointed in the direction they wanted to travel.

From within the envelope, Dave pulled out a sealed baggy containing a small square of torn and battered silky red material. Dave hadn't followed protocol to ask for permission from his supervisor, but then he had already skirted the rules when he took Sarah and her dogs to search for the original child's femur.

"Here ya go, boy," Dave cooed to the dog as he lowered the opened baggy.

Smoke pushed his long, black snout into the opening of the container. The dog sucked in the article so hard, the baggy collapsed around him. They gave Smoke as much time as he wanted to study the scent on the small patch of material. His tail continued to whip back and forth with intensity.

After the dog had enough of the article, Smoke turned around to look at Hein as if asking, "You ready?"

Hein gave the command, "Let's go, boy," and Smoke put his nose to the ground for a second and then turned. He went out to the end of his line, made a circle and looked back at Hein again. "Okay, buddy. Do your thing. Let's go. Search!" Hein shouted with enthusiasm.

The dog began to move forward slowly and methodically.

"Backtracking is pretty much a newly developed technique, and this really isn't what you would call backtracking. If he does happen to locate her trail, it's going to be pure luck." Hein bent down as he followed the dog and gave him some encouraging words in a high-pitched voice as the men trudged behind.

Dave gave Hein and Smoke space to get their game in gear. Once the dog figured out which direction they were heading in, Hein let the line feed out. Dave needed to stay out of the way, but also keep up with the pair, so he stepped in behind Hein.

Smoke took off at a slow jog. The dog cast back and forth, moving side to side as he progressed forward. Hein did his best to keep him from getting tangled in trees and bushes blocking their path along the edge of the cliff. Occasionally the dog would stop and turn his nose toward the sky and take in the scents around him. Smoke was a serious worker and although he hadn't found any human tracks or scent matching the article, he continued to work, moving forward with intent and endurance. Dave was impressed by the dog's drive and work ethic.

After almost an hour into the task, Hein suggested, "Let's take a break for about ten minutes. I need to water Smoke and check his paws."

It had been slow going and frustrating cutting along the ridgeline with all the summer overgrowth. Several times they had to stop so Hein could untangle Smoke's longline from low lying brush or branches.

"Okay, no problem. Do whatever you need to do to keep him fresh," Dave replied.

They had gone over a mile so far without luck. But if Smoke did locate a trail, Hein would have bragging rights and a story to tell. Both Dave and Hein kept their eyes peeled for any clue— footprints, clothing, broken branches, whatever they might find.

They were coming up to the bridge where Dave and the swift water rescue team had put in their boats the day before. Dave figured it would be a good stopping point for the day. If they hadn't found anything by then, they might have to try another day and another strategy. *But what fucking strategy?*

Hein readjusted Smoke's harness after watering him, pulling it a little tighter around the dog's body. They were getting nearer to roadways and he wanted to make sure his dog was secure.

Smoke hadn't slowed until he had been forced into momentary downtime. His nose was like a vacuum constantly seeking out his surroundings for scents which belonged and those that didn't. Normally, a human would be at the end of the trail, which was satisfying to the dog. But today, even if Smoke succeeded in locating the scent trail, there would be no human reward at the end.

Hein, Smoke and Dave continued to work north along the riverbank. The ridge had slowly disappeared as the bank and river became mere hills. They approached the bridge area and the slope took a steep grade down.

"Easy," Hein told Smoke. He didn't want to be pulled forward on the decline. The dog looked back at his handler but obeyed. Smoked eased up a bit.

Closing in on the road and bridge, the dog's body language began to change. He became more animated. His tail went up like a flag, stiff and ridged except for the white tip swaying back and forth as he moved forward.

Dave and the swift water team had just been there the day before so there were fresh tracks and scent everywhere.

Smoke hunted around the area, checking out Dave and then sniffing hard around the area some more.

The men waited patiently, while Smoke spent time checking the roadway and bridge exhaustively. The dog picked up a trail he really seemed to be interested in. It was evident he had finally locked onto a specific scent.

"I'm not sure if it's just a fresh trail from someone who's recently passed this way, or if he's picked up the victim's trail. I just need to let him work it out," Hein offered up.

"No problem, let him do what he wants."

Smoke followed the trail slowly over the tarmac on the bridge. He went about twenty-five meters and stopped. The dog sniffed hard, keeping his nose pretty much in place as his back legs and back end circled around.

The dog stopped again for a moment, indicating the trail seemed to go in two directions. Then he picked a direction and focused on the invisible trail. Smoke continued sniffing hard until he followed his nose to the side and up the concrete barrier of the bridge. The dog broke out in a howl, pulling his handler with excitement and force.

Dave and Hein looked at each other. They knew the dog had located the subject's trail.

Smoke began following that same trail back the way they had come. *Back the way the girl must've come.* He followed until it crossed back onto dirt and headed into the woods and up a hill still heading north. Then the trail turned and started to bear northeast.

The sun was fully up in the middle of the sky now. Temps had risen several degrees, and the men started to sweat through their clothing. Smoke was still working well but was beginning to show signs of fatigue.

"We really should get another trailing canine out here," Hein told Dave. "This trail is still hot. Who knows where it might lead? And we need to do this soon before we lose it completely."

"Okay. We're pretty far from our vehicles now anyway. Good stopping point. I'll see if I can call someone to come pick us up," Dave said, reaching for his cell phone. "But I don't want to wait until tomorrow to continue running this trail. Do you have any suggestions on another team close by who would have a good trailing dog?"

Hein thought for a moment. "Well, there is a civilian about thirty minutes out. I've run dogs in the past with her and she's attended several of my seminars."

"Would you trust that handler with this old of a trail?" Dave asked.

"I'd trust her dog. Good working animal. And she's pretty accurate at reading her dog."

Hein gave Dave the handler's contact info.

As Dave put the call in, he wondered if he should let the sheriff know where he was and what he was doing.

It was getting late when the civilian handler and her bloodhound arrived. Dave tried to raise Kasey but the call went straight to his voicemail. In the meantime, he was able to reach Felding. Dave gave the deputy sheriff a quick version of what had transpired and let him know exactly where they were.

"You're trespassing. Did anyone give you permission to access that area?" Felding sounded miffed. It caught Dave off guard.

"No, not really, but we were following the hound."

"You need to be real careful, Graves," Felding replied. "It's miles over hard terrain through that mountain. Only a few homes and abandoned shacks. A couple back roads, pretty desolate area."

"I know, I looked over the topo map," Dave stated dryly.

"Well, some folks don't take kindly to having their privacy invaded and will go to whatever means necessary to protect it... if you know what I'm saying. I think you need to drop this."

Dave understood perfectly—moonshiners, drug labs, illegal plants. "Will do," he answered. "I want to see how much farther we can run this trail and if it leads us to any other clues. We'll only be out a few more hours and call it quits."

"You're on your own time and dime," Felding reminded him.

Dave heard static and realized the connection had gone dead. *Maybe the reception. Or did Felding hang up? Where was Kasey?* Felding was the only one, aside from Deputy Brooks, who knew what he was up to.

Dave shoved the cell phone in his pocket.

After speaking with Felding, Dave realized exactly where he was—the bridge was located directly on the other side of the mountain from the mass burial site.

Dave had a foreboding feeling but was excited to be figuring out a piece to the puzzle as well.

Hein and Smoke had gotten a ride back to their vehicle, leaving Dave with the civilian handler and her canine. Her dog was only a little over a year old but had shown a lot of promise in one of Hein's seminar.

Before pulling the bloodhound out of his crate, Dave laid the map out on the hood of his cruiser. They discussed how difficult the steep grade of the mountain was on this side. It would be rough going up, especially following an exact subject's trail behind a dog. You couldn't walk it at an angle or pick your path.

Once they discussed the situation, the handler pulled her dog out. She readied him with his harness and long, leather lead. Dave pulled out the scent article and showed it to the hound. He rolled his large nose over the small piece of material. He huffed a few times then put his nose to the ground.

"Hope you're ready," the handler laughed at Dave, "'cause once he gets going, he's hard to stop, and he moves out fast!"

The dog circled around, backed up a few steps, inhaled deeply, then caught the trail and off they flew. Dave had to jog to keep up at first. Once they hit the tree line and the terrain changed from tarmac to soil, the dog slowed. He took his time checking the area and then found what he was looking for and bolted forward. Dave quickly tied a small piece of fluorescent flagging tape to a tree where they entered the woods.

The hillside took a harsh turn upward. Dave started to fall a little further behind as he grabbed onto trees to help hoist himself up. They moved on toward slightly more stable, level ground for a few hundred meters. Suddenly, the hound stopped. Dave caught up to the team.

"He's found something," the handler said in a quiet voice.

They watched as the dog worked hard at the scents he could detect. He huffed loudly at a spot, sucking in a scent over his receptors. Then he lay down and looked back at his handler.

She and Dave approached the spot. Under the dog's paw was a small patch of red, pushed into the ground by what looked like a large boot track. Beside the material and boot track was a small print of a bare foot.

"Good job, Bruno!" the handler lavished on the dog. She pulled out a handful of chopped up treats—freeze-dried beef liver. "Jackpot!"

She gave the dog a few more handfuls and then released him from his down. Pulling out a nasty looking dirty towel with holes all through it, she got the dog into a tug session and let him win and have his favorite toy. The dog lay down beside her, engulfed in pulling on and trying to shred his towel.

Finally, a clue that shows the tracking dog was on the right trail. Dave was excited. He stood back and looked down the mountain. He turned around, so he could see what direction the pair had come and which way they were headed. He pulled out his phone to take pictures and make notes.

Retrieving a plastic baggy from his pocket, he turned it inside out. Using it like a glove, Dave reached into the dirt and removed the torn red material. He pulled the baggy right side out then zipped it closed. Using a pen, he marked it with GPS coordinates and the date. He also marked the area with flagging tape.

Dave made additional notes in his phone as to which direction and bearing the footprints were heading and had come from. He took a few sticks and poked them into the ground around the imprints then laid several large leaves over top to try to maintain the tracks' integrity.

"I think it's time to call it quits for the day. I need to take this information back to the station and regroup, to see where we go from here. Appreciate your help today. You guys did a great job." Dave reached down to pet Bruno on the head and told him what an awesome dog he was.

Dave stayed several feet behind the team as they descended the steepest part of the trail they had followed up. He was exhausted. As he lagged behind, he imagined the subject—the young girl running for her life—barely dressed, no shoes. He stopped every so often to try to imagine the scene. If she was barefoot, there had to be blood somewhere along the ground. If she was running blindly down the mountainside, she would have left other clues to what she had endured and where she had escaped from.

But he was still dumbfounded no one had reported her missing yet. He had scoured the reports over the last few days, starting locally, then spanned out regionally, and finally when nothing showed up on the radar, he expanded to the whole country. Weird. Just didn't make any sense. Hopefully, forensics would've gotten a sketch done of her by now, or soon. That might help determine an ID. They were also going to enter her DNA into the national system to see if any information was available. They had found semen in her vagina and could enter that detail as well.

The trio continued down the mountainside until it leveled off. They took a quick break for water. From where they stood, you could just make out the river flowing below. When a car crossed the bridge, the metal reacted with a loud echoing sound. It was easy to tell you were getting close.

If the girl had headed this way, did she know where she was going? Did the sounds draw her near the bridge? Or was she being chased and thought she would be rescued if she made it here? But the biggest question was whether she had jumped or was murdered.

CHAPTER 51

SARAH

Sarah woke to the tantalizing aroma of coffee wafting up through the farmhouse's floorboards. Comfy, she lay still, listening to the old house come alive. Eventually, the clattering of dishes and ruckus below brought her fully awake.

Hearing Kellee call to the dogs out back and the screen door slamming, Sarah decided it was time to crawl out of bed. Morning sun splashed through the window panes, warming her as she yawned and stretched. Smiling, she felt whole... happy for the first time in ages.

Few words were spoken as the women pushed food around their plates picking at their breakfast. Both dreaded the nearing departure. They had stayed up talking into the early hours of Sunday morning. Kellee filled her in on what she had been keeping busy with and Sarah brought Kellee up to date with the remains search and the state's investigation.

Shyly, Sarah confided in Kellee her feelings for Dave.

Looking up from the table, Kellee stared at Sarah with a smile a mile wide.

"What?" Sarah blushed, looking away.

"I'm happy for you. And Dave. You know he's a good man. Not perfect, but no one is," Kellee replied. "You two are good for each other. You stand up for yourself, but you learn to compromise as well."

Sarah nodded. She looked out the sliding glass door that led to Kellee's large backyard and garden. "I know," she voiced just above a whisper.

"Are you feeling okay, Sarah?"

"Yeah, why? Just a little fatigued from working the remains site, Dave getting hurt... the barn fire. But even so, I feel more complete, relaxed. I'm not sure how to put it."

"I know you're tired, but you look great. Almost as if you radiate from within." Kellee reached across the table and gently held her friend's hand.

Embarrassed, Sarah smiled sheepishly into what was left of her cup of coffee.

After loading the dogs into the SUV, the women said their goodbyes, promising they would see each other again soon. With tears in her eyes, Sarah drove out the farm lane.

At the first rest stop, Sarah called Dave. They discussed how the meeting with the forensic artist had gone. She told Dave the artist promised to email her "aged" sketches soon. She also brought him up to date on how Kellee was doing. Dave filled her in with the clues he found while utilizing the trailing dogs. He went over his speculations about where the victim may have gone in the river and in what direction she had come from.

Conjuring up a mental picture of the young girl escaping from her situation, trying to evade her captors, Sarah was sure the girl had jumped from the bridge. She knew that's what she would've done in that same situation.

"I think Kasey is somehow involved," Dave said.

The red flags and uneasiness Sarah had felt reemerged. She had a knack for reading people and if it weren't for Kasey being Dave's boss, she would've avoided him all the time. The man's body language cautioned Sarah that he had a hidden agenda, but she hadn't been able to figure it out. But why? He was a sheriff, for hell's sake. And yet... a badge was the perfect place to hide behind.

"If he's tied into the compound and has something to do with the operation, then you may be in danger," Sarah voiced with concern.

"Promise me you'll call the feds. Promise me," Sarah pleaded with Dave. "I don't have a good feeling about this."

"I plan to, Sarah. It'll work out," Dave replied.

Hours away and feeling helpless, she worried Dave would try to handle the situation on his own.

CHAPTER 52

DAVE

Trying to ease Sarah's worries, Dave reassured her he would be careful and watch his back. But truth was, he was leery as hell. Dave was still new to the area, to the agency. He didn't quite know where the line would be drawn between the law and loyalty.

Heading to the station late Sunday, he knew there would only be a light crew on duty. He wanted to do more research on the property and surrounding area where the bodies had been located.

Dave scoured over maps of the area. He had researched the landowners on that side of the mountain, and found names of those who still held acres near the state-owned parcels. Racking his brain, he tried to find a connection between Sheriff Kasey and any of them—but hadn't found the link just yet.

Most of the area wasn't occupied, or at least it wasn't knowingly occupied. Old deserted mine shafts, deep-rooted overgrown farms and settlements had been long abandoned, left to rot. Most of the area had been timbered at one time and used for pasture land, but had set so long, mature trees now resided there along with low-lying scrub growth. The land, the terrain was very rocky and currently unsuitable for either farming or grazing livestock.

Several unimproved dirt roads led up the mountain, but only a few had been maintained. There appeared to be one well-traveled dirt path leading to a few houses but then dead-ended into what seemed like a large compound. Evidently an older family lived there who didn't socialize or come to town very often. Their children had been home-schooled and never left the property. Apparently, the family was said to be somewhat backwards—

hermits that kept to themselves. No one seemed to know much about them.

Over the years, there had been several minor infractions tied to that family: overdue vehicle registrations, late property tax payments, and complaints from the bordering neighbor. Those complaints had been logged over the past twenty years by one neighbor on the east border. Dave decided to look deeper.

Only a fraction of the complaint reports had been entered into the system. Most were on file either at the old records house or in the basement of the sheriff's station where he worked.

Of the reports Dave was able to pull up in the computer, most dealt with loud music, parties, trespassing, or reports something suspicious was going on. The neighbor noted vehicles coming and going at all hours of the night. *Doesn't sound like a family living like hermits. More likely manufacturing or selling drugs.*

The north, west and south side of the compound were surrounded by state game lands. This included the back side where the adjoining property coming down met up with where the bodies had been discovered. "That would've been a difficult trek to carry a body," Dave suggested out loud. *Unless they used some type of all-terrain vehicle.*

Deputy Grimm, who had also been working the remains site with Sarah, overheard Dave in his office. Seeing the maps splayed out on Dave's desk, he pointed out some of the information from the search on Thursday.

"Here is where Sarah and I covered by horseback what we think is the perimeter of the burial site." Grimm used the tip of a pencil to pinpoint. "Over here is where several rough and primitive trails were found which look like an ATV would have made. And here is where we were riding when we figured out we were being observed by an unknown subject."

Thanking Deputy Grimm for the info, Dave made more notes in the margins of the maps. He knew he had everything in front of him to figure out the mystery of the young woman's body, the burial site, and probably even what happened to the missing children from Sarah's foster home. But something was eluding him.

His cell phone rang. Pulling it out of his pocket he frowned but answered the call.

"Well," Kasey cleared his throat, "I think this is all speculation and you're rushing things. No one gave you permission to run those trailing dogs, Graves."

"Other than speculation I'm not sure we have enough to merit a search warrant for the compound." Dave drummed his fingers on the table. "But between my barn burning down, being shot at in the recovery boat, and searchers getting spied on in the woods... I think we need to act on this quickly. And I think it's time we spoke to the FBI."

Dave paused and waited for Kasey's reaction. Hearing none, he continued.

"If this is all tied together," Dave continued, "it means this has been going on for a long time right under your nose. And if there are children involved, we will need more than just our support to take this on. I'm not well versed in human trafficking, especially when it involves children."

"I'm telling you to back off, Graves," Kasey hissed. "I don't appreciate a deputy who isn't obedient. No one gave you permission to run those dogs. This is no longer your case and I want you to stay away from it. I mean it. You back off, you hear me?"

Dave didn't know how to respond. Hearing the line go dead, he sat at his desk for a few minutes holding the phone. Although he thought Deputy Sheriff Felding was far enough removed from the situation, Dave got this empty feeling there was something more going on with him as well. How far did hometown loyalty go? How far would Felding go to protect Kasey if he knows the truth? Dave could no longer trust Felding either.

"You know they're connected, right?" Grimm asked.

"What?" Dave replied as he made his way out of his office.

"I overheard your phone conversation."

"Connected? What do you mean connected?" Dave asked the other deputy.

"Felding is tied to the compound. Those are his estranged relatives. Kasey and Felding are related. You should watch your back," Grimm warned, then added, "Sarah's as well."

CHAPTER 53

DAVE

Staring at the cell phone in his hand, Dave was torn. He was wrestling with an internal struggle whether he should make the call outside his agency or confront Sheriff Kasey directly about how the latest incidents were connected. And what if Kasey was involved?

Dave found himself at a stalemate. There was more than enough circumstantial evidence regarding the burial site and the compound to warrant the Bureau's attention, but he also wondered how this might affect him. And Sarah. Would he lose his job over this? What was the right thing to do?

Dave mulled over the situation. Deciding what he believed was the right thing to do, he made the call, going over both of his superiors.

The Bureau put him in touch with the agent who covered his area and who headed up the FBI's Human Trafficking Task Force. Over the phone, Dave brought the agent up to date on everything that had transpired in Nelson County and how it might be tied to human trafficking and a special investigation in Pennsylvania. Somewhat reluctantly, he even shared that he believed Sheriff Kasey was tied to the compound.

The agent asked Dave to meet with him and his partner at The Lovingston Cafe near the Sheriff's Office. He was given instructions not to speak to anyone regarding the situation and to bring whatever records he had kept on the incidents.

Heading to the office to collect his data, Dave's thoughts pulled him in different directions. Not knowing how this would affect him and going behind Kasey and Felding's back left him stressed. He felt like he was being squeezed in a vice. He didn't like being in this position.

"Dammit," he uttered under his breath, pulling up to the station. Kasey's Excursion was parked out front. Short on time, Dave hoped he could make his way in unnoticed, avoiding Kasey and the other deputies. Entering the building, he greeted the receptionist and headed down an empty hallway to his office. *So far, so good.*

Reaching his office, he peered through the rectangular side window of the door to see if the sheriff was sitting at his desk. Releasing a deep breath, he wasn't aware he had been holding, he entered an unoccupied office. Pulling open the bottom drawer of his desk, he reached to the far back, grabbing files he had secretly been creating on all the recent incidents.

Dave pushed the desk drawer closed, stalled and looked around. A few deputies passed by his office, but no Kasey so far.

The station was close enough to walk to the diner. Putting the files under his arm, Dave readjusted his holster belt, made sure his shirt was tucked in properly, and headed out the door. He told the receptionist he was going to lunch and would be unavailable for an hour.

Walking along the shoulder of the road toward the diner, Dave looked across the street where the cafe stood and spied a deep maroon Crown Vic parked by the side entrance. The angled glass made it difficult to see inside the building as he passed the front of The Lovingston Cafe.

Dave scanned the entire restaurant the moment he walked in. Peering over several patrons, past the register and take-home desserts in refrigerated cases, his gaze stopped abruptly. He locked on three men sitting in the back corner. Two of them were obviously agents from the Bureau in sharply dressed gray suits. The third one took him by surprise. All three glanced up as he stood by the front door.

Swallowing hard, Dave's legs felt heavy and leaden. He didn't like knowing he wasn't in control. Suddenly he was unsure of the situation he had gotten himself into. Dave slowly made his way to the back-corner booth.

"Afternoon gentlemen, afternoon Kasey," Dave stated. "I didn't expect to see you here."

"I'm sure you didn't," Kasey growled back, moving his large self over to make room for Dave on the bench seat beside him. Dave hesitated.

"It's okay," Kasey said looking at the agents as he spoke. "You're a pain in the ass and don't follow orders, but I'm not gonna get rid of you just yet."

Dave sat down. Both agents introduced themselves.

"Can someone fill me in on what's going on here?" Dave asked.

"Well, to begin with, the area—that compound you've become so interested in lately—has been under investigation for several months," Kasey started. "No one from our department was supposed to know about our efforts." Kasey glared at Dave. "Then you came along."

"You know about all of this? I mean... you're not involved, you're not part of the compound?" Dave spouted.

"Hell no, Graves. But Felding is and you had to go and almost blow the cover on everything. Felding is onto you. If you hadn't made the call to the Bureau, we were going to pull you anyway." Kasey's face grew red as he pressed Dave. "Felding would've taken you out. You put this investigation and your life in danger, dammit."

Dave shifted in seat, uncomfortable as the sheriff berated in him in front of the agents. "I had no idea..." Dave halfheartedly responded.

"What we didn't know," Kasey continued, "was how this all tied into the Pennsylvania investigation, and, I believe you have some information on that?"

Recovering from the shock of seeing Sheriff Kasey sitting with the Bureau agents, Dave pulled his notes from his research. He went through each incident, explaining how it all connected to the compound—Sarah's foster family and their ties to the Nelson

County area, the children who had gone missing over the years from the Pennsylvania foster home, and how he believed that several of the remains on the side of the mountain behind the compound would likely reveal these missing children.

One of the agents made phone calls substantiating Dave's research regarding the foster home and the internal investigation that was taking place in Pennsylvania, while Dave sat idly by and Kasey worked on his lunch.

"It all confirmed," the agent reported to the other one. "We've got the go ahead."

The second agent nodded. "Time to put the plan into action."

"What plan?" Dave inquired.

"Sorry," one of the agents explained, "but we will be handling this case from here on out."

Dave eyed Kasey questioningly. "What? Did you expect to be involved in the take down?" Kasey looked at him.

"Well, yes," Dave replied.

"You've down your part," Kasey spoke between bites. "More than your part. Let them handle it. I'm sure the Bureau will need our department at some point. Let them make that decision."

***

Several hours later, a specialized task force descended upon the outer edges of the compound. Utilizing high-powered scopes and binoculars the team was able to get a good look at the layout. The area inside the compound was active as several inhabitants moved about packing vehicles.

With darkness descending, the agents decided it was time to make their move. Coordinated efforts between the FBI's Human Trafficking Task Force, the ATF, and the state police, had put together a plan of attack.

A heavily armed SWAT team turned out in bullet-proof vests and helmets fitted with face masks wound around the fringes of the compound. Troopers sat near the entrance of the road and blocked off outside access.

The teams bordered the wood line, facing in, toward the center of the compound where the main house and a few trailers were situated. As the teams strengthened their forces in the wooded areas, several hounds within the compound began to bark, straining against the end of their heavy chains.

A handful of men outside one of the trailers stood alert. Appearing confused, they scanned the compound in all directions while the dogs continued to bark and jump at the end of their tethers.

"Who's out there?" one man carrying a sawed-off shotgun yelled. He fired a round in the air.

There were at least a dozen cars situated across the compound. With the sound of the gunshot piercing the air, startled men tumbled from the trailers. Pulling on clothing as they fled, the men ran to parked vehicles.

Law enforcement teams lay in wait in the safety of shadows. With armed officers in place, and recovery teams on the way, the agent coordinating the incident gave the SWAT team the go ahead.

In single file, the SWAT team entered the compound. Swinging around in the direction of movement, the man on the porch pointed his gun toward the armored men and started shooting. Returning fire, the SWAT point-man took the shooter out.

The man on the porch flew backward into the railing. Other men dropped to the ground or scattered in different directions within the compound.

Moving in closer, the team tightened their grip around the buildings. There were voids and debris—several places to hide and ambush, the teams took time to check carefully as the officers moved deeper into the compound. Several broke away from the fold and entered the house trailers to clear them.

Numerous captives were found in each building—girls, women and boys. Some were hiding, some were crying. Most were dazed and confused... under the influence. All but the young lady who had gotten away, gotten away to her death last week. The recovery teams moved in quickly to assess and help the victims.

One lone old woman was taken in without incident. Remaining silent, she wouldn't give up the name or the whereabouts of the man who had been her partner for years. But the teams were sure they had the correct subject. She matched the aged version of the forensic drawing they'd been given.

Her accomplice was still out there... somewhere.

CHAPTER 54

SARAH

Relieved, Sarah was thankful the raid on the compound was over and Dave was safe. She was satisfied the horrors of her foster home would also be resolved. It would still be months before the remains were completely unearthed and attempts at identification could began. Maybe years.

Sending up a silent prayer for the deceased woman who Dave had recovered from the river, Sarah felt connected, spiritually, to her. She saw the woman in her dreams occasionally. It was as if she knew that she was the missing link to the mystery. Her trail was what had finally led to the captives' safety.

The young woman had yet to be identified, but Sarah's soul was at peace knowing she had played a part in solving this ugly crime.

A twinge of fearfulness still stirred in Sarah. The male counterpart from the compound remained on the loose, but there was hope his whereabouts would be confirmed as the investigation continued. It didn't help alleviate Sarah's uneasiness. He was still out there, somewhere.

Time to get on with her life—her and Dave's life. The internal investigation into the foster care system was on-going. Somehow, she knew it would be for years, but at least the mystery was solved as to what had happened to several of the children from the Pennsylvania foster care system who had disappeared over the years.

There was still the possibility she may get called back one day to endure a retrial. But none of it mattered at the moment. She was ready to concentrate on the work Dave had begun...

researching her past. Sarah wanted to find out more about the brother she may have and what had happened to her daughter. DNA was her only hope.

So far, her daughter hadn't appeared to be among the children found within the compound. Maybe she'd be located among the remains, or maybe she was still out there somewhere. Either way, Sarah wanted to know.

It would hurt, but part of her past could be laid to rest. It was time to move on and get back to the life she and Dave were trying so desperately to build together.

Deputy Sheriff Felding was found to be tied to the family dealings from years ago. There was a possibility he had been involved with illegal adoptions. Although he had been arrested, he had been able to make bail. With Felding free for the time being, the barn fire unsolved, and the river shooter still unidentified, Sarah knew Dave worried about their overall safety. They took whatever precautions they could, but life still had to go on.

Deciding it was time the horses returned to the farm, Dave gathered a few of his work buddies and raised a run-in shed so the horses would have cover. There was still much work to be done clearing the destroyed remnants, so they could rebuild their barn. An on-going arson investigation into the barn fire continued, but so far hadn't yielded any solid leads.

On a warm inviting morning, Sarah and Dave headed to the vet clinic where Sunny and Tank had been boarded for the past few weeks. J.C. was meeting them there with his rig to haul the horses home.

Sarah and J.C. had become close friends over the last few months. J.C. was someone she trusted, completely. She felt lucky to have him in her life. He was like a father figure in many ways.

They pulled up to the clinic and could see J.C. already there with his truck and trailer.

"We're going to have to invest in our own truck and trailer eventually," Dave told Sarah as they exited the Explorer.

"When we win the lottery," Sarah joked back. With only one person in the household working full-time, it would be a while before they could afford anything extravagant like that.

They found J.C. in the barn speaking with the vet and his wife. Sarah gave J.C. a quick hug when she saw him. He introduced them to the couple who had cared for their four-legged friends.

"Thank you so much, Dr. and Mrs. Costa," Sarah said as she shook their hands. "Dave and I really appreciate you caring for the horses. I'm sure Sunny and Tank have enjoyed their short vacation."

Sarah admired the Italians' olive skin, dark hair and strong European attractiveness. They were a striking couple who had immigrated to the states when they had graduated and married.

"Oh, no problem. We're glad we could help. So sorry about your barn. It had to be devastating to you both. At least the horses weren't there when it happened."

Mrs. Costa continued to stare at her, making Sarah self-conscious. "You look so familiar, dear. You're not from around here?"

"No, I'm kind of new to these parts," Sarah replied. She hoped they hadn't read about her or seen her picture in the newspaper back during the trial. It suddenly made her feel uncomfortable. She wanted to get the horses and get out of there.

Sarah and Dave grabbed lead ropes and snapped them to each horse's halter after they paid their board bill to the couple. They had just headed out of the aisle toward the horse trailer with Sunny and Tank in tow when a young girl barreled out of the house.

She looked to be around nine or ten. Running toward the horses, her curls flew in every direction as she sprinted to the small gathering.

"Oh, Sunny and Tank, I hate to see you go! Can't they stay a little while longer? They were so much fun to take care of!" The freckle-faced girl rambled on unabashed, displaying her dimpled cheeks and vivid green eyes.

Sarah froze. She watched as Dave looked at the young girl and then back at her. The dimples, the hair, the freckled ivory skin tone. Her facial expression. It couldn't be. Or could it?

ACKNOWLEDGMENTS

Insert acknowledgment text here...

ABOUT THE AUTHOR

M.C. HILLEGAS worked in private industry until resigning to care for her family. She worked as a 911 Operator and ran background checks for firearms for the Pennsylvania State Police. Her main passions include equines and canines. She's ridden horses most of her life and has been involved in air-scenting search and rescue canines since the early nineties with the American Rescue Dog Association (ARDAINC.org). She is also a member of a mounted search and rescue team, TrotSAR (TrotSAR.org). She resides in southcentral Pennsylvania with her family, canine partner Roo, and riding partner Chex.

OTHER TITLES BY THIS AUTHOR

Payback
The Canine Handler, Book I

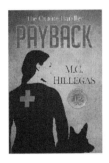 Sarah Gavin believes she has left her dark past behind. College diploma in hand, successful in her job, she is now aiming for the FBI Academy. But as a volunteer search and rescue canine handler, ghosts from her past come back to haunt her. In conflict with herself and surrounding events, Sarah must fight to hold on to her sanity.

COMING SOON:
Comeback
The Canine Handler, Book III

Made in the USA
Columbia, SC
29 October 2018